'**Scintillating** . . . *Berlin* is **wonderfully funny**, and
Daphne's observations about modern life, men and the
challenges facing young women always hit the nail'
– *FINANCIAL TIMES*

'**Uncommonly funny, cinematically vivid, and refreshingly
honest** about how we deceive others and ourselves'
– LISA HALLIDAY, author of *ASYMMETRY*

'Anyone who's started over in a new city – let alone a
new country – will relate . . . **One for Sally Rooney fans**'
– *SUNDAY TELEGRAPH*

'**A compelling, raw, and thrillingly strange
outsider tale** of loneliness and deception. Setton
is a wonderful writer who, with this sharp debut, **adds
to the great canon of contemporary anti-heroines**'
– MONA AWAD, author of *BUNNY*

'Setton builds her growing paranoia and sense of dread
to **terrific** effect **in this unsettling, compelling read**'
– *OBSERVER*

'[An] engagingly self-conscious debut . . . **our attention is
firmly held by the wry wit of Daphne's voice** . . . the
book's success lies chiefly in its line-by-line charm'
– *DAILY MAIL*

'**Enjoyable and astute** . . . Daphne's impressions
are rendered in **precise, lively prose**'
– *TIMES LITERARY SUPPLEMENT*

'In this **dark and twisty debut**, Setton crafts a clever thriller-cum-expat
narrative for fans of Ottessa Moshfegh's *My Year of Rest and
Relaxation* . . . **Raw thriller meets darkly funny coming-of-age**'
KIRKUS REVIEWS

www.penguin.co.uk

Berlin

BEA SETTON

PENGUIN BOOKS

TRANSWORLD PUBLISHERS
Penguin Random House, One Embassy Gardens,
8 Viaduct Gardens, London SW11 7BW
www.penguin.co.uk

Transworld is part of the Penguin Random House group of companies
whose addresses can be found at global.penguinrandomhouse.com

Penguin
Random House
UK

First published in Great Britain in 2022 by Doubleday
an imprint of Transworld Publishers
Penguin paperback edition published 2023

A CIP catalogue record for this book
is available from the British Library.

ISBN
9781804991039

Text design by Couper Street Type Co.
Typeset in Adobe Garamond Pro by Jouve (UK), Milton Keynes.
Printed and bound in Great Britain by Clays Ltd, Elcograf S.p.A.

The authorized representative in the EEA is Penguin Random House Ireland,
Morrison Chambers, 32 Nassau Street, Dublin D02 YH68.

Penguin Random House is committed to a sustainable future
for our business, our readers and our planet. This book is made from
Forest Stewardship Council® certified paper.

2023

In loving memory of my grandmother, Aimée Setton.

For my mother, my Samwise.

For your birthday.

Dad & Joy xxx
xxx

I

A Fresh Start

I ARRIVED IN BERLIN at the beginning of February, before the shame and guilt brewing somewhere low in my stomach turned symptomatic. These feelings were disproportionate to the events that had engendered them: the unreciprocated drunken confession to a man I had pined after for a year; an argument with a flatmate about a neglected kitten; an unexplained resignation followed by a refusal to even read my boss's hurt emails. Nothing that will loom large in the retrospective of my life, nothing I will remember much longer – just the kind of routine negligence and behaviour that slowly taints everything. I was ruining my life a little every day, and although I see now that these things were redeemable, I've always found starting on a clean page more inviting than amending an imperfect first attempt.

I moved from London without telling anyone that I was leaving, without saying goodbye to the people I knew there. Berlin is an easy place to start anew, as everyone seems to have just arrived. People even dress as if they are perched on the sill of a long journey, with belt bags and bandanas and tin bottles clipped to rucksacks with complex infrastructures. When I first arrived, I found the city shockingly dirty. Not in a picturesque, old-fashioned way – don't think of mud or pastoral dung, the kind of organic crud that calls for a thorough satisfying scrub-down with a hard bar of soap after a long cheek-reddening day. I mean depressing, modern trash, the quotient of the paradox of too little and too much: ugly corners of yoghurt pots and immortal plastic bags, trainers and soaked old spongy mattresses covered in glittering bottle shards.

My first flat was in Kreuzberg, a poor part of the old West, a *Szeneviertel* (cool neighbourhood) near Kottbusser Tor. Berliners affectionately nicknamed the area 'Kotti', which came in handy as a mnemonic when I was trying to remember the German word for vomit: *kotzen*. The flat was above a methadone clinic, and my comings and goings were witnessed by a quiet group of straw-haired addicts with strong blue pupils that rolled loosely in quivery egg-white eyes. They didn't smell of anything, and never tried to catch the door as it swung closed behind me. They would shuffle together or stand to let me past, and then re-settle in the warmest configuration the doorstep allowed.

It wasn't nice there. The staircase had no windows at all and smelt sewery. The shower curtain dragged, as if weighed down by mould, and the toilet flushed only half-heartedly. The plumbing was so old that the water tasted of blood. There weren't any cupboards, only repurposed ladders stacked with clothes and books, with a few rungs cleared for me. The boy I rented it from was an Austrian ballerina, who had once been at university with someone I knew vaguely from the London coffee-circuit. He was the same size as me, and so I wore all his shoes and jumpers, and quickly felt at home as a raven in Kreuzberg's dark flock of Adidas and bad-boy sweaters.

In the first days there, my existence was very narrow: I took the U-Bahn eastwards to my German class. The first two hours were grammar, then we had our break, and the last two hours were dedicated to hearing and speaking exercises. There were only seven students in A1.1, the absolute beginners' class, and three of them were called by some variant of the name Catherine. Katya was from Saint Petersburg and winkingly referred to her Spanish baker-boyfriend as her 'Chorizo'. When I first met her, she had thick, waist-long chestnut hair that she played with constantly – picking out split ends, or fluffing it up like a restless, glossy sparrow – but after a few months she bobbed it, and looked far more 'Berlin', though she had lost her gestural preening charm. There was Catalina from Caracas, who had escaped Maduro's communism with her boyfriend, Luis. He was her physical opposite: she, small and dimpled and voluptuous; he, tall, angular and sparse. They were both doctors but didn't have the license required to practice medicine in Berlin, and so instead worked alternating shifts in the McDonald's on Hermannstraße, a busy intersection close to our language school in the working-class district of Neukölln. The old woman from whom they rented a room was intolerant of smells, and had forbidden them from cooking anything in oil. Frying was the only kind of cooking they knew, and in those first weeks they looked so depleted that Katya took to bringing them leftover bread rolls from Chorizo's bakery. And then there was Kat from Sweden, with a fringe clipped to the quick, and an uncomplicated sexless body. She only became important later.

After class I would ride the U-Bahn west towards home, and memorize ladder lists of words in the ballerina's bedroom. When I was bored, I would go down to Karma Rösterei, the coffee shop around the corner. It was an unremarkable vegetable-milk kind of place – though it stood out on the street of shisha bars and kiosks, which all sold reliably average coffee for a third of the price of Karma's espressos. I would go to Karma and order a foamy oat latte, half mortified and half thrilled by my solitude. I memorized sentences that I found poetic – '*Ich konnte den Glute des Feuers spüren*' (I could feel the glow of the fire) – hoping to delight future German interlocutors. I repeated slang-y sentences I overheard on the U-Bahn – '*Ich flitze mal zum Spandau rüber*' (I'm popping by Spandau). I liked the sound of places in Berlin, particularly the consonance of Pankow and Spandau, the ends of the U-Bahn line that to this day remain only names to me. I arrived in a winter I found too cold to walk around in, so for the first couple of months I knew the city in skewed constellations of U-Bahn stops. It was only later, when the weather turned warm quite suddenly on the night of the 3rd of April, that I started to colour in between the lines.

But I'm getting ahead of myself. I was describing my routine in those delicate incubative months. After coffee, I would very often go to the cinema and practise how to ask for a single ticket: '*Ein Ticket bitte! Und ein kleines süßes Popcorn.*' I would always eat dinner late, after the cinema. Always the same: *Rotkohl* (pickled cabbage) with mustard, followed by raw oats and sweet oat milk, all from Denn's Bio Supermarkt. I spent a lot of time on my phone, clicking and swiping and refreshing, pacing the reassuringly familiar landscape of apps. This was my life when I first arrived. I relived the same day each day, the possibilities corseted by my taut German. I enjoyed myself very much. I liked repeating precisely the same thing, feeling like a powerful ballerina or horse, knowing how much youth shimmers and lust fizzes close to the surface – but keeping it in check, turning in early and alone, delighting in the precision of the coming day's choreography, choosing to do only this, with symmetry – over and over.

Not ad infinitum, however. By now it was March and my lease was nearly up, the ballerina was returning from Vienna, and I had to find a new place to live. I thought it might be a good idea to live with other people, so I had applied for a number of *Wohngemeinschaften*, or WGs.* Most of the ads were the standard kind of thing you'd expect: 'Looking for someone clean and responsible, professionals only (sorry, students), 420-friendly',† and I quickly found a spacious room around the corner from Kotti. I shared the two-bedroom apartment with a Polish woman called Ewa who was very nice on the days she didn't take crystal meth. The rest of the time she was either absent, thrashing to techno in a dark room somewhere, or too present, pacing the flat during her horrible comedowns. The meth made her paranoid and accusatory. She would send me texts in the middle of the night – 'Hey, have you seen my red hoodie? If you borrowed it I hope it isn't lost, my dad gave it to me. Also, I'm missing a jar of sunflower seeds. Did you take it?' She would check the stove was off and the door was locked and scrub the sink as if she were scouring her soul. I made the mistake of googling 'side effects of meth addiction' and came upon an article about meth-induced psychosis and violent behaviour. After that, I began to lock my bedroom door at night, waking from sleep to check it was properly secured, increasingly unsure which of us was more paranoid. After a two-week 'trial' period, I gave up on the idea of a flatmate, and started looking for a place of my own.

I soon found out that the ease with which I'd found the ballerina's apartment and Ewa's room had been a bit of

---

* This is what Germans call a flat-share, though *Wohngemeinschaft* literally means a 'living-community', which sounds rather utopian.

† Slang for cannabis.

beginner's luck. I visited a number of flats, and had to suffer countless odd interactions and conjure convincing false smiles in places that stank of sweat or thawing frozen prawns. A tall man with pale legs covered in black hairs showed me around a luminous studio while his girlfriend hid herself beneath a tipi of bedsheets. A beautiful eyebrowless Italian man showed me a flat he had gutted and furnished from IKEA. Finally, I met a woman who, for the purposes of this story, shall be referred to only by her initials, EG. She was looking for someone to take over her studio for six months, while she moved to Seattle to attend a Blood Spatter and Distribution course at the University of Washington as part of her criminology degree. She advertised a 'cuddly nest in a nice neighbourhood' near the Hermannplatz U-Bahn. She claimed that the flat had a wooden floor and '*Hinterhof* charm', meaning that it looked on to the inner courtyard rather than the street. The old buildings in Berlin are several courtyards deep, and living in a *Hinterhof* is a trade-off of sorts – the flats are sometimes quieter, usually safer, but little sunshine penetrates the entrails of those courtyards. EG specified, however, that not only was her flat very quiet and safe, it was also very light, because it was lined with three very large windows.

There was a whole lot of planning and scheming I had to do in order to secure the flat. It began with this email.

Dear EG,
My name is Daphne, and I am a PhD student in Philosophy, moving to Berlin from London.* I am interested in your flat, am responsible and I take good care of people's homes and

---

* A lie. I was at the time recovering from a round of rejections from master's programmes in Philosophy. I had been accepted nowhere.

possessions.* I am non-smoking and quiet.† Let me know if you are still looking for someone.

With best wishes,

Daphne Ferber

P.S. I apologize for the email in English. My German is very basic.‡

This email was well received, as I knew it would be. People always seem to trust philosophers. Belonging to that particular faculty is a kind of stamp of respectability. What most people don't know is that philosophers (who are mostly men) are dirty maniacs. If a philosopher responded to an ad of mine, I wouldn't even answer. I would assume that he was aesthetically stunted and sexually frustrated, and that he ate horrible, fishy, bristly things for breakfast.

In this case, I took full advantage of the misplaced credit given to my faculty, and EG granted me an interview. I visited her place at night, and so I couldn't really tell about the light and the windows. The flat was on the first floor. The entrance smelt of raspberries and white chocolate. EG was very beautiful: she had dark-red hair and extraordinary green eyes that looked painted with acrylics – thick and dauby with glistening whites. She was a head smaller than me, with a round, friendly face that made her seem kinder than I would later find out she was. She was originally from Münster and in the last year of her PhD in criminology, but her secret, dearest wish (I discovered later, when I read her diary) was to become an actress.

'Daphne, right?! Do I pronounce it well?'

---

* Aspirationally true, but in fact, a lie.

† True, except when someone I find attractive offers me a cigarette.

‡ At this point in the story, very true indeed.

7

'Yes, that's absolutely perfect.'

She stretched out her hand; it was tiny and bony and a little moist, and fluttered nervously in mine like a bird caught in a trap.

'Please come in, welcome to my cosy nest.'

Apart from the corridor and a small windowless bathroom, the flat consisted of one large room lined by three very tall windows facing – as promised – the inner courtyard. It held a small kitchen outfitted with very specific equipment – something to heat chocolate, a device to core apples, a special saucepan in which to cook asparagus. Germans are very particular about asparagus. They wait impatiently for the first appearance of the white asparagus, which marks the start of *Spargelzeit*, the harvest season between April and June. EG explained how to steam the white asparagus lightly to preserve its scallop-y texture, and then showed me her cookery book.

'This is the best asparagus recipe, my Oma's *Spargel* with bacon croutons and cream sauce. I will leave this for you. Please don't get any stains on it, but if you look after it, you can use it.'

'Yum! Looks so good! I definitely will!' I lied. It was full of recipes for apple and cream dishes that I wouldn't cook even if my life depended on it. Her cupboards were crammed with heirloom-esque items – thick-bottomed, ugly crystal things, painted plates and tureens. The rest of the room comprised a table-cum-desk pushed up against the window, a plain wardrobe and a double bed. The lampshades were made of pink polka-dot material, the general mood one of cosy frou-frou. We ate heart-shaped chocolates and drank mint tea. I told her about my philosophical interests and my German language ambitions. She suggested that upon her return from abroad, we could set up a language tandem together: she would help me with my German and I would help improve her English. I sensed that she liked me, and the next day she told me I could have the flat if I wanted.

But the flat did not belong to EG, she was only renting. It belonged instead to a Frau Marie Becker, of 42 Cicerostraße, 10707 Berlin-Lichtenberg, whom I had to meet before I was given the final blessing. I arrived flustered, five minutes late with a runny nose. Frau Becker offered me a tissue immediately and kept pressing more on me. At first glance her sitting room looked cosy and full of the markers of a happy life: surfaces cluttered with photographs of grandchildren, pencil marks on one of the doorframes marking their heights over the years. She had gone to some trouble to prepare for my visit, and had readied a lace-lined tray with a jug of apple juice and a bowl full of Kinder Eggs. But the flat was cold, the sink in the toilet was full of frothy spit-out, and when I sat at the kitchen table, I found myself absentmindedly scratching flecks of old food off the greaseproof tablecloth. She began to peel one of the Kinder Eggs and asked me where I was currently living.

'I live just around the corner from Kotti – Kottbusser Tor?'

'Ah *ja*, *ja*, I know Kotti.' She made a face. 'Not many Germans there!' She corrected herself, remembering that I was not German: 'I mean, not many Europeans, like English and German. And you came to Berlin to learn German, no?! You're not here to learn Turk! You are moving to the better Kreuzberg, the European side.'

She offered me some apple juice and poured it into a wine glass, filling it to the very top, so that I had to lower my face over the glass and suck it up to avoid spilling it. While I drank, she told me about her visit to London, and asked me about the state of various famous museums. She wrongly attributed my dishevelled appearance to a bohemian chic. She clearly thought I was some kind of artist, even going so far as to praise Bridget Riley and the op art movement, which I knew nothing about, but urged me to refrain from painting directly on to the walls, and told me where I could buy good art supplies. I could not think of how to correct her politely in German, and so responded instead with a vague smile and bewildered silence. This seemed to have been effective, because EG told me a few days later that Frau Becker had decided to accept me as a sub-tenant. I think the real reason she wanted to meet me in person was to make sure I was a 'real', white European. For all the assertions people made that Berlin is a 'diverse' and 'accepting' place, there are still shameless racists here.

EG and I celebrated my new sub-tenancy the following week, with *Sekt* (German sparkling wine) from the supermarket, and the rest of the heart-shaped chocolates which she had somehow not touched since the last time I had visited her, exhibiting the kind of self-control I've never been capable of. I found out that she had a boyfriend and was on the pill, that she loved *Harry Potter* and *The Lord of the Rings*, that her favourite person in the world was Audrey Hepburn (followed closely by Elizabeth Taylor), that she was an avid cinema-goer, and that her grandfather had been in prison for war crimes after World War Two. She asked about my own family, and I was vague, mentioning London, French parents, a big brother. I asked her about the neighbours. She knew the men directly above and below her. Her relations with them were friendly, and she claimed that they were both quiet. This was a lie, I was to discover the third night after I moved in: the man upstairs, Günter, regularly had very loud sex. He was so theatrically loud that I feared he might have been playing some kind of one-sided erotic game with me.

The man downstairs played heavy metal music most evenings, which filled my room with a low-grade malevolent buzzing. EG did not warn me of these disturbances, but she did mention a slightly awkward incident involving the downstairs neighbour.

'It was the day I moved in, and my boyfriend stayed. We were in bed and then I heard someone knock on the door. We ignored it because, well' – she broke into a rather coy smile, from which I surmised that they had been enjoying an 'intimate moment' – 'well, because it was late, but then I heard it again and I got up and asked who was at the door. A man – I don't think he was German, but I'm not sure – shouted through the door, and said he lived downstairs, and that he wanted to give me a welcome gift. Well, I shouted through the door, thank you, but it's nearly midnight, I won't open the door for a stranger at night. And then I saw him once in the staircase and I said hello, but he ignored me. I mean, maybe he was offended but he can't expect a woman to open the door to a stranger late at night. I mean, this is a good building with professional people living in it, but still. What would you have done?'

'You were right, I wouldn't have opened the door either,' I told her, but I privately judged her behaviour as very unneighbourly. I made a mental note to go and introduce myself to this neighbour, perhaps even to bring him a small gift. I wanted to make it clear that I am a much friendlier kind of person.

I moved in on the 3rd of April, which was the day the weather turned suddenly warm. I trekked several times backwards and forwards on the U-Bahn like a solitary mule, laden with supermarket bags stuffed with running socks, proud, independent and self-contained. I was glad to be rid of Ewa, whom I planned never to speak to again. I love a fresh start.

It was magic to feel my self-reliance, and these strongly muscled legs and tight bags swinging against my torso as the train rattled. What a compact adult package I had become!

As I was coming and going, I noticed that there were small brass plaques on the pavement outside EG's building. Each square was engraved with the name 'Cohen', a date of birth, a date of deportation and Auschwitz as the place of death. I looked them up on Google and found out that the plaques are memorials called *Stolpersteine*, or 'stumbling stones', and that they identify each building from which Jewish families were deported. Once I'd noticed the *Stolpersteine* outside my door, I realized they were everywhere, a seemingly random scattering of bronze squares outside bars, cinemas, run-down flats and grand old buildings. It was jarring, at first, to see Berlin's lively streets filled with so many little graves, but after a few weeks they became part of the scenery and I stopped noticing them altogether.

105 Huberstraße is the first place I have ever moved into in which I did not feel the urge to douse everything with 100 per cent alcohol. I unpacked all my clothes and hung them obediently on the hangers that EG had cleared for me, next to her dirndl Heidi-dress and her shoulderless dresses which were too small for me. I put my running shoes next to her woefully tiny Converse, and then I threw away the contents of her fridge and store cupboards. The bins were in the courtyard. I have always had a lot of anxiety around waste disposal and found it embarrassing that the bins were so exposed, making furtiveness impossible. I am convinced that not only do I consume the wrong kinds of food, but also that I dispose of my waste in quite the wrong way, too. I cannot figure out if a yoghurt pot can *really* be recycled and if the smooth soft mirror lid can go along with it – or whether it belongs somewhere else altogether. So I threw away her packets of biscuits

and pasta and a full jar of raspberry jam under the cover of darkness, and I felt purged, with the fridge and cupboards wonderfully bare.

EG had told me that her flat received a lot of natural light. I was not able to corroborate this claim until I had moved in, but she hadn't been lying. In the mornings the room was dark, but in the afternoon the sun was so powerful that the air seemed to swim. At times the flat was so flooded with light that it looked like those cells we slid under the microscope's lens in biology class – the ones that seem empty, or to contain only an inanimate smudge, until you get the focus right and suddenly you can see something moving, and you can identify the freshwater zooplankton *Daphnia magna* – its pulsating heart and quivering digestive organs terribly exposed. On sunny days all the crumbs and smears I had made would spring into unforgiving relief. Then I would feel a little guilty, and try to make the flat as clean as I had promised EG I would keep it. The problem was that I am not a gifted cleaner. It isn't that I don't notice things. I always notice that odd cluster of hair that people overlook on the back of the toilet seat, and I hate the feeling of my skin kissing the sticky surfaces made by greedy hands closing kitchen cabinets. I'm also not a phlegmatic cleaner. I am a good hooverer, and a good mopper because I actually *lift* the chairs and tables, and push furniture around, while most people make do with going respectfully around them, as if weeding around a sacred tree. The problem is that I just can't make sense of cleaning products. I'm always rubbing the windows with Pledge, scrubbing the stove with something for the toilet. This is strange, as I was a rather talented chemist at school, but somehow these various solutions and functions remain opaque and I seem to rub dirt into a chemical permanence, rather than to scour it off. The point is that with regards to the light, EG was true to her word. That first afternoon the room was graced by a spotlight of sunbeams. I lay on EG's bed until dark, full of a nervous and giddy optimism for this new chapter, the true start of my new life in Berlin. The ballerina, Ewa, the missing hoodie, all that was behind me. I slept soundly. I had no presentiment of what was to come.

2

An Enemy in the City

A T 3 A.M., I WAS woken by shattering glass. First an undiscriminating clumsy *clap*, and then a delicate tinkling of shards falling to the ground. The reverberation of the smash was inside my body as well as outside, and I knew straight away that something violent was happening. My curtains were drawn and so I could not see if my window had been broken, as I suspected. I didn't know whether the noise was directed at me personally, or whether this sort of thing often happens in Berlin apartment buildings.

This probably has nothing to do with you, I repeated to myself as adrenaline bled into my lower abdomen and started to congeal. The smokers are not scrutinizing the contents of your bins while pretending to smoke. The Austrian ballerina is not ignoring your last email because you ate some of his cooking chocolate. Ewa has not come for you on a meth-crazed killing spree. Not everything is about you, and this loud noise is none of your business. It is probably a generic disturbance. I did not move from my bed to try to get a view of the courtyard because I hoped that if I just lay there and waited, time would do its work quickly, and string together enough moments that the terror of the present would end.

I reached for my phone and googled 'how to call the police in Germany if you don't speak German'. My phone reception was poor, and I couldn't move near the window for better reception in case the smashing started again. Sweat was trickling down my ribs and my fingers were numb. The prospect of having to call the police distracted me from the fear of the incredibly loud noise. How could I explain what had happened? I knew the words for 'window' and 'accident', but not 'stone'. Could I try to speak to them in English? I started googling 'very loud explosion in the night' and discovered a series of threads about a sleep disorder called exploding head syndrome:

> If you have exploding head syndrome, you'll hear loud explosion-like noises as you're drifting off to sleep or around when you're waking up. The former is a type of hypnagogic hallucination, and the latter is a type of hypnopompic hallucination. Although they're only hallucinations, which are imagined, the noises in exploding head syndrome feel very realistic at the time they occur.

The cause of the syndrome is disputed – it is unclear if it is neurological or psychological. It is often treated with antidepressants. I have been fending off prescriptions of antidepressants for most of my adult life, because, as W. H. Auden said, 'I don't want to get rid of my demons, or my angels would fly away too.' But if I have exploding head syndrome, maybe the time has come to give them a try . . . At some point the train of these thoughts petered out into sleep – and suddenly it was morning, and everything was boring and normal again, my terror in the night as foolish as a child's nightmare. I drew the curtain, and saw that the window was indeed smashed, which refuted the exploding head syndrome hypothesis.

I still went for my scheduled run first thing that morning. I ran four 2.5km loops of the Hasenheide, a wonderful patchwork park that EG had recommended. It had an open-air cinema, a skate park, a smelly petting zoo and littered lawns, threaded together by dusty paths. It was much warmer that day. After months of frost, the air was gentle on my skin. I checked my time and distance and number of calories burnt once a minute. The Gambian dealers drank coffee from thin-skinned plastic cups and unzipped their parkas and swivelled their heads to the rhythm of my loops.

On my return I ran into the upstairs neighbour in the courtyard.

'Hi . . . I am Daphne,' I stammered, embarrassed by my childish German, and the sweat rings and the dark hairs visible between my leggings and socks.

'Günter, a pleasure to meet you. Ah, you run? Me too, this year the Berlin Marathon. So you are from America, or where?'

He was blond and handsome, but he looked a little piggish, as if someone had scrubbed him pink before sending him off from the farm to the big city. He was a close-talker, and I could smell something meaty on his breath. He was friendly, however, and when I made an excuse to leave he told me to knock on his door if I ever needed anything.

I had a shower and took my time combing a chemical-smelling conditioner through my hair. I felt light, purged of the night's drama. The 4th of April must have been on the weekend, because I did not go to German class. Instead, I let my thoughts drift on waves of social media. I never posted anything on Facebook or Instagram. I worried that my pictures or status updates would go ignored and receive no likes or comments and that I would fail at being 'visibly popular' on the internet, something I thought was beneath me to want but which I craved like everyone else. Instead, I lurked on the pages of others, mainly women, old romantic rivals from school or university whose photos I would scroll through, terrified that I would accidentally 'like' one of their pictures and they'd know that Daphne Ferber had nothing better to do. That day, I spent hours stooped chimp-like over the glowing shell of my Mac, opening and closing internet windows automatically, repeatedly boiling the kettle to top up paling dregs of Nescafé. I had by this point examined the spiderweb scar on the window, and used Google to formulate a new possible cause: 'fracturing in glass induced by sudden temperature change'. With this in mind, I composed the following email to Frau Becker:

Sehr geehrte Frau Becker,
I am the sub-tenant of EG (April–September).
Last night the outer glass layer of my rightmost window exploded. I am not sure why . . . maybe the sudden change in temperature overnight broke the glass. How should I proceed? Do you have someone you can call for repair?
Please excuse my rudimentary German!
Yours sincerely,
Daphne Ferber

She answered me the same morning, with a promise of a visit from the repairmen three days later. That same evening, students from my German class came over for a small housewarming party. Kat arrived early, and everyone else arrived very late. She wore tight black jeans and a halter top. Her hair was tied back in messy bunches, revealing an elegant neck.

She brought stick-shaped pretzels called *Salzstangen* as a housewarming gift. As soon as she came in, she went straight to the window, tracing the scar with her index finger.

'What the fuckkkkk, Daphne, *krassssss*.'*

I didn't like Kat much. I found the way she scrunched up her nose and pouted unconvincing, given her X-rated vibe. She swore often but ineffectively, so that everything she said sounded contrived. When I poured her some *Sekt* she knocked it over nearly immediately and let it dribble on to EG's parquet, unconcerned. I didn't show my irritation, dropping a dish-towel on to the puddle with feigned nonchalance. I poured her another glass, and we both drank fast, inhaling the froth before the bubbles had time to settle. Kat seemed nervous: she began to tell me something about her boyfriend, but lost her train of thought, her eyes darting between my face and the broken window as if the sight disturbed her. I did what I always do in situations I find awkward – I prostituted my soul for the social good, and told her laughingly of my night of terror, drawing out the story a little, mocking the madness of the exploding head syndrome hypothesis. I watched her as I spoke, and noticed her reactions were slightly off; she looked concerned in the moments of comedic relief, and disinterested during the story's climax, the lag between my words and her expression like an out-of-sync TV. 'But I would rather die than ask a friend for help in English,' I finished, expecting her to laugh or at least smile, but instead she sighed, and said, '*Ja*, well, I think English isn't a very friendly language, and it isn't as useful in Berlin as I'd hoped.'

---

* *Krass* is a great German colloquial expression. It is used for emphasis and it means something is *really* something; *really* good or *really* bad or *really* delicious or *really* disgusting.

The Venezuelans arrived at long last, with corn *arepas* sweating into kitchen roll, and *cuajada*, which tasted similar to mozzarella. Kat ignored the food but took a great interest in Catalina and Luis.

'So, you guys are from Cuba?' she asked in English.

'Venezuela,' they answered in unison.

'Oh, I've heard it's amazing?'

They both nodded and smiled. 'Yes,' Luis replied, 'there's some very beautiful parts of the country, really we have—'

'Did you know they don't allow advertisements there?' Kat interrupted.

'Oh yeah?' I replied. 'Really, Luis? No advertisements?'

'Well, we have some, but not as much as in Germany.'

'Uh, it's so much fucking better,' Kat said, ignoring the plate of food Catalina pushed towards her. 'Honestly, here it's just like, people pretend to be socialist or whatever, but then they go home and they buy their houses and they buy their stuff and it's so much shit coming at you all the time, and you take the U-Bahn and it's just Nike Nike Aldi Aldi blah blah Cola. You know?' She took another sip of her *Sekt*. 'Even, like, people say the healthcare system is much better there? Right? And I think, maybe I'm wrong but I think that women there are fucking crazy liberated, like Chávez was a feminist way before his time, right?'

I waited for Luis to respond, but he busied himself spreading the *cuajada* on his bread and avoided eye contact.

'I don't know anything about Chávez, but I get what you mean about ads and that kind of thing, it's over-stimulating, isn't it? All those colours and slogans . . .' I trailed off rather feebly.

The conversation continued this way for an uncomfortable quarter of an hour, with Kat's leading questions about how 'amazing' Venezuela must be going entirely unanswered by Luis and Catalina, who studiously focused on their food, and occasionally looked at each other with raised eyebrows. This was not the first time a Berliner had told them how lucky they were to come from a communist regime and how much better life in Venezuela must be. In general, I was to learn, Catalina and Luis despised anyone even vaguely left-wing. They hadn't moved to Europe to enjoy the free-love YOLO Berlin experience: they were economic immigrants, there to capitalize on Germany's higher standard of living. It was easy to forget, in a city full of squats and anarchists and anti-capitalists, that we were living in the strongest economy in Europe. The Venezuelans saw hippies, hipsters and social-ists as a bunch of ungrateful hypocrites: if they didn't like capitalism, they should move to a communist country like Venezuela and see how they liked it there. They, for their part, were grateful for every job opportunity they were given, no matter how gruelling or 'unfulfilling'. Already, they were earning enough to send money to their families in Caracas, who were struggling to survive the worsening food shortages and power outages. Catalina and Luis responded only mono-syllabically to Kat's questions, and I tried to change the subject but the Venezuelans seemed uncomfortable. The evening was saved by Katya and Chorizo turning up very late, raucously drunk.

I was revising grammar a few days later when the men came for the window, wearing neat matching blue overalls like workmen from a picture book. It was an intricate job because the window was built with three layers of glass. I mumbled something about 'mögliche Temperaturänderung?'* and the older of the pair shook his head and delicately tapped the

---

* Possible temperature change.

nucleus of the explosion. '*Stein,*' he said. '*Geworfen.*'* I tried to offer them a glass of water, but this led only to confusion, and I finally had to pour a glass from the tap and mime drinking it and point at them. They shook their heads without thanking me, and returned to their work. They were completely silent so as not to disturb me, and so I felt I ought to return to my severable verbs. I pretended to concentrate but was silently thrilled. This interaction was a confirmation that I had done the right thing in moving to Germany. Until then, I had always been very wary of IT men, driving instructors, electricians, key cutters or any category of man who has knowledge that is integral to my survival, which I will be dependent on but never possess. Such men tend to ask to use the toilet and leave the seat up. They shout and clump around in big boots. They are, all in all, very bad for feng shui. These German handymen, on the other hand, were like house elves, quietly getting on with it with a light footstep. They vacuumed and dusted and carried the shards away with them. The only time they broke the silence was at the very end, when the younger man asked me: '*Hast du einen Feind in der Stadt?*'

I misunderstood at first, and thought he had said *Freund*, meaning boyfriend, and for a moment I was happily outraged (How dare he! Am I that irresistible?) and a little disappointed that he had ruined my German Handymen Are Different theory. But I asked him to repeat himself, and finally I understood – he'd said *Feind*, meaning an enemy. No, I said, shocked. Of course not. I haven't been here long – I have only just got here – I haven't even had time to make a friend yet, let alone a *Feind*.

---

* Stone, thrown.

The question made sense, of course, given the final diagnosis of a stone-induced smashing. I lived on an inner courtyard. It was impossible to blame a drunken passer-by. Two different keys were required to access the inner courtyard, and so the stone-thrower's presence outside my window was no accident of fate. This realization left me to formulate three possible hypotheses to explain the night's events:

i. An over-enthusiastic Romeo, looking to wake his girlfriend, had mistaken my window for hers, and confused the large stone for harmless pebbles.

No such person exists in the age of Hinge, Tinder and restraining orders.

ii. A homeless person had somehow managed to follow one of my neighbours into the inner courtyard, and had smashed my window out of general malevolence rather than targeted hatred.

To someone who knows Berlin, this scenario sounds possible, as the homeless sometimes tried to infiltrate buildings in order to steal glass bottles from the bins and return them for the deposit money (Berlin had a recycling scheme that paid up to twenty-five cents for every bottle). However, this seemed far-fetched, as the homeless population in Berlin was neither violent nor threatening: they lived in a parallel world, resented by everyone for the 'eyesore' they presented, but ignored and isolated from the rest of Berlin life.

iii. One of my neighbours with access to the courtyard had done it.

This third hypothesis presented three further variations:

a. A neighbour could have done it in a fit of drunken high spirits.
b. A neighbour could have done it as a vendetta against EG.
c. A neighbour could have done it because they had (inexplicably) taken against me.

a. I discounted. The aim was too sure for somebody who'd been drinking.
b. Seemed possible, given how unneighbourly EG had previously been. She was also a criminology student, so she had probably met many disreputable characters in her line of research. Perhaps someone wanted to avenge themselves against her for having found some crucial evidence, or lost some crucial evidence. I also thought that few people would have noticed she'd moved out, and that one woman had been replaced by a slightly bigger, uglier one.
c. Seemed unlikely because I am a very good neighbour. I eat only raw food and adding milk to something is the most cooking I'll do – so I am never at the root of a shocking smell. I also never play music, and usually go to sleep by ten. Even if I wake up early, I never vacuum before a respectable time. I might be a bad friend with a penchant for ghosting, and a flaky employee, and a controlling girlfriend, but I am a good neighbour. Of this I am still certain, despite everything that happened to me in Berlin.

3

Estella

T HE WEATHER CONTINUED to tilt precipitously spring-
wards, and intrepid green spots began to emerge and
disrupt the monochrome. I still remember that first spring
in Berlin, with far more specificity than the stacks and stacks
of other springs that linger only as a hazy wash of black
manure and optimistic snowdrops. This time, I tracked each
change in nature with dogged attentiveness. This had, I am
sure, little to do with what happened next, and far more to
do with the fact that I was so unoccupied, and that the over-
dose of sterile grammar had starved my brain of organic
pleasures.

I tried not to think about the smashed window in the following weeks, but my sleep was shallow and my nights were
full of anxious, muddled dreams: in one, I ate soup full of
shards of glass and vomited blood; the next night, I dreamt I
threw a wine bottle through the ballerina's window. I began
to grind my teeth in my sleep and woke up with a painful jaw
which clicked every time I opened my mouth. But once the
novelty of the bricking story wore off, and I'd run out of
people to tell it to, I tried to forget the unpleasant events of
the first night in EG's flat. I was busy making myself at home,

and re-established my narrow routine: run, coffee, class, grammar, early to bed, never deviating. I was starting to find it boring, though it didn't occur to me to go out more, to try to make friends, or try to find work. In London I had waitressed in a coffee shop near Angel called Knights in Black Satin. It was a good coffee shop, mind, with career baristas proud of their trade, who could smell the difference between Ethiopian and Colombian beans. I loved working there and did all I could to fit in. I liked and feared my co-workers, who were tattooed and nonchalant and far cooler than me. I copied how they dressed – oversized shirts, septum piercings, beanies – and I adopted their lifestyle: working hectic shifts and then drinking in underground bars in Dalston till morning, dulling the ache in our legs with Dark and Stormies and showing up to work still buzzing from the night. I learnt to use the particular language of third-wave coffee people. I watched videos on latte art and studied caffeine-extraction curves. I lectured customers who ordered 'extra-hot lattes' about the optimum temperature for milk-protein stretchiness (65 degrees Celsius), and brewed V6os and AeroPress with the same sombre ceremony of a priest preparing sacramental wine.

But then, one night, I'd made a mistake. I had gone out drinking with one of my customers, a Norwegian guy called Stig. He was part of this notably cool group of guys and girls who lived in Islington. They wore Doc Martens and Everlast hoodies and hoop earrings and wire-rimmed glasses, cultivating a street-smart bookish aesthetic that I found irresistible. Stig was very tall, with close-shaved ash-blond hair, and dark circles under his clear, emotive eyes. I had known him by sight for a while, but we'd only spoken a few times, about trivial things. I had somehow developed an obsessive, painful crush on him. One day he asked me whether I'd like to go to a bar with him. I had too much to drink, and confessed my obsession: 'Ever since the first time I saw you, Stig, I wanted something to happen between us. I knew it would, one day.' We ended up sleeping together, and the next morning he brought me breakfast in bed. When I left for work, I was elated. Sex with Stig had given me zero physical pleasure – it had been incredibly hurried and frantic – but our night together had done wonders for my ego. I sent him a text thanking him for breakfast, and he answered straight away:

[11:35:12] Daphne: Thank you for coffee and croissant! Have a lovely day :)
[11:36:12] Stig: Hey Daphne. I actually have a girlfriend and we are coming 4 Koffee into Knights later. Please, be discreet!

I wondered how he had thought I'd behave. Did he think I would slip him a note, 'Thanks 4 frantic sex'? I spent the whole day trying very hard to be discreet, but I felt like a lumbering elephant, spilling cappuccinos, forgetting orders and sweating profusely. Stig and his girlfriend didn't show up that day, but I lived in constant fear that they would, and I imagined the humiliation of having to take their orders and fuss over them with sugar and napkins. The anxiety became too much to bear, and I quit without notice the following week. I let my boss's reproachful emails accrue in my inbox, and never spoke to anyone from Knights in Black Satin again.

Since moving to Berlin, I couldn't bring myself to try to find work. I didn't need the money. I had doting parents who sent me enough to live on each month. I'd somehow convinced them that learning German would be very good for my career as a philosopher. (I had not told them about the graduate school rejections.) From time to time I would be beset with shame about my circumstances: twenty-six and still dependent, educated expensively but fruitlessly, failing at this crucial stage to get my foot in any professional door. I thought about all the students I'd known from Oxford who'd had to work as well as study, my friends who were paying off enormous student loans, and those who were using their first salaries to contribute to their parents' expenses.

I was grateful to my own parents, who had always made my life incredibly easy, but I also blamed them for many of my failures. I thought my failure to thrive might be due to my privilege, the blanket of security which smothered my creative impulse and removed all necessity from my life. There was nothing I had to do. My co-workers at Black Satin were far more independent and well adjusted than I was, despite the fact that they were constantly teetering on the edge of financial disaster. I pretended to be in the same situation as they were, and always felt like a sham. I acted as if I cared when our boss deducted the price of broken cups from our wages, or failed to pay us on time. But it made no difference to me. I didn't really need the money.

But these self-indulgent, my-privilege-is-a-burden kinds of thoughts would recede soon enough, especially since no one I knew in Berlin, apart from the Venezuelans, seemed to be doing any work either. Kat didn't work. Katya waitressed at an espresso bar, but only for ten hours a week. All the students on my language course were either 'freelancing', receiving unemployment benefits, or doing the same as me, covertly living off their parents while remaining vague about the source of their income. This idleness was a city-wide phenomenon and was part of the strange, disorienting social fabric of Berlin. Weekends and weekdays had much the same texture, as the streets were always full of people with no place to be and nothing much to do. People did not discuss their work, or lack thereof, as both the rich and the poor were scared of being exposed. If anyone did ask what I was doing, I'd lie and say I was au-pairing for a French family, or on a funded PhD programme researching Schopenhauer's influence on the early Wittgenstein. This usually shut down any further questions.

The only major change in my routine that spring was that I stopped taking the U-Bahn and began to ride the bicycle that EG had encouraged me to use. It was far too small for me, and when I draped myself on to it, I looked like a crumpled daddy-long-legs. Nevertheless, I began to ride through the Hasenheide park to German class, and the branches above me looked like clenched fists slackening into the weather, the leaf buds unfurling to dapple the light. The Gambians had abandoned the sheltered bushes which now pulsed thickly with the electric chirp of sparrows. The men got in my way, tried to catch my attention, but I answered their gentle incitation – 'You all right, my friend? You need anything?' – with the detached, benevolent smile of the Buddha. The hill between Hermannplatz and Boddinstraße was too steep for me, so I would nonchalantly wheel the bike up the hill with one hand while pressing my phone against my cheek with the other, and pretend to be engrossed in conversation by uttering vaguely Germanic-sounding noises. Then, I'd lock up the bike outside the language school and wipe the smudge of beige foundation and sweat off the screen. I always sat in the same spot, between Russian Katya and the teacher. I always brought a big thermos of Nescafé with me, and Katya and I would share it, wordlessly pouring cups for one another, negotiating with our eyes, *no, no, you finish it, last one is for you*.

Yet all this gives a terrible impression. I was not *quite* so bereft of company. Although, properly speaking, that early spring was a solitary performance, men inevitably drifted into the orbit of my life. This is not because I am a beauty – although I do have nice ankles and an expensive colourist – but because I am such a brilliant bullshitter that I can blow air into the holiest of egos. I don't do this because I *want* these kinds of men around me – I mainly like to be left alone – but because my soul is very nimble when it comes to conjuring enthusiasm for mediocrity. I think, all things considered, that this is one of my best qualities.

The point is, there were men around, and one of them was called Callum, a Glaswegian whom I'd met one day at Karma Rösterei. Callum was perfect, physically speaking. He was tall, and heavy-set enough to make me feel feminine, but he was nothing like those iron-pumping men who look like genetically modified cattle. He had geometric tattoos on his biceps and long golden-blond hair. He cared for his muscles and eyebrows and clothes, but he still somehow looked nonchalant and very masculine.

Let these statements hang as an overarching and justificatory foil to all the horrid things I am about to say about him. I don't like rhetorical questions, so I will just *state* that it is a mystery to me why the knowledge that someone who I do not like is attracted to me turns me into Estella from *Great Expectations*:

Estella: 'Am I pretty?'

Pip: 'Yes, I think you are very pretty.'

Estella: 'Am I insulting?'

Pip: 'Not so much so as you were last time.'

Estella: 'Not so much so?'

Pip: 'No.'

She fired when she asked the last question, and she slapped my face with such force as she had, when I answered it.

'Now,' said she. 'You little coarse monster, what do you think of me now?'

It's also rather ironic that in these situations, Estella's character emerges in me, because to be frank, in my heart of hearts I am *overwhelmingly* Pip. I am always wretched and pining and romantic and heartbroken. I still hanker after my university love, Sebastián, a beautiful, beautiful boy from Colombia. Even after three and a half years of silence from him, and my emails going mostly unanswered, and a very emphatic one in which he wrote:

Daphne – thank you for your email and I apologize for taking so long to reply. It isn't that I don't care about you – I do, but to be completely honest, when I think of our time together, it's as if I were trying to remember a bad dream. I don't understand the person I was during that time, and our whole relationship is associated with so many things I wish I could just forget. I imagine you feel something similar.* I wish you well, but I think it would be best if we didn't communicate any more.

---

* (No, I did not feel the same way at all, but of course I wrote, 'Yes, yes, I feel just the same!')

But sometimes I am Estella. I am relieved that I have the capacity for such edge and cruelty. It isn't that I think I am too good, but I do worry that I am weak.

Callum came over one day, around the same time the white asparagus started to appear in supermarkets. I was glad to see him, because he was British and we could speak without my having to rehearse what to say before opening my mouth. It was nice to take a break from German. My German class had a pact never to break out of the language together, and though the Venezuelans broke the rules with me, my Spanish can only muster the colours and names of fruits and simple sentences like, 'I don't love him now, but I do miss him.'

Even though I was not interested in Callum romantically, I instinctively did what I do when 'Boys' come over. I put on make-up, but not too much. A key part of my charm rested on giving the illusion I was a 'natural beauty'. I pretended I was one of those 'relaxed' girls who didn't care about her looks. But secretly there was little I cared about more. I was embarrassed by my enormous hoard of cosmetics. My concealer, the colour of dead skin cells, had leaked into my toiletry bag, which I kept in such a dirty, crusty state that it probably contained florid colonies of acne. I hid it under the bed, and tidied, but not too much. I left things out to make it seem as if the boy in question was only an afterthought, as I had a *very full life*.

I filled the kettle because Callum did not drink, which theoretically I do not mind, or at least pretend not to mind, because what kind of a person would mind about a person not drinking. But in fact I do mind, it actually really bothers me, because I doubt people who don't drink really know *how to enjoy things*. Of course, I can't be sure of this, nor can I assert that I know how to enjoy things either. But someone who feels out of control around alcohol may not be the best at managing their own pleasures, and that leaves me very unconvinced that they will allow me to enjoy pleasure myself, let alone give it to me.

He arrived and asked for a caffeine-free tea and we spoke about books. He had not read *The Secret History* or *The Bell Jar* and I noticed that his nails were crescent-shaped and full of milk spots. At one point, he picked up my copy of *The Magic Mountain*, flapped it in my face, and ejaculated loudly that his greatest fear was 'not being able to produce one of *these*!' He told me in great detail about the plot of his first novel. It was an original idea about a group of pregnant women protesting against climate change by live-streaming late-stage abortions, told from the point of view of the would-be fathers. He spoke about different possible endings, and then at great length about his other writing and aspirations. He might be a good writer one of these days, he might even produce something *Fight Club-* or *American Psycho*-esque, and garner much admiration from male critics. But whatever bright literary future awaited him did not compensate for his complete lack of curiosity in me. Not that I complained. On the inside I was Estella, full of seething disdain, but on the outside I just smiled demurely and egged him on: 'It sounds great! So then what happens?'

He stayed over because it was very late, and he lived far away. At 2 a.m. we changed into pyjamas – I lent him a pair I'd stolen from the ballerina's – and chastely brushed our teeth. This reassured me that we were on the same platonic page, because personal hygiene is not, to my mind, a prelude to something erotic. We got into bed and lay side by side under the covers and I didn't feel a thing. Well, I actually had a terrible, terrible stomach ache from eating so many raw carrots and celeriac with mustard and sriracha before he arrived, and of course couldn't really get comfortable because he was there. He asked me about the faint throbs of music coming from downstairs and I told him it was just the neighbour, and that I barely noticed it any more. My stomach hurt and I felt I might be sick, and I was too hot, but my skin felt icy. I was so unpleasantly, inescapably present.

I could feel every particle in the space between us tingling expectantly, but it didn't feel right and delicious in the way it can when you want something to happen, that precise *sharpness* of magnets clicking or scissors nipping. At one point he put his arm across my shoulder and I could not bear how time inched on. I hadn't drawn the curtains, and I kept looking at the window, half expecting it to shatter. We both lay there in complete silence, pretending to sleep, and I really was amazed by the depths I had sunk to again, lying in bed in spring in Berlin with a boy who I did not like, unable to sleep, and not saying a single honest thing.

Morning finally showed up, and I didn't wake so much as gradually realize I didn't have to pretend to be asleep any longer. Callum was awake too, and I asked him a question I already knew the answer to, whether he had slept well, and he lied and said he had. I prepared coffee on the stove with Ethiopian beans that smelt of buttered toast. I've always enjoyed how the Bialetti sputters and spits, and I like myself when I prepare coffee. It is such an unmistakably normal thing to do. Callum stirred the dense liquid and said very little while I washed up and crumbled the disc of coffee grounds in my hands. I had a shower – the tension of the night had given me a rather peculiar smell. I watched the soapy scummy water rise up my ankles, quite aware that Callum had not begun to dress next door. It was only seven, and my German class didn't start until nine, but I hurried him and pretended that I had to leave. He walked towards the U-Bahn, and I walked in the opposite direction and ducked into a doorway around the corner. Only after I was sure he was gone did I hurry home, feeling like a survivor, running past a man in the staircase who I correctly assumed must be the downstairs neighbour, he of the heavy metal music. His flat was on the ground floor and his windows faced the courtyard. I had never seen him before, as he had draped blue and grey towels over his windows, and never seemed to move them. He did not respond when I said *Guten Morgen*, but stared unseeingly back at me. I hurried up the stairs and hated Callum for interfering with my morning routine. I smeared foundation under my eyes and on the spots near my hairline and left for class.

But this was only one night, of course, and spring pressed on and things got a little more expansive. I learnt to leave glass bottles in the street for the homeless to collect instead of throwing them in the bottle bins. In mid-April I skipped a level in German – I jumped from A1.1 to A2.1 – and left Russian Katya and Venezuelan Catalina and Luis behind. Kat came with me – her German was even better than mine – but apart from her all the students were new. We spent the first hour doing *kennenlernen* exercises: *Ich bin Daphne, ich bin sechsundzwanzig Jahre alt, meine Eltern sind Franzosen und ich habe einen Bruder. Ich bin in London geboren und aufgewachsen. Ich habe Philosophie in Oxford studiert.** We started on the genitive case and learnt how to use the letter S to string together words to make elephantine compound nouns, my favourite being *Gewissensbisse*, bites of conscience. A few weeks later, one of my new classmates, Gabriel, invited Kat and me to a party.

---

* I am Daphne and I am twenty-six years old. My parents are French and I have one brother. I was born and grew up in London. I studied philosophy at Oxford.

Gabriel I liked very much. He wore big, lovely Patagonia jumpers and had the complexion of a young fawn, light-blue eyes and olive skin and soft curls of the same colour but threaded with gold. He had been a pilot in the Israeli air force, and in the hordes of self-hating angsty people I know, he was refreshingly sure and fond of himself. He was studying to become a filmmaker. At the party he went from cluster to cluster of guests to make sure that everyone was sufficiently fed and watered, as benevolent and generous as a bumblebee. He offered me flatbread and hummus, which he told me had been made by his girlfriend, Nina. (I know, I was disappointed too.)

Apart from Gabriel, the party was charmless, full of too many cool people too cool to eat his homemade hummus, and the neighbour's huge stinking dog running around, stuffing his snout into everyone's crotch.

Kat arrived late. It was hard to look at her and hard not to. She was exquisite and captivating in a way I will never be. I am fine-looking, attractive to some, but I don't have that kind of arresting beauty. She wore her hair loose, and it looked lighter, as if she'd washed it for the first time in weeks. It was the exact shade of blonde that my hair colourist tries to synthesize in me. She wore a black T-shirt as a mini-dress. She was bare-legged, with black studded boots and skilfully made-up eyes. She walked over to the drinks table and began mixing herself a complicated-looking cocktail. I felt everyone noticing her – slight pauses in conversation, surreptitious glances over shoulders – but she seemed unaware of the effect she had, or was so used to it that it barely stoked her pride. I went over to pour myself another drink, and she looked relieved to see me: 'Good, Daphne, thank fuck, I don't know any of these people. How are you? Did you eat something? Stay near me, please?' I led her over to Gabriel's group, but she barely greeted him, and the others – a group of French guys – studiously ignored her. They were just the kind of men who take great pains to ignore beautiful women. They knew they didn't stand a chance with her, and pretended they weren't interested, focusing their energies instead on more attainable girls like me.

'Where are you from?' one of them asked.

'My parents are from France, but I grew up in London.'

'Oh, so you speak French?'

'No,' I lied. Kat looked at me curiously – she knew I spoke French. But she didn't contradict me. I didn't repay her show of complicity, however, as shortly after that I left while she was in the toilet. I hadn't enjoyed my first Berlin house party.

On the way back from Gabriel's flat I walked past the Tempelhofer Feld for the first time. Tempelhof used to be an airport: its curved terminal building was designed by Hitler's favourite architect, Albert Speer, but ten years ago the air traffic was moved southward to Schönefeld, and gardeners and skaters and runners have reclaimed it. That evening was warm, and so the park was full of groups of friends lighting early-spring barbecues and couples twisted in blankets. I felt full of a kind of illicit hope, witnessing such human-scale pleasures taking place on a site designed for Machines and Industry and War. The Tempelhofer Feld still looks like an airport; the runways are intact, with obsolete signs warning of the perils of approaching aircraft. The line of the horizon is unbroken by trees. I rested my bike on the ground and took out my phone. I watched the sun drop down in slow motion. The windows of the terminal building flared, as if on fire, the guiding lights of the runways flicking on as the light faded. I took a picture, and set it as my screensaver, replacing the one of Pringle, the kitten I'd adopted in London.

*

I biked home and got into bed, but I couldn't sleep. I was hungry. I had nothing that I really liked to eat in the fridge, and the cupboards were intentionally bare, because Day Daphne knows that Night Daphne's resolve is weak. Occasionally, Day Daphne would throw off her shackles, and I would have a kind of midnight feast. That night I ate a rectangle of this strange thick protein-rich yoghurt the Germans have, called quark, with stevia and dusty carrots, and I slept a few hours.

The next morning, I woke early and ran across the Hasenheide park but barely noticed it or my Gambian watchmen, heading for the grander pleasures of my new discovery, the Tempelhofer Feld. I had it all to myself. The sky loomed low and close, a lovely dense proton blue above me, weakening to white along the horizon. I ran loops around the circumference and then down the central runway. On the western part of the circuit, the air smelt of brioche, apricot jam and coffee which, I later learnt, came from the Leibniz biscuit factory outside the park.

4

Richard Grausam

WHAT I WROTE IN the previous chapter is not completely true. The bits about Callum, the party and the midnight feast are true, but I omitted the most important part of the evening. On the way home from Gabriel's, I bumped into Richard Grausam, who was walking home alone from the Tempelhofer Feld. I've wanted to obliterate a most shame-inducing character from my narrative. But if I can't be honest in writing, when will I ever *really* be honest?

A few days after I started my new class, Gabriel invited me to attend a 'philosophy workshop' being held at his girlfriend Nina's yoga studio. I was dubious about both the crowd – philosophers, fishy maniacs – and the venue, but I went along. Richard Grausam was the leader of the seminar. He was attractive, I suppose, to some women closer to his own age, which I imagined to be around forty years old, even though he looked, in retrospect, much older. He split us into groups, and assigned us different philosophical themes to discuss. Mine and Gabriel's was about social media and 'the self'. Gabriel was too shy to talk in front of the group, and so I dredged up some mumbo-jumbo concepts from my degree course, and discussed Heidegger's essay on *The Question*

Concerning Technology. The others in the seminar – mainly white men with septum piercings, dreadlocked hair and baggy trousers – were not particularly taken by my presentation, but the seminar leader was, and he gave me his card so that I might send him the Heidegger essay in full.

I titled the email 'Our Automated Souls' (which is poetic, not flirtatious) and he replied immediately, telling me how '*tense*' my email had made him feel, and could we meet so that I could share my knowledge of the philosophy of technology with him, please. I cannot remember our exchange and I can't present any of his emails as evidence, because I deleted them from my inbox, blotting him out from my digital biography. So, I'll have to rely on memory alone. This part of the story won't be drawn out. There will be no sketching of his face or prolonged description of the kind of food he ate, nor will I relay the line of conversation. I do remember that I sincerely thought he wanted to speak about philosophy, and so I spent a few hours reviewing my notes on Heidegger's *The Question Concerning Technology* to make sure I could really be helpful. But despite his professed interest in my brain he never, ever asked me a single question about myself nor about my take on Heidegger's critique. And I gave ear to his monologues with unfeigned enthusiasm and genuine engagement. Where had the Estella in me gone?

The best thing about him was his enthusiasm for the spring, and his introducing me to two things that I love dearly: Hans Fallada and *saure Zwiebeln* – a kind of pickled onion. The worst thing about him was absolutely everything else. Despite our age gap he never spent a cent on me, and he even refused to give the glass bottles to the homeless, taking them to the collection centre himself and pocketing the twenty-five cents to spend on the chilli cheeseburgers from the Burgermeister near Kotti, with extra onion, *bitte*. He was a substitute yoga teacher. He was a conspiracy theorist and eschewed WhatsApp, as he was terribly paranoid about privacy. (It is chiefly men who are narcissistically worried about this issue, who layer masking tape over the lens of their webcam – as if these men are of any interest to anyone.) When he found out I went to Oxford, he was frightened and started asking me about Secret Societies, and Freemasonry, and when I joked that I was a high-ranking lodge member, he showed the lack of humour that is the hallmark of even the best German men I know – he took me very seriously and looked quite unnerved. He thought, as many intellectual men do, that ceaselessly pointing out everything that is bad in the world was enough to make him good.

Nevertheless. I kissed him, and spent several hours in his company, a passive floor-to-ceiling Woolfian mirror.* His kisses were horrible. I have dreamt of them since. His jaw clicked with tension. He seemed to want to suck my soul and youth through my mouth. But, you see, he *was* very, very good at German – being completely German – and he had once been a semi-professional handball player, and he came from Leipzig – the birthplace of my favourite philosopher, Gottfried Leibniz – and all this somehow worked together to impress me.

My dislike of him very quickly outgrew my loneliness. I told him I did not want to see him any more but he kept *insisting* that I had misunderstood him, and that we should talk about it more next time we met, because I owed him more of an explanation – say, tomorrow? At first, I could not understand what was going on, nor why my *I'm sorry* and *no*s and my *stop* and eventually my desperate *please, please leave*

---

* Virginia Woolf, in *A Room of One's Own*, writes: 'Women have served all these centuries as looking glasses possessing the magic and delicious power of reflecting the figure of man at twice its natural size.'

me alone were so ineffective. And then when I realized he *was* actually pretty clever, because he used words in a careful manner which always gave the *impression* that he was answering me, but he was in fact ignoring my lines, and reading from his own much-rehearsed script which came from a story in which he always, *always* gets what he wants, I started to be really frightened, and told him, 'This is beginning to scare me, please respect my right not to see you any more, please stop all further contact with me,' to which he responded, 'What is wrong with you, what drugs have you taken? Don't you think you owe me more of an explanation, shall we meet tomorrow to discuss it?' At first I kept answering, trying to put my foot down ever more firmly, to no effect at all. After a month of back and forth, my profound unease started to turn to livid fear, and one hot afternoon I sat in a cell of light in my sunlit flat and I turned to my trusted Google and looked up 'what counts as harassment', 'how to get someone to leave you alone for ever', and discovered a book called *Stalkers: A Survivor's Guide* by Santiago Álvarez. In the first chapter, he writes:

> *Every day, every time you meet someone new, you are called upon to make decisions — can you really trust this employer, employee, teacher, taxi driver, friend, lover? However much you might hope that this question will fall to the police, the doorman, your boss — the decision and responsibility to keep yourself safe is no one's but yours. No one else has access to the only power which can truly protect you from violence, and which can tell you who deserves your trust: your intuition.*

My intuition about Richard Grausam was, and in fact still is, that he contained the potential of real violence beneath a very thin surface of left-wing eco-post-proto-righteousness. I pressed on with Santiago Álvarez's text, and recognized Grausam in the list of 'the biggest tell-tale signs that a man is dangerous': won't take no for an answer (check), no close personal friends (check), denies your reality or claims that you are delusional (check), narcissistic (check), controlling (check).

In Chapter 2, Álvarez advises that the best way to deal with stalkers is to ignore them. Despite the urge to do something dramatic in response to threats and harassment, it is best not to respond.

I stopped reading the deluge of emails and texts he continued to send. For the next few months, he would call me at least four times a week, once tricking me into answering on a private number. I was tempted to answer his messages, I fantasized about revenge and cold cruelty I have never been capable of. I even drafted the perfect revenge email, which included nothing except for the name of a prominent Berlin law firm, a screenshot of all his insane emails and messages as a PDF attachment, and the line *if you don't leave me alone, I will sue you*. This email still lies in my draft folder, ready. I continued to follow Álvarez's advice. I still do not answer unknown numbers to this day, and he continues occasionally to send me emails, which I delete from my spam folder so that I will never be tempted to read them for a kick of adrenaline. On the night of Gabriel's party, I biked away from him as fast as I could. He was on foot, and tried to run alongside me to keep up. He looked ridiculous, running in his jeans and leather jacket, but I was frightened, not quite sure what he was capable of. He was surprisingly fast, but I soon left him behind. I heard him shout 'I miss you!' in a sad, broken voice, and then his footsteps dropped away. I left the Tempelhofer Feld behind and crossed the Hasenheide park, unable to breathe. I got off the bike, and sat on a bench next to the smiliest Gambian dealer. I grasped my chest, checking that my heart was still beating. I felt dizzy, freezing in the fading sunlight, my fingers were numb, and I was terrified my heart might stop. 'Everything good, my friend?' he asked. Does he know CPR? I wondered.

5

New Friends and Old Loves

I T WAS AROUND THE start of May that I began to make real friends. I started seeing Gabriel every few days, and the barista from Karma Rösterei – a redhead with spider tattoos on his knuckles – finally learnt my name. I discovered a running group on Meetup.com, and rose early one Saturday to meet at the Grunewald, from where 50,000 Jews were deported to extermination camps. The only other runners were two men. This is just the kind of scenario I often hear about on crime podcasts and think, well, that could never happen to me. I would never arrange to meet up with two adult men I had met on a forum in a secluded forest in a foreign country.

But as soon as I arrived, I realized they weren't a threat at all. Ollie was tall and in his early forties, and had an Essex accent, so instead of name he said *nayyyyme*. All of his features were mismatched, but his smile and beady blue eyes pulled the whole lot together. He hunched his shoulders and turned his left leg inwards when he ran, and he wore heavy-looking shoes because of his flat feet. He ran very fast all the same. Evan was from Arizona, with dark-brown velvety hair and eyes. His body did not appear to move as he ran, his feet hardly lifting off the ground, as effortless as a coasting frigate. I can't remember what I told them about me. I've now lost track of what lies I'd told about how I was earning my living in Berlin. The variations on the au-pair job and philosophy PhD stories all got so confusing that in the end I referred obliquely to 'my work' whenever anyone asked. We didn't speak much anyway, as the path was sandy and sloped and we had to fight for breath.

I rode the S-Bahn until the Jannowitzbrücke station, and then switched to the U-Bahn, which is effectively a transition from Heaven to Hell. The S-Bahn is overground and heated in the winter. The seats are arranged into small compartments, an anachronism in which one might conceivably have a *Strangers on a Train*-type encounter. The U-Bahn is underground and more reminiscent of the atmosphere of *Midnight Express*, poorly lit, with plastic patterned seats. It is full of heroin addicts with swollen hands who pace up and down the rattling corridors on the catwalk of the doomed.

I was passing Der Kaninchenbau, an infamous twenty-four-hour bar a few minutes from home, when I saw Sebastián, my boyfriend from university. At first, I was sure it must just be some kind of mirage. I've had countless false sightings of him in all kinds of unlikely places. But then, rather than dissipating as I drew closer, the likeness grew sharper and sharper until the blurriness resolved itself, and he was five metres away and it was plainly him. Disordered brown hair, strong Roman nose, broad forehead. And a beard!* He was walking towards me, talking to a girl wheeling a bike. She spoke loudly, and though I couldn't make out

---

* Sebastián had wanted to grow one when we were at university, but at the time he could produce nothing more than a thin curtain of wispy hairs.

what she was saying, I was gratified to hear that they were speaking English. He clearly wasn't integrated in Berlin life, if he had a foreign girlfriend. I don't recall what she looked like, but if she had been particularly beautiful, I would have remembered. I called his name, reflexively, without thinking. He didn't hear me, and my survival instinct kicked in. I sidestepped into Der Kaninchenbau and they passed without even glancing in my direction.

Inside the bar, everyone was smoking cigarettes, sweating and grinding their teeth. The bartender was a woman with a dark veil of foundation and mackerel-blue eyes. She pointed to my running shoes approvingly. 'So healthy!' I sipped my tea and searched for Sebastián on Facebook. We weren't friends, but his privacy settings were lax, so I could see that yes, he was living in Berlin. Well, this wasn't a surprise. He was a hipster, he spoke German, and he'd told me several times that he wanted to move to Berlin when we graduated. I'd expected to run into him, perhaps even hoped I would.

Before logging out again, I scrolled through his timeline. He was in the first year of a PhD in Economics at the Freie Universität of Berlin. I saw him in the Tempelhofer Feld, at the Brandenburg Gate, and I saw lots of pictures of him with an American girl called Emilia. I saw a picture of them together, in Medellín. I'd been desperate to go but he had never asked me. She was uglier than I am. I'm not even gratified by this. It's just a fact.

I considered sending him a message, of course. It did feel like too incredible a coincidence to ignore. I worried that, by ducking into the bar, I'd sidestepped my destiny in a way fate would find displeasing. But even if I did contact him, he would probably not answer, since he wasn't exactly enthusiastic about keeping in touch with me. He had ignored the reply I had sent to his last email. He'd probably think I'd followed him to Berlin, and would delete my message just as I deleted Richard Grausam's.

Or he might actually answer, and we might meet again. He would be cordial and I would be crushed, and somehow this whole story would become all about him. He is actually not at all important; his character certainly does not warrant the attention I have given him until now. I was the more interesting one in the relationship. Cleverer, too. When we were together, I wasn't that keen on him. I lied to him all the time. I found him weak and easy to dominate. I developed a much greater attachment to the scar that formed around our break-up than to his actual person. There is nothing awful about him – he was kind – but he just wasn't *that* great, and if I've made him sound like something special until now, then all the credit ought to go to the writing. Certainly not to him. Though I do wish him and the American girl nothing but the best.

Back in the flat, I decided it was time to clean, and I began to empty and rearrange the drawers I'd stuffed with old receipts from the supermarket and grammar sheets. I pulled out EG's stack of diaries. The writing was cramped but legible. I had tried to read them within the first week, but my German hadn't been good enough. Now I could understand most of it. I'd hoped to discover something dark about her – wicked sexual proclivities, accounts of stalking an ex-boyfriend, or at the very least a confession of lies or deceit – but the diaries contained nothing but long boring lists of her weekly expenses, and ideas for self-improvement: 'Nothing sweet after 4 p.m.!' and 'Moisturize every day!'

Later that afternoon I biked to the Tempelhofer Feld and lay on the grass with *The Magic Mountain*. It had been Sebastián's favourite book. He'd told me over and over again that I just had to read it, that it was just my kind of thing, but I was on page 15 of 1,200 and it was so boring that I wished I'd brought the German grammar. My tyre was flat, and I couldn't summon the wherewithal to have it repaired. The day had turned soupy, grey, hot and irritating. I read twenty-five pages, and then checked my phone. No Facebook messages, no WhatsApps.

I checked my spam and saw an email from an unknown sender:

> Daphne . . . let me know how you are?! And where . . . you were in my dream yesterday, and in my meditation. Shall we go to a yoga class together? Please . . .?
> Miss you . . .

It was from Richard Grausam. Just when I thought my store of adrenaline must be out, my body managed to pump another good round of it into my abdomen. God, was he watching me at that very moment? Was I overreacting? Was I paranoid?

I read his message again. I could hear it in his voice. The ellipses reminded me of the way he spoke in open-ended sentences. He had sounded ironic whenever he spoke English, as if the entire language was a big, trashy American joke. He had sent the message forty seconds ago. He was nowhere near me but still, he was snapping his fingers in my face, frightening me and commanding my attention. How could I ever have listened to him and acted so interested in him?

Yet again, I followed the advice given by Santiago Álvarez, which is to say I did nothing. I deleted his message without answering it and put my phone away as if nothing had happened.

I looked out towards the west of the field. The wind had picked up and heavy grey clouds were amassing in the far distance. I heard someone call my name, and recognized Kat. Her hair looked unkempt and greasy, and she was wearing a low-cut top with faded jeans, and a pair of dirty red Converse. She looked fantastic.

'Heyyyy Daphne, whatssup!'

'Hey! How are you?'

'I'm OK!'

'Did you enjoy the party at Gabriel's?'

'No, not really after you left, I didn't really talk to anyone.'

I felt guilty remembering how I'd sneaked out while she was in the toilet, and I stammered an apology, which she interrupted to ask me if I wanted to go over to her house.

I wondered how I could make my excuses, *a meeting, a dinner, an essay due tomorrow*, but Kat knew I had nothing to do – I had told her that I occasionally babysat, but she knew it wasn't a proper job, and she didn't have one either. And though I didn't like her much, I needed company, so I found myself saying yes, and following her out of the Tempelhofer Feld.

I knew that she lived with her drug-dealer boyfriend and I probably only went with her because I was curious about him. I wasn't interested in being her friend at all. We wheeled our bikes down a dirt path so narrow that we couldn't fit side by side. She spoke very quickly and expletively over her shoulder. I couldn't hear much, and I wasn't concentrating. I was trying to keep track of where we were going, memorizing a sequence of landmarks – an Aldi supermarket, a mattress with POST-ANAL spray-painted on to it – because my phone was soon going to run out of battery, and she was leading me into uncharted South Neukölln territory and I was worried I'd lose my way home once it got dark.

We stopped at a *Späti*, because Kat wanted to buy salt sticks. *Spätis*, or *Spätkauf*, which translates literally as 'late-shop', are one of my favourite things about Berlin. They are something between a New York bodega and a Parisian *épi-cerie*. In Berlin, the *Spätis* are mostly run by Turkish men, and they are one of the reasons I found them so great, because first-generation Turks often speak pretty simple German, so I could always understand them, and they tended to understand me as we shared the same linguistic struggles. They were far friendlier than the gum-chewing ex-Stasi agents who work in German supermarkets and who looked at me with scorn and incomprehension if I mispronounced anything.

This particular *Späti* on the way to Kat's would become a significant place to me, one where I would live moments of pure terror. It was run by an Armenian man who was originally from eastern Turkey. He was aided by two beautiful teenage daughters who dressed like toddlers, with plaited hair and frilly white dresses. They ignored Kat and me as we went in to buy her salt sticks, and she told me what an incredible relief it was to speak to someone who really understood and thought like her, which was absurd considering I hadn't heard a word she'd said. Her flat was in an ordinary, nondescript building. The *Hausmeister* was mopping the entrance; the staircase was sparkling clean and thick with the smell of his grapefruit-scented cleaning product.*

Kat's flat was on the ground floor, and not nearly so clean as the entrance. It was composed of a sitting room with cracked black faux-leather furniture, an overly bright kitchen, and a narrow bedroom with a single, unmade bed on the floor. It looked indecent, like something Tracey Emin

---

* The *Hausmeister* is another Berlin feature. They are similar to a New York super, or the French concierge, though often (but not always) friendlier. In EG's apartment building, Frau Becker took on the *Hausmeister* duties herself. I'd seen her a few times in the courtyard, flopping around ineffectually in an apron and yellow rubber gloves.

could photograph and make a fortune from. Here and there, I could see some wholehearted attempts to create a functional adult household: a well-stocked spice shelf, cheerful brass trays, a few carefully framed prints, and a blackboard to keep track of what was running out. Yet these hopeful gestures were eclipsed by great patches of neglect: bare light bulbs, stacks of bowls used as ashtrays, old bongs sloshing with fetid water. Kat offered to make me tea. She pulled out a Tupperware full of *kunafa*, those stringy bird's-nest pastries which look better than they taste. They were squashed to a pulp of syrup and pistachios.

'I love the Arab foods with all the nuts,' she said, which seemed hard to believe, because she was so incredibly thin. 'The Arabs are really generous with the nuts, they're not Jews about it at all!' Her casual, throwaway anti-Semitism was bewildering, but familiar. Kat reminded me of a group of students I'd met while I was at Oxford, who thought that vague anti-Semitism and 'saying it like it is' when it came to 'the Jews' was somehow avant-garde and chic.

She pinched up some more pastry threads and explained that she had met her boyfriend, a Swede named Lars, when she had bought drugs off him in a bar in Stockholm. They had moved to Berlin a year ago. They went clubbing together, and had a rotating diet of MDMA, cocaine and ketamine, but she was sick of this, and of the kind of phoney people she met in the Berlin underworld. Lars was possessive of her, but she felt that she could never abandon him after everything they had been through, but we couldn't talk about it then, she added, because he would be home soon. She was trying to finish her master's thesis in Art History about Fascist architecture, but it was impossible for her to get any work done around Lars and his friends. She wanted to hang out with other kinds of people, *real* people, like me.

'Please eat,' she said. 'Don't tell me you're on a diet. Eat before the boys come home because they won't leave you any.'

I accepted a small plate of pastry. I told her that I, too, was sick of the party scene (a lie, I've still never been to a club in Berlin), that I was lonely too (true), and that I was tired of the superficiality of all my relationships. I told her how the predominant state of my early twenties was loneliness, how it all often felt like a fake life, how I couldn't escape the feeling that my real, *good* life was happening somewhere else, and how frightened I was that I might never find out where, and that I'd miss the whole thing loitering off stage. I told her about the Venezuelans and Russian Katya and Gabriel, but how they really didn't know anything about me at all, and how they didn't have much time for me, but she interrupted:

'Well, don't bother with Gabriel. The Jews are mean with their time, aren't they, they don't make good friends.'

Lars came home then. He was tall and very broad-shouldered. We hugged rather carefully, because he had injured the middle finger of his right hand and swaddled it in a huge white bandage. He asked if I wanted coffee, and he ground it and made it with an *ibriq* on the stove. He seemed unhealthy, but he wasn't unattractive. In fact, he was charismatic, and looked like he was capable of some truly wicked fun. I was very aware of his smell; I noticed it as he leant in to hug me. I sat downwind from him and kept inhaling it as he doctored the coffee. He sat very close to me and my forearm kept brushing against his. I said *no, thanks* to sugar and to more nest-pastry and to salt sticks and to the blunt he rolled, but *YES* to the double vodka with Red Bull, which was lukewarm and anaesthetizing. Just what I needed.

I don't do well on weed at all. The last time I'd smoked was the week before my graduation, in May two years earlier. I had visited a great friend of mine, a good-natured Bostonian who we all called Google Greg. He was something of a maths genius, and had already published his work in a few academic journals, and attributed most of his breakthroughs to his copious inhalation of Alaskan Thunderfuck. He made me smell the enormous IKEA baggie of weed, and began to explain his final-year dissertation thesis as we passed the vaporizer back and forth. Something to do with programming language and language mathematics. I remember nodding emphatically, as if I understood. At one stage he demonstrated some point by asking:

'What does a cow drink? Answer quick!'

'Milk!'

'What do you put in a toaster?'

'Toast!'

'Bread and water. See the way that humans assimilate language . . .'

I was completely astounded by this and wondered if it meant I had lost my mind. He seemed to be speaking at a manically high pitch, and I excused myself and fumbled down the corridor to the bathroom. I stared at myself in the mirror. My face was normal, but my heart beat incredibly fast. My armpits were soaked. I went back to his room, acting as if everything was normal, and he resumed his explanation. After a little while I was so seized by panic that I suddenly stood up, and said I had to leave immediately – *Thing with a graduate student, it's been in my calendar for ages, sorry sorry, I just remembered!* I made it across the street and into my apartment. The touch screen of my phone seemed strange, and my hands were so numb and trembling that I could barely type. Who can I call, I thought. Definitely not Sebastián. He'd broken up with me by then. I can't remember the reason he gave – he did his best to invent some

explanation that wouldn't hurt me – but I knew the real reason was that I'd been a terrible girlfriend and lied to him
constantly. I called my mother, who was asleep, and told her,
'I'm having a bad high,' and she told me to toast some bread
and drink a glass of milk, that it would be fine, these things
happen to everyone. I kept pacing and pinching my skin to
make sure I was physically still there, checking the time
obsessively. A few hours later, I felt better, but I vowed never
to smoke weed again.

I finished my drink quickly, downed a second one, and
poured myself a third. Kat left to go and buy more drinks
and I found myself alone with Lars. He pressed his legs
against mine. I pretended not to notice, and began to tell
him all about the bricking story. He stared at me very
intensely, and I avoided his gaze. I wanted to turn to him and
kiss him, but I was scared of Kat. She soon returned, came to
sit next to me and offered me a drink, and I found myself
putting my arm around her, overcompensating for my evil
intentions.

'So, little K? How are you doing?' I slurred.

'Ermmm, very good, very good, are you OK?'

'Yes, I'm great! I'm great. Want to do a shot with me?'

'No, thanks!'

'Come on!'

'No, sorry.' She shrugged my arm off her, and I did a shot
of vodka, my face burning. I felt embarrassed, overly effusive
and drunk. She looked bored, and began to pick at her hands,
pulling at the skin around her nails which was already pink
and raw.

'Something crazy happened to me today!'

I told the story of running into Sebastián as I always told
stories – embroidering, exaggerating – 'And then, I had to

jump into this shitty bar, and have a drink to steady my nerves. We broke up ages ago, but I always had this feeling that he would re-emerge in my life somehow. I can't explain it really, but I always felt there was something unresolved between us, some kind of unfinished business, you know?' She nodded. 'I had no idea he was in Berlin,' I lied, 'but yeah, now I'm not sure, maybe I should reach out to him, I mean it's quite weird to just pretend I never saw him. What do you think I should do?'

'Message him, for sure!'

'You think so?'

'I mean, it makes sense. You're in a new city, you don't have any friends here, you might as well write to him. Worst-case scenario he doesn't answer, right?'

'Or he replies with something horrible . . .'

'Yeah well, if he does then you know that he isn't worth caring about after all.'

'OK, OK, you're right. How about this: Hey, Seb, how are you? I'm living in Berlin now, and I think I might have spotted you in Kreuzberg? Let me know if it was you. Hope all is good with you.'

I found his profile, pressed on the message icon and sent it. By then the haze of skunk had grown so dense that it was stinging my eyes. Kat was saying something, and I managed to answer her, but I kept thinking about Sebastián. My heart was thudding, my breath quick and shallow. I took another shot of vodka to try to calm down. Steady the nerves. Steady the nerves. Lars came over with more drink. It tasted like dish detergent. I took another sip and realized I was going to be sick. I got up, still smiling, my teeth clamped together. I managed to make my way out of the front door before vomiting in the hallway, all over the floor the *Hausmeister* had cleaned only a few hours earlier. I got out of the main front door and was sick again. I stayed there, bent over for several minutes, retching, waves of nausea and then relief. I'm purging the past, I told myself. I wiped my mouth with the back of my hand, and went into the *Späti*, where I bought a cellophane-wrapped bag of sugar-coated nuts, a giant bag of skinny popcorn, M&Ms, a bottle of Diet Coke, and a family-sized jar of Nutella. The *Späti* man bagged everything for me, and I balanced the two rustling orange plastic bags on my bike handles as I made my way back through the dark, following the way from the *Späti*, past the POST-ANAL mattress, over the bridge and towards Aldi and home.

In the flat, I kicked off my shoes and unpacked my snacks. Standing at the kitchen counter, I ate the nuts first, licking off the sugar and then crunching the cashews, almonds, rather soggy pecans. The popcorn packet popped open with a belch of that sickly-sweet cinema breath, and I ate it in handfuls between spoonfuls of Nutella and gulps of Diet Coke. My curtains were open. I wondered how visible I was, and whether anyone would know what I was doing. I felt as if I was watching myself from the courtyard, staring up at the bright box of my window, clear as an illuminated cell. I saw myself there, as naked as a *Daphnia magna* under the microscope, reduced to a feeding thing, all trembling intestine and fluttering heart. Soothed and mortified all at once, mechanically chewing without tasting anything at all. Pack to mouth, jar to mouth. I mixed the blue and yellow M&Ms in a cup with an entire pot of quark, and added big spoonfuls of stevia, making a sweet impromptu granola. I wished I could do something to pull her out of it – anything – reach up and tap on the window, throw a stone, startle her. Sit down and eat like a normal person. Make yourself a real meal. Block Sebastián before he can answer.

I checked my phone. No answer. I scrolled through Facebook. I saw a picture of Katya and Catalina, presumably taken by Luis. They'd all gone out together without inviting me. I threw away the Nutella jar, the packets, cleaned the counter. I fell into bed, my mouth still full of chocolate. My sticky hands stained the sheets. I waited for sleep, but the wave of exhaustion was receding. I wondered whether Kat, Lars and I would be friends. I found it strange that Kat hadn't texted me, as I'd left without saying goodbye. But she was used to me giving her the slip.

The neighbour above me, Günter, was having his weekly loud sex session, and the weirdo downstairs was playing his terrible music again. Günter's girlfriend was obviously faking her orgasm. No one screams all the air out of their lungs like that. But then again, I've only had pretty average sex, and maybe Günter was a formidable lover. I found it almost funny at first, but after twenty or so minutes I began to feel seriously annoyed. Sandwiched between two men, passive as always, helplessly subject to their oral secretions. I *have* to do something, I thought, my poor German be damned. I got out of bed, slipped on my running shoes and paused on the landing. Upstairs or downstairs? Although Günter was friendlier, I couldn't face interrupting him *in flagrante delicto*, and I worried that he'd realize I'd been able to hear him having sex for months and suspect that I'd been deriving some creepy voyeuristic pleasure from him. So I decided to ask the guy downstairs to turn down his music.

His front door was closed, and I knocked once and waited a good minute, but no one answered. I knew he was home; I could hear him in there, opening kitchen cabinets and banging pots and pans around. I knocked again, a little less meekly, and I sensed him standing still to listen. I stood back a little, expecting him to open up, but after another pause it became clear he wasn't going to. We both waited on either side of the door, and I could feel his attention as he listened for my presence. I was about to knock again, but something stopped me. I just suddenly had a feeling that whatever was going on in the mind of the person on the other side of the door wasn't something good. I backed slowly away, shuffling my feet so as to muffle my footsteps. He still didn't return to his dishes. I could hear him breathing. I started to feel quite frightened and began to back up the staircase, careful to keep quiet, still facing his door. I double-locked the door behind me, and I tried to listen for some sign of life from downstairs, but Günter was still going strong upstairs, so I couldn't hear a thing. After the malevolence I'd sensed through the door, I was actually grateful to hear Günter upstairs, glad that some-one with so much lively endurance was awake only a stone's throw away if ever I should need help. I checked my phone again – still no answer from Sebastián – then got into bed.

6

Men

I WOKE TO A room swimming with heat. I had a dry mouth and a tight jaw. I checked my phone and saw Sebastián's answer:

> Hi. I don't think it is a good idea that we meet up. I am with someone here in Berlin so please don't contact me any more.

The impact of these words hit me with the smart of a slap. I deleted the message and blocked his account before he could block me. I thought I might be sick again, but I went running anyway, vindictively going for even longer than usual, doubling back on myself, running up and down dead-end paths so as to hit exactly 18km on my distance tracker. An ineffective attempt at absolution. I wondered why Kat had encouraged me to write to him. I sensed some malice in her. Perhaps she was taking revenge for abandoning her at the party. Or perhaps she'd sensed that there was something between me and Lars. I'd certainly got her back by vomiting all over the apartment building entrance.

From time to time, my despair overwhelmed me and I'd come to a full stop. I hadn't drunk anything since the previous night, and my throat was still sore from being sick. I picked at my shorts and pinched my thighs. It was at least twenty-nine degrees, and my T-shirt chafed my skin, leaving a strange pattern of marks on my chest that looked like a piecrust pricked with a fork. I thought about all I'd eaten. So ashamed, I wanted to cry out, or bang my head against a lamppost. I imagined Sebastián's reaction. A thrilling moment of ego boost – perhaps a text to a friend, 'guess who messaged me again?' – followed by irritation, and then the pleasure of the rebuff: 'please don't contact me any more'.

Running back towards the flat, I was filled with a terrible sense of dread. I pictured letting myself into the courtyard, staring up at my flat and seeing a broken window again. Or perhaps someone hiding in the flat. The downstairs neighbour. Or, even worse, Richard Grausam. My fear of him was so visceral that the thought of him made me want to run and hide like a hunted animal. It was inconceivable to me that I had ever been in a room alone with him. But it was true, I had, and from time to time I would remember things. Holding his hand. Kissing his neck. Sharing a beer (which I'd paid for). These flashbacks – which would come to me out of nowhere – were far more disturbing than his harassing calls or emails.

I was too tired to finish my run, and walked the last few kilometres home. I unlocked the door and was surprised by the chaos in the flat. I couldn't remember having left it in such an awful state, with stacks of washing-up on the counter. The bedsheets were on the floor, and food wrappers were strewn around. I piled my sweaty clothes and those stained with vomit and/or Nutella into the washing machine, and stood at the sink for a long time, scrubbing the leathery tannic stains out of EG's mugs, using hot water and a load of noxious-looking neon-pink dish-soap, which I inhaled deep into my lungs as if I were in a hammam. I gawped vacuously out of the window on to the courtyard below. Even if I do nothing but continue this minimal existence, I thought, time will keep moving past me. Even if I remain as immobile as a paperweight, time will still stack up the days and pin the receipts of all of them to me until I find myself with a thick wad of them in my forties, and a hefty pile in my sixties. I'm sure they'll tot up to something that feels weighty and satisfying, and that I'll feel rich at the end – no matter how impoverished my days actually were, I thought, as I dried the dishes.

I needed distraction. I took the U-Bahn to the cinema and saw two films, one after the other. The first was awful, a French comedy, which the Germans found hilarious but which was not in fact *at all* funny. Or perhaps it was – I just couldn't concentrate on the film. I was caught up in what Germans call a *Kopfkino*, which literally translates as 'head cinema' but which means a daydream or day nightmare which loops over and over in your mind: the night Sebastián made you try *aguardiente*, the pride with which you introduced him to your family, the day he broke up with you when he caught you out in a lie – these clichéd moments that you ought to be immune to but which have held you captive for two years, eight months and a few days – but who's counting?

The second film was *Call Me By Your Name*, and seeing it renewed my resolve to put Sebastián out of my mind and make the best of my time in Berlin. Something about the routines of a middle-class family – attention paid to food, proper three-course meals and clean sheets – all this civility worked on me like those tanks of oxygen administered to the gravest tubercular cases in *The Magic Mountain*. After months of gasping the befouled breath of my solipsistic bubble, I remembered that there are some great lofty things in this world: decorum, pathos, fate, honour, love. Somewhere along the way, I'd lost sight of this fact. I'd fallen into worrying whether the supermarket stocked my favourite sweetener, if Rewe or Aldi was cheaper, if it was important to buy organic, whether or not identity politics is actually a good thing or if I just feel compelled to *think* it is because I want to be considered a good person, whether all my personal failures can legitimately be blamed on parenting and patriarchy or if this is just the coward's way out.

At some point, the stakes of my life had sunk appallingly low: I lived and died by the length of the line at the supermarket and hairs in my sandwich and the volume of my downstairs neighbour's music. I had constructed the rudiments of a mollusc-y, bottom-feeder kind of existence – one in which words like decorum, pathos, fate, honour, love could have no purchase at all.

Yet, as I rode the U-Bahn home, elation swelled in my chest and forced my face into a smile. I still might have that kind of life. True, it hadn't seemed so promising of late, but I had had a good start. I'd grown up around exquisite people of great taste and impeccable moral fibre – the frumpiness of my dress and mind, the terrible raw food and the interminable lying was probably just a phase. The seeds of greater things were latent in me somewhere, just waiting to bloom.

Yes, there is hope for me still, I thought, as I unlocked the outside door and then the door to the inner courtyard, and made my way up the stairs. I can't carry on living on a diet of grammar and early nights and platonic friendships. I'm young, and I've blossomed as much as I ever will. I should enjoy it while I still can. I'd been going about Berlin all wrong, I thought, as I put the kettle to boil. Only I would be so perverse as to have turned this city into a sanatorium. I spent every evening on Reddit and Google's barren land-scapes, or stalking people I no longer spoke to on Facebook. Long before midnight, I shrouded myself in EG's lily-white sheets, while all around me, people were going out, lighting cigarettes for one another in the night and pairing off to sleep together just as I was waking up alone.

I made myself a decaf instant coffee with milk and stevia. I was inspired. I hadn't had much luck with friends – none of the ones I really liked were quite as lonely as me. Russian Katya had Chorizo, Venezuelan Catalina had Luis, Gabriel had Nina, and Ollie and Evan from the running meet-up had partners. The ones who *were* lonely – Callum and Kat – were as useful to me as a pair of drowning sailors. All these relationships did not come close to fulfilling my fantasy of a trusty band of German friends. The next best thing to a big conniving plotty gang of bosom buddies, to my mind, is romantic love. I'd been single for almost three years.

I couldn't allow my Sebastián obsession to fester any longer. What if I ran into him again? What if I ran into him and the American? Then he'd have officially won. We'd been compet-ing since the day we broke up. It wasn't a publicly acknow-ledged, openly recognized contest at all, but still, we both knew it was happening. If you don't marry your first love, you will be stuck in a lifelong, distant arm-wrestle with him, car-ried out in that nebulous place between your mind and your social media account. You might not think of it consciously, but believe me: every success will feel sweeter because it will be a small revenge. Every time you get a promotion, a great haircut, a memorable orgasm, you will think of him and feel a special, satisfying, vindictive happiness. Of course, forget-ting about him would be the ultimate revenge, but social media and the internet make that impossible. Even if you have it under control now, in a few years you'll give in to the itch to look him up on Google.* The competition ends only when you are both dead. Sebastián was winning the contest so far: a PhD in Economics in Berlin (8 points), a girlfriend (5 points), nice beard (2 points), horrible answers to my messages (5 points). I needed to up the ante if I was going to catch up. A tall, Germanic man would be ideal. One who adored me and wanted to pamper me at his chalet in Bavaria.

Tinder, however, proved too radical a leap. I found it very intrusive; the moment I downloaded the app the room suddenly throbbed with suitors. I deleted it after a few frightened swipes, and signed up for a MatchTime A-list account, for 9.99 euros per month. I also preferred it because it seemed more computer-y than phone-y, and communicating with someone through a laptop while sitting at a desk seemed less promiscuous than doing so while lying in bed, swiping on a sleek tactile phone.

The profiles of potential matches are fanned out across the screen in a semi-circle like a set of cards. The page of the person currently under consideration is in the centre. It sort of works like one of those big rotating conveyor belts in sushi restaurants, where the dishes are prepared in advance, and you just snatch whatever catches your eye on its way around.

One man called Henrik, 28, living in Schöneberg, had the following profile:

Basics
Straight, Man, Single, 178cm, Fit
Speaks
German, English, some French, some Danish, Attended University, Atheist (but it's not important), Doesn't smoke,

---

* This is NOT STALKING. It is run-of-the-mill NORMAL EMOTIONAL DETECTIVE WORK!

Drinks sometimes, Doesn't do drugs, Vegetarian, Doesn't
have kids, Scorpio

I could probably beat you at:
Bench press

I value:
Curiosity

I spend a lot of time thinking about:
Thinking

When I die, I will:
Probably stop painting

What I'm actually looking for:
Big butts & ghostly thin wrists.

I admit that was a *particularly* terrible one. But I didn't
cherry-pick – I just logged back into MatchTime to refresh
my memory of what it looked like, and Henrik of the big
butts & ghostly thin wrists was just the first profile I happened upon. The very next profile to come up belonged to
Farouk, 27, of Prenzlauer Berg, 180cm, 'A little extra' build.
Other ethnicity, speaks German, Arabic and some English,
Dropped out of University, Smokes sometimes, Drinks
sometimes, Does drugs sometimes.

Self-summary:
If you are racist, fuck off 🖕
I'm so against racism, sexism and homophobia
Love wins 🖤

My golden rule:
Sweet is often fake!

A movie I've watched over and over and over again:
Classics only!

Not for the faint of heart. At the start I was very dutiful and went through profiles slowly, carefully giving each boy his due, reading all about his favourite films and following the links he posted to YouTube videos and memes. Another reason I was slow was that I worried that, in a sleight of hand, I'd accidentally click past the perfect person. Once you've clicked the big red cross, the discarded profiles disappear for ever (unless you have the 14.99 euros a month subscription). After a few hours, however, I became rather skilled at judging whether or not I should pause on a profile. I became a kind of expert, a kind of MatchTime anthropologist, if you will. In fact, I began to classify the men into various categories. The eight most common varieties are:

1. **Readers of *The Little Prince***
    Big egos, shallow intellects. This type is easily recognized by the extensively filled-out 'cultural' section. These men are keen for you to know all about what films they've been watching (lots of film noir and *Twin Peaks*) and which books they've been reading. You won't find anything much longer than 250 pages on their list – just lots of short novels for clever boys. Charles Bukowski and Milan Kundera feature prominently; Murakami is pretty typical; maybe Hesse (*Siddhartha*), something by Chuck Palahniuk (*Fight Club* or *Invisible Monsters*), some Bret Easton Ellis (*American Psycho*) and always,

always, for some reason that I can't fathom, *The Little Prince* by Antoine de Saint-Exupéry. I suppose it *is* 'French', the shortest book which brushes upon themes of alienation and loneliness. They say things like, 'My thoughts on life lie somewhere between Dostoevsky and Chernyshevsky, Nietzsche and Marx,' and 'I'm filthier than Bukowski!' These guys enjoy 'deep talks', they worry about 'authenticity' and claim to hate social media – they are using MatchTime 'ironically' or for 'experimental' purposes: 'I'm not really into dating apps, but I guess I'd give it a try,' or 'Just gonna see if this works cos dating sucks, but I prefer to talk IRL.' They also like to explain things; for example, James, 31, a Straight, Fit, Monogamous man, helpfully discloses that 'contrary to popular belief, coffee or techno are not lifestyles. I would appreciate if you had more going for you in your life.' They hate truly beautiful women, and this secret rage creeps in via rejection of 'fake girl bullshit', apparent in such comments as 'no superficial stuff, no selfies, no I don't want to follow your butt on Instagram'.

2. **Men with Sisters**
Men of this category do not have quite the same intellectual aspirations of *The Little Prince* guys, as they don't necessarily want to be *cultured*, but they do want to be seen to be very *emotionally intelligent*. They often have sisters, and they'll keep mentioning that they have sisters, and if they don't have a sister, they'll have a female best friend, one they 'really literally grew up with, she tells me everything, you know?' Their profile pictures will be full of

women, sometimes with babies and children too, and they have a tendency to curate their reading list to include at least one female author (bell hooks features prominently). They're like those people who think that having a Black friend means they aren't racist – they think that being *related* to women lends legitimacy to the claim they respect women. They'll keep tampons in their bathroom. They think this makes them saints.

3. **'Allies', 'Anti-Fas'**

They call themselves 'anti-fas'. They apply the prefix 'post' and the verb 'decolonize' to the most unlikely collection of nouns: Facebook; Europe; the Collective Conscience; Dating; the Homeless; Psychology; Books. They are very like the Men with Sisters, in that they think political commitment insulates them from being chauvinistic and imbues them with an aura of irresistible piety. For a good example of this sub-type, consider Jonas, 28, 181cm, Average build. His profile consists of the following:

Self-summary:
I'm currently focused on projects supporting post-capitalist and justice-led ways of working and living. We need to decolonize the internet and our minds and learn to think post-structurally.

I spend a lot of time thinking about:
What unalienated/decommodified labour might look like.

You should message me if:
You love to talk about anti-fascism, feminism, post-capitalism, just write me.

<u>I value:</u>
Sarcasm, critical thought & anti-capitalism.

4. Conspiracy Theorists

Richard Grausam, the stalker's category. They like Julian Assange and think the allegations of rape against him are part of a US-led 'honey trap' conspiracy. They, like *The Little Prince* sub-type, are pedagogically inclined, in the vein of 'you don't have to be a vegan/Greenpeace addict but *be aware* about the environment and that the consumer society is a form of implicit manipulation, feeling the urge to buy something at Black Friday, Cyber Monday, Christmas, birthdays, anniversaries, Easter, all this contributes . . . please don't do it'.

5. Men Who Overtly Dislike Women

The title of this category is self-explanatory. Take Tobias, 33, Straight, Man, Single, 184cm. He displays many of its characteristic features:

<u>Self-summary:</u>
i don't care for randomness. i value my time, and i will value yours. spending time chatting about nothing just for the sake of it is not my idea of existence. i don't play games. if you don't have a picture that shows your body, i won't message you.
i am very open in what i want, and who i do it with and don't want it with.
i'm self-employed and work mostly in live music . . . the rest of the time i'm happy to fill on my own, because i like myself. and you should, too, because otherwise we won't get along.

when people don't know me, they think i'm the most egotistic. when they know me, they think i'm the least egotistic. i think both is true.

if i texted you, then it's not because i need another lay, but because i want to.

if your thin in your pictures & fat in real life then bye bye.

I value:

women who actually think for themselves and might think of challenging gender dynamics and messaging first for once.

6. GI Joes

Americans with big arms, straight noses and steely eyes. The GI Joe is a good old-fashioned MAN in your conservative grandma's understanding of the term. They don't ask you to 'hang out' or 'chill' in an ambiguously worded invitation that might be platonic, might be romantic, or might be purely sexual; they ask if they can take you out for a date. They won't let you split the bill, and they'll walk you home if they don't have a car to drive you (GI Joes are not too worried about the environment). Of course they can drive – that goes without saying. They are good at all sports. They watch ESPN and scream at the TV. They make corny jokes. They eat a lot of meat and Cheez-Its and drink Bud Light and vanilla-flavoured cola.

7. Clever, Cultured Boys

The main differences between these guys and *The Little Prince* readers are: a) they won't mention *The Little Prince* and b) their profile will be a lot shorter. They don't shy away from using 'cute' emojis and don't deny their taste for consumer culture. They like sunshine and brunch and football and The Strokes. They're clever but they do not, unlike *The Little Prince* readers, sublimate their sexuality with intellect. They've tended to have some success with women, so they're not quite so cross as some of the other sub-types.

8. Lovely, *Wonderful* Men

These probably constitute 25 per cent of the men on MatchTime – there are simply loads of them, and they more than make up for all the rest. They tend to be very bashful, they find it difficult to talk about themselves, insisting that they are just 'normal' and 'friendly'. They often admit to having asked their friends to help fill out their profile, and these friends describe them as 'loyal, positive, slightly nerdy, supportive'. The 'first thing people notice' about them is that they are 'always smiling', or 'introverted but kind'. They have a tendency to list their faults as well as their qualities, determined not to oversell themselves. Although they aren't pushy, they're not pushovers either – they have broad shoulders and successful careers and interesting jobs, in things like humanitarian aid or engineering. They like to cook: 'all kinds of things! But especially savoury dishes, quiche and risotto. And *Kartoffelkloesse*, a delicious kind of potato dumpling.' They are modest but passionate about their interests, open to vegetarianism but not militant about it. They're good guys, they smile fully in their profile pictures, gazing straight into the camera, not striking an ironic pose, or pretending to be captivated by something outside the frame. They are the only sub-type of men who fully commit to the MatchTime experience. They don't pretend it is a game; they are brave enough to admit to having high hopes of meeting someone. I'm very tempted to copy and paste a few of their profiles to prove just how wonderful they are – I won't, out of respect for their privacy – but take my word for it, they are lovely. Discovering hordes of such men did much to raise my spirits, and just the knowledge that they were out there was worth a million times more than 9.99 euros per month.

Of course, the above categorization is by no means exhaustive, and plenty of men straddle several genera at once. It should be noted, too, that the category a man belongs to in the incubator of MatchTime does not always reflect his personality in the wild, although it often does. Most of the men who liked me were categories one (*The Little Prince* readers) and four (the Conspiracy Theorists), which made some sense, because I think I mentioned studying philosophy and maybe even name-dropped Murakami. I got a decent amount of attention from category sixes (the GI Joes). Most of them were out of my league, and would have had their pick of the crop in another city. But many women in Berlin are feminists and cannot handle the contradictory feelings these hypermasculine men produce, and so competition for category six is low.

The men I liked tended to belong to categories one (*The Little Prince* readers) and seven (the Clever, Cultured Boys). I tended not to go for category eight, the Lovely, *Wonderful*

Men. No, not because 'girls like bad boys', but because I know myself too well – when I go on dates, I disconnect from how I am feeling, surrender my sovereignty, pass the reins of my free will to my suitor. I become a mirror, the Woolfian mirror I mentioned before, and often an even worse kind, the Harry Potter Mirror of Erised: some primal reptilian part of my brain somehow discerns what my date wants from me, and who they want me to be, and I completely shift shape to mirror what it is they most desire. If they want someone stupid, I'm stupid and I ask them what it actually *means* to be an engineer. If they want a French girl, I start to talk fondly about the Left Bank and my grandmother's flat near the Sorbonne. If I intuit that they are a closet Conservative (and all Conservatives in Berlin have to be closeted), then I start to complain about the trash, and how awful all these people are for just feeding off the great German state, and if they are Communists (although I really try to avoid these), then I start picking at loose threads in my sleeves in a discontented manner, and tell them I am considering moving to a commune in Pankow, so overwhelming is my concern not to contribute to the gentrification of Kreuzberg. The craziest thing I do is to actually contort myself physically. I'm not sure if I've mentioned it, but I am freakishly tall, and if a guy is too close to my height, then I hunch over or hold a tiny squat for the whole evening, which is pretty exhausting. This does not tend to happen too often, however, because I will never go on a date with a man who doesn't include his height on his profile and I say no to anyone shorter than 178cm. I don't like hulking over a potential lover.

This might make me sound cunningly manipulative and controlling. If I am then it is despite much purer intentions. I like people to feel comfortable and accepted for who they are. It is true that sometimes I can channel Estella and become haughty and cruel, but all in all I don't like displeasing people. I don't want to shatter a German man's lifelong fantasy about French women. I don't want to emasculate a man by towering over him. Sometimes I feel protective of literally everyone.

So this is why I would never knowingly go on a date with a category eight man. Because what I haven't said about my desire to please is that it is not sustainable either. I can protect and please for an evening, perhaps a few months. But it is simply not possible to hold a squat for my whole life. And when I begin to stand a little taller, to admit that I actually hate Paris and never eat croissants, the problems start. Friends begin to feel thwarted, men feel disappointed. I've sold myself on false promises and they all start crawling back, receipt in hand. I start feeling solipsistic, misunderstood by those who claim to love me. I punish them ruthlessly for being so willingly fooled by my facade. There is always a breaking point, usually someone calling me out on an inconsistency – 'But I thought you loved France? Wait, but didn't you say you were doing your PhD already?' Usually I know when this is coming. I am practised in reading the signs by now and I tend to just pick up and leave before friends or boyfriends properly understand what happened.

Of course, I could just come clean. No, I got rejected from graduate school, I was ashamed to admit it; and no, I'm not actually a vegan, I just really wanted you to think I am a good person – but I'm not different from anyone else. I'm weak, and my need to be liked is stronger than my liking for the truth. And so category eights are off-bounds, as are category eight friends, because disappointing lovely, wonderful people is something I've done before. I swore I would break this habit in my new life in Berlin.

7

Perfect Pitch

THE DAY AFTER I downloaded MatchTime was a Monday at the end of June, and the start of a new module in my German. We were starting the B2.2 level, where we would learn 'to interact with a degree of fluency and spontaneity that makes regular interaction with native speakers quite possible without strain for either party'. There were a few familiar faces that day – Kat, who was picking at the skin around her nails with the aggression of a vulture tearing into a carcass, and Gabriel (the paradigmatic category eight) but also the Venezuelans and Russian Katya who had been promoted a level to our class. There was only one new student, a girl called Leila. She was handsome, with black hair and exquisite dark-brown eyes. She seemed to want to talk to me at the end of class, but I had to hurry off. I was scared Kat was going to say something about my vomiting all over the entrance to her apartment. I also had a waxing appointment I had booked to prepare my body for my MatchTime dates. On the way I thought I saw Sebastián again, this time on an Uber Eats bike, and I began to worry that the Richard Grausam stalking was turning me into a medical-grade paranoiac. I didn't dwell on the sighting, I just put it down to pre-waxing nerves.

I hate going to the waxing salon. Paying women from Turkey or the Maghreb to deal with the grotesque flaps of my soft white body makes me feel like a colonial oppressor. Even worse, it makes me feel like I'm oppressing myself. I lighten my hair, I repress my hunger, I smear beige chemicals all over my face – isn't paying forty euros a month to remove the velveteen down gracing my form just a step too far? No, I thought, as I pushed open the door to Waxing Dreams, in my case, it isn't. As I've mentioned before, I'm very tall, and I have very broad shoulders and rather large hands. My femininity is already tenuous, and certainly not established enough for me to get away with being hairy. I'm a feminist, sure, but I want to be attractive.

I was quickly shown to an impeccable booth and told to undress. Şengül was my wax artist, and she could sense my unease when she told me that I needed to take my underwear off, too.

'We're all women!' she said. 'We all look the same down there. It's just like the bones, you know, under the skeleton. Spread your legs, *mein Schatz.** Hold the skin tight. No, more like this. Who made this mark on your chest? Not a man? You're very thin, did someone break your heart? No? Homesick? I don't miss Turkey at all. Gaziantep. You know it? Near the border. Too hot! Terrible! But very good food, much better than here. You know gözleme? Baklava? If you go there you will get more fat. Ha! Maybe it's better we stay here! Ha! Turn over now, *mein Schatz*, bend your leg like this.'

On my way out, I ran into Venezuelan Catalina, who was tying her bike up just outside Waxing Dreams.

'*Hallo!*' she exclaimed. 'What are you doing here?'

---

* *Schatz*, or *Schatzi*, means 'treasure' or 'darling' in German.

'I was just visiting a friend,' I said. 'What are you up to?'

'Come with me, I'm having coffee with Katya, please come!'

I followed her into Markthalle IX, a beautiful, nineteenth-century covered market just around the corner. Russian Katya's boyfriend sold bread at the Italian bakery there, and Katya had recently started working at the espresso truck just opposite. I think she found that job mainly to keep an eye on him, because she was extremely possessive. It seemed to me that he was doing all he could to encourage her jealousy – kneading dough in a needlessly sensual manner and offering up samples of focaccia to the lithe German girls who crowded around him, placing the slivers between their lips like a priest administering the sacrament. Venezuelan Catalina bought a mozzarella and pesto sandwich, and kept offering me bites. Russian Katya made me a double espresso and sat down for her lunch.

'Look at her – see the one with dark hair? With the blue skirt? If she tries something with him, I know he'll finish with me.' She took a bite of her sandwich. Pesto, mozzarella and tomato. The sight of it made me faint with hunger. 'He's always just waiting for the next upgrade. You know, last week I saw he was on Tinder. It broke my heart, it hurt so much. And he lied to me, told me he bought it to explain how it works to a friend.'

'It's free,' I corrected her.

'What?' she said, her mouth full of bread.

'Tinder. It's free.'

'Ah, OK. But look at her, I think maybe she's too beautiful for my boyfriend. But I don't know, for a one-night stand, maybe she'd do it.'

'Listen, Katya, *you're* much too beautiful for him. And if he wants her, just let her have him. They probably deserve each other. You can't go out with someone who makes you feel so insecure. You're young, you've got everything ahead of you.'

Both women nodded in agreement with my platitudes, the kind of thing my female friends always regurgitate to each other when we're together. Chorizo was a sleazy scumbag, not worth her time – but I knew that she'd go home and order some expensive underwear online, or go for a full Brazilian wax at Waxing Dreams, anything to hang on to him. All I was doing was telling her how she ought to react and now she would feel a double failure: failure for not being able to hang on to a mediocre man, and failure for not having the appropriate independent liberated woman response to this loss.

I got home and passed the downstairs neighbour in the courtyard. He was leaning up against the wall and smoking, facing towards my window. We ignored each other without acknowledging our silent, fervent, through-the-door tango. I put the kettle on and logged into MatchTime. I'd left my window open and the flat was full of the neighbour's smoke. I lit some incense and began to scroll.

I had two new messages. The first was from Hans, 26, Straight, Man, Single, 180cm. Living in Friedrichshain. His pictures were pretty nice – one of him at a lake, one with a group of friends at the Tempelhofer Feld and one of him holding a picture of himself using a mirror to take a selfie. I liked his clothes, hipster but with clean lines. He had black hair, pale skin and a few old acne scars which made him less handsome and much more likeable. His profile was very on point, very category seven, Clever and Cultured:

Self-summary:
An artist of motions, notions and emotions.

<u>I like to make:</u>
Cookies and cakes, especially before Christmas. Stollen, for example. And *Pickert*, which is a kind of Westphalian pancake.

<u>What I'm doing with my life:</u>
Don't get philosophical on me, you!

<u>My partner should be:</u>
Alive and ideally not imaginary.

<u>I spend a lot of time thinking about:</u>
How I can stop overthinking everything.

<u>The most private thing I'm willing to admit:</u>
I'm on MatchTime.

We texted back and forth a little and set up a meeting for Friday night. The other message was from a guy called Milosh, 26, Straight, Man, Single, 180cm, whose profile was also the epitome of a category seven:

Born in Poland, raised in Freiburg. Study the Birds, Bees, and History 📖, DJ. Deutsch, Polish, English & a bit of French.
Ich liebe Hummus!*

The first picture was a close-up of his profile, with a snowy park stretching out in the background. He was wearing a black beanie with big strands of dark-brown hair swept across his eyes.

The next picture must have been taken during the summer – he was wearing round John Lennon sunglasses, and he was staring into the camera, his hair long with a messy

---

*   I love hummus.

parting and a heart-shaped face. The third picture was a little less promising – he wore one of those snapback skater caps that I consider a hallmark of idiocy and the same sort of wife-beater shirt that Kat's boyfriend, Lars, had worn. His message, which I've translated from German, read:

Hey Daphne, how you doing? That cocktail in the picture looks delicious 😊 Do you also like to drink wines? Red or white?

I drafted a few answers, checking that my German was correct using Google Translate, typing into the textbox without sending them, to see how they looked on the page.

Hi Milosh! Yes, only Deutscher Riesling these days!

Hmmmm, but he probably doesn't know what Riesling is, which will be embarrassing, or else he will, but my liking of it will make him think I'm pretentious, and that I'm a high-maintenance kind of girl who will expect him to pay for things. I liked the exclamation marks, though – they conveyed the breathlessly enthusiastic vibe I was trying to project. Maybe something more:

Hello Milosh!
White in this weather!

But then I thought that sounded as if I was screaming. Without exclamation marks?

Hello Milosh.
White in this weather.

No, absolutely terrible, that looked like a haiku. A smiley was in order.

> Hello Milosh 🙂
> White in this weather!

Or:

> Hello Milosh!
> White in this weather 🙂

In the end I went for:

> Hello Milosh 🙂
> white in this weather 😊!

The lightness of tone obviously worked, because Milosh suggested a date on Saturday, the day after the date I had planned with Hans. It would be the first busy, social weekend I'd had since moving to Berlin.

People always say that the most important moments usually glide by unremarked upon, as invisible as fish in a flowing stream. You don't notice them at the time, they say, you're too busy going with it. But I don't find this to be true. I always know when the day I am living will come to tower high above the others in the landscape of my past, and whether someone I have just met will play a starring role. This probably says something about me – I've never been very good at 'going with it'. I don't think I ever fully immerse myself in anything. My body is in the stream, true, but I've always got my head a little above the water. I'm always looking down at myself, watching how my legs thrash about, and how the fish and weeds flow all around me.

The point is, when I woke on the 24th of June, I knew the forty-eight hours ahead would be the kind I would pause at when parsing the heavy tome of my past. In the future, I'd have my monkish illuminators decorate these pages with either gold-leafed angels, or lots of those terrifying devils they liked to draw in medieval manuscripts. I just wasn't sure which it would be yet.

I went for my run in the Tempelhofer Feld as usual. The windows of Albert Speer's airport terminal caught the colour of the sun, which had not yet fully risen. When I arrived it was still a discrete red disc, but as I finished my first loop it was pumping the sky full of light and losing its shape.

I always feel somehow exorcised after a run. I feel I've breathed and sweated out all the impurities that have been building up in me. I'm not sure where my concern with feeling pure comes from. It's not like I grew up with strict sexual mores. Anyway, if my concern was being pure in the 'Christian sense', then I'd be fine. I mean, I was basically living the chaste life of a nun, except without any of the convivial community aspects of being in a convent.

The kind of purity I'm concerned with is more . . . clinical. It has more to do with feeling unclean and contaminated, a creeping suspicion that my mind and body have been blighted. The kind of feeling that makes me wish I could scour my organs and brain with bleach. I told a therapist about this once, and she got all excited, and started speculating about my having a long-repressed childhood trauma.* There might be something dark and awful, she said, festering

---

* She also diagnosed me with penis-envy.

nastily somewhere in my subconscious. She tried to badger whatever it was out of me through hypnosis, but nothing was uncovered.

I just don't like the idea of something outside my body getting inside my body without my explicit permission – be it food, glass, drugs, blood or semen. The fear goes the other way, too. I'm scared of too much blood or an organ falling *out* of my body somehow. Before I stopped getting my period, I was terrified each time it came that I might haemorrhage. In a way, my subconscious is probably like some sort of stressed-out US border control agent, except whereas her tools are guns, tasers, batons and sniffer dogs, I've only got running, calorie restriction and cleaning products.

I'm also an extremely negligent border control agent, the kind who shows up with a stained and crumpled uniform, and who falls asleep during her shift and lets ten tons of cocaine past. I'm always slipping up and losing control over myself – l let hair build up and clog the shower, I don't wash my hands after riding the U-Bahn, and, most shame-inducingly of all, I eat thousands and thousands of oat flakes, in the middle of the night, by the light of the moon. Often, when I woke up in EG's flat after one of these 'midnight feasts', I couldn't bring myself to even look over to the mess of half-filled mugs of porridge, spoons smeared in coconut oil or quark, empty sugar packets. It was only after I'd run and showered, when I felt I'd settled my debts, that I would clean everything carefully, opening the windows and lighting some incense. Cleaning up the mess on those occasions felt optimistic, like starting on a perfect blank page.

When I returned from my run my legs were covered in dust. I washed it off and it ran down my shins like melted caramel. The big toes on both feet were very bruised and the nails were starting to fall off. I remember being a little concerned about how much hair I was losing. My brush caught thick bunches of it when I combed through my conditioner. I wrapped my hair tightly in a towel and rubbed coconut oil into the wounds on my chest, which were sore and bleeding again from rubbing against my sports bra. Applying the coconut oil always felt like a kind of self-anointing. It was one of the nicest things that I did to take care of myself. I opened the window and the curtain fluttered in the light breeze. I dried my hair, and on that particular Friday, I took ages doing it, running my fingers through it like a mother chimp grooming its baby. I dressed, and all in all, I looked pretty good. I was wearing an enormous shiny shirt which left the illusion that I wasn't wearing anything underneath. Deodorant, foundation, powder, mascara. Hans and I had arranged to meet around 8.30 p.m. and I left with plenty of time, stopping by a *Späti* to buy a pack of cinnamon gum which I nervously chewed through and spat out as I rode the S-Bahn towards Ostkreuz. Looking back on it now, I feel nearly nostalgic about that person I was then, a trusting lamb, surrounded by malevolence but blind to it, trotting along, looking forward to the future and what it held for her, worrying only about her date and whether he would find her pretty.

The other passengers seemed stranger than usual and distant, as if a rift was forming between me and everyone else. They were still on earth, tethered to normality, while I was drifting off into space. This might sound very melodramatic, but I should add that I was a) extremely nervous about the date and b) wearing my noise-blocking headphones, which are so effective that they always make me feel as if I am in some kind of shadow-world. I wasn't listening to any music, because I was trying to save my battery. All I could hear was the sound of my own swallowing, and the beating of my heart in my ears. I often give myself panic attacks when I pay too much attention to my heartbeat. It just seems so unlikely that the entire lofty wonder of my being, my imagination, spirit, soul, should be tethered to *this*, a steak-sized bloody pump. The more I think about my heart, the faster it beats, and then I can't think of anything else. Google Greg had once explained to me something he called 'quantum weirdness'. Physicists, he told me, have discovered that subatomic particles display different properties when they are being measured, as if they were conscious of being observed. Ever since he'd told me about it, I constantly worried that this 'observer effect' might apply to my heart, and that if I thought about it too much, it might just give out.

My train pulled into Ostkreuz at 8.25. I quickly realized that it had been a stupid idea to meet there, like planning to meet someone you don't know at Times Square or Oxford Circus. I spent a good fifteen minutes searching for the station's main exit and checked my phone.

'I am a bit late, sorry!' he had written.

'*Kein Thema!*' (no problem!) I answered, and replaced the phone in my pocket, and then proceeded to enact one of the most strained five-minute performances of my life. Anyone who has been on a MatchTime or a Tinder date will know precisely what I am referring to – I can only describe it as the Act of *Pretending* That One Is *Not Pretending* Not to Be Waiting for a Blind Date. Such a performance requires you to cast a nonchalant unfixed-yet-not-unhinged gaze in the general direction you think the date might be coming from. The field of vision ought to be fairly wide both horizontally and vertically, although completely open spaces are to be avoided when possible, as it might result in you spotting your date when they are still a few minutes' walk away. Then you will be forced to stare at them like a gormless creep until they reach you. If you do spot them, try to pretend that you have not yet seen them. Failing this, it is better just to begin to walk towards them at a moderate pace.

Ideally, you ought not to have your phone out – it will make you seem overly dependent on social media, and like the kind of person who is never able to just BE with yourself. If you can't manage to hold the nonchalant unfixed-yet-not-unhinged gaze for the entire performance, bring some other kind of prop. In Berlin you might be able to get away with knitting or something crafty, but ideally it should be a dog or a cigarette. At a pinch, a book will do. NOTHING that might look like a prop, however – this rules out anything by Proust, the depressing Russians (Tolstoy, Dostoevsky, Bulgakov, etc.), and, sadly for me on that day, *The Magic Mountain*. I brought *Der kleine Hobbit* instead. I knew the English version nearly by heart, so it was easy to understand. I interrupted my pretending-to-read about every two pages or so, swiping my eyes along the horizon to see if I might spot someone who looked like a Straight, Man, Single, 180cm. While it is important to seem charmingly engrossed in one's own world, one must not look unapproachable. I was interrupted from my fake reading by a gentle tap on my shoulder:

'Daphne? *Ich bin Hans.*'

I knew in that instant that nothing serious would happen between us. I liked his height, and the lightness with which he touched my shoulder. He was kind, not too shy, pretty educated. But I just knew that I could never *ever* be 'romantically involved' with him. I know immediately whether or not I am going to be able to have sex with someone, and I am always faithful to this instinct. It's not about how good-looking they are. In fact, I'm never attracted to dazzlingly gorgeous men. My border-control subconscious keeps too tight a leash on my heart and so has done much to protect me from the heartbreak and humiliation of falling in love with the Sean Connerys of this world, despite the fact that Connery was the colostrum of my sexuality. As a child, I hoped to grow up to be Bond himself. When I realized I was female, I focused my energies on becoming a Bond girl. When I realized I was not nearly as beautiful as Honey Ryder or Jinx Johnson, I started working hard at school so that I could go to university and become brainy like Moneypenny, and just catch glimpses of Bond on his way to meetings with M and Q. At university, I tried to project Bond-like qualities of suaveness and style on to the puny hipsters in my philosophy classes, with limited success. So it wasn't anything to do with Hans's looks, which were perfectly decent – it was something else, something 'chemical'.

The details of our evening together are unremarkable, and are cast into shadow by the events of the next thirty-six hours, so I will describe them briefly. Hans had clearly given some thought to where we should go. He led me along the strange Ostkreuz harbour, and on to a peninsula of the River Spree called Kap Stralau. The peninsula was an overgrown and empty pocket, yet only a few minutes away from the megastation and the concrete-bunker nightclubs of the old East. He had brought a picnic blanket, and a delicious smoky derivative of Club-Mate for me to try. He was from Münster, the same town as EG, and he spoke just like she did. He blinked rather a lot, like a frightened rabbit, and had square-clipped nails. He was studying something dire, something like 'management of hospitality relations', but only because his parents had forced him to. What he really wanted was to go to the conservatoire in Berlin, as he was a very talented pianist. In fact, he slightly bragged he had something called an 'absolute ear', which meant he could recognize the pitch and name the musical note of absolutely any sound. This skill, which I put to the immediate test by making all kinds of strange shrieks and noises, acted as a kind of refrain to the date. We kissed and it wasn't unpleasant at all. At around 2 a.m. he accompanied me to the S-Bahn platform. I was flustered, speaking nonsense to cover my fear that he might try to kiss me in front of the crowd on the platform. But he didn't. He hugged me and breathed, '*Komm gut nach Hause,*' (get home safe) into my ear, a little forlornly. Or maybe it was I who was forlorn, full of caffeine from the Club-Mate, but with an empty stomach, speeding off alone to an empty flat.

8

Under Siege

I REALIZED PRETTY QUICKLY that I was on the wrong train. That's the thing about the S-Bahn. However much I've praised it, I failed to add that it is really difficult to navigate. I'm sure it would take some kind of Alan Turing to find some logic in it. The lines have completely arbitrary names, composed of letters and numbers which seem whimsically assigned.

Until then, I had only taken a couple of lines and I mistakenly believed that all the S-Bahn lines looped. It took me about seven stops to realize that I was not going to end up in Kreuzberg just by hoping, and so I got off at the next stop. I was in Marzahn, the 'deep East' of Berlin. I was a little concerned by the unfriendly-looking tower blocks, the very dim lighting, and the fact that the next train back to Ostkreuz was not coming for fifty-two minutes. By then it was 2.30 a.m. and I was exhausted and starving. So I walked out of the station, braving the streets with nothing but *Der kleine Hobbit* to defend myself with, hoping I would stumble upon a bus which might carry me home.

I see now, of course, that this was classic murder-victim behaviour, that all the elements were in place for a good juicy true-crime story. Bare legs, blonde hair, internet dating. The police would accuse Hans, of course, and he might look like a realistic suspect in the tabloid press, with his big square hands and blinky eyes. They would interrogate him, ask him, 'What was the musical pitch of her final screams, you Westphalian bastard!' Hans is so wonderful and lovely that he might have made a false confession just to give my family closure.

Yet although I was scared, especially when the battery died on my phone, it was the kind of delicious, contained fear you feel when you curl up with some popcorn to watch a horror film. I didn't think anything truly terrible would happen. This might seem stupidly naive, but to be quite honest, life so far had given me plenty of reason to be naive and stupid. Ever since I can remember, the world has been generally indulgent and benevolent towards me. I was never left to cry as a baby and never denied anything I wanted as a child. When I was a teenager, I would get drunk and walk home alone in the dark and arrive unmolested at a warm and peaceful apartment. If I left my credit card in a bar, it would be waiting for me behind the counter when I returned to retrieve it. I tended to have luck with tangerines and oranges – I somehow always got pipless ones. So this behaviour, taking the S-Bahn without checking where it was going, and my confidence that I would find a bus home at 2.35 a.m., wasn't really folly at all. It was based on lived evidence and empirical data. True, perhaps I had not been paying close enough attention to the recent surge of misfortune in my life: abandonment by boyfriend of three years, rejection from graduate school, acquiring a stalker, an inability to find friends, complete social and intellectual isolation. Nevertheless, if I took stock of all the events of my twenty-six years, it still made sense to be optimistic.

Miraculously, a bus appeared, and I rode it all the way to my cinema in Mitte, and then took the U-Bahn, the familiar stops eastwards to the Hermannplatz U-Bahn station. By now it was 3.30 a.m. I bought one packet of yellow and three packets of blue M&Ms from the station's vending machine and ate them all by the time I got home, pouring them into my mouth as if they were Tic Tacs.

I pulled out my keys and let myself into the courtyard of 105 Huberstraße, feeling as exhausted and relieved as Bilbo on his safe return to Bag End. The upstairs neighbour's light was off, which meant I would not be lulled to sleep by his rhythmic thrusting. The downstairs neighbour, however, was very much awake. His ground-floor flat was a veritable cell of light and oozing a mist of hash-smoke, which I knew would have drifted up and through the open window into my bedroom. It would reek of weed for days. I saw the neighbour's bed on the floor, and a nightmare of dishes and overflowing bins. He turned towards me, and our eyes met very briefly as I walked past. I thought I saw him licking his lips, in a crude and pointedly lascivious way. But it could have been a trick of the light. I was so tired I could barely keep my eyes open.

I dragged my weary body up the stairs and let myself into my flat. I kicked off my shoes and padded barefoot down the corridor, when I felt a stabbing pain in the heel of my foot. I turned on the light and wanted to scream. The whole room was glinting with white crockery and transparent glass. The cupboards were open, and half-moon discs of smashed plates lay over the counters and kitchen floor.

I heard something on the stairway. I ran into the bathroom and closed the door behind me. I guessed that whoever had broken into the flat was somewhere nearby. Perhaps they were still in the flat. I felt dizzy. I sank to the floor, cradling my head in my arms and pressing my face down between my legs, biting down on my knees and pushing my tongue against them to make sure I was still alive and that I could still feel my body. I didn't scream. I waited for the door handle to turn.

I was straining to listen but desperate not to hear anything, my instinct to face the situation wrestling with the more practised reflex of denial. The corners of my mouth were tight and clenching into a grimace. I was sweating coldly into my shirt. I fumbled for my phone. It was out of battery. I waited a while longer, and then crawled out of the bathroom, pressing my knees into the shards, and grabbed my charger. I plugged it in and waited for the screen to light up. I regretted then all the times I had picked over the details of crime scenes and found out as much as I could about murder victims. This time it was me, and in a few hours, I would be autopsied by rough-handed strangers with sharp scalpels. The astonishing contents of my stomach would be scrutinized and displayed, my semi-digested midnight feast of M&Ms used to estimate the time of death. My screen came on, and by its light I saw that the floor was covered in blood from the cuts on my knees and foot.

I dialled the police number, 110, and a woman picked up at once:

'*Polizeinotruf, hallo.*'

'*Hallo, ich wohne in Kreuzberg, Huberstraße.* I think someone has broken into my flat.'

'Are you in immediate danger?'

'I don't know, but I think so, yes.'

'What is your address?'

She made me repeat myself several times.

'Can't you move? The reception is bad.'

'No, I am sorry, I can't, I think I am in danger.'

I heard her typing, and then she said, 'OK, they will be with you in a few minutes. Do you need me to stay on the line?'

'Yes, please.'

And so we sat still and breathed together in silence, until the doorbell rang.

'They are here,' I said, and she hung up before I could say thank you.

The black courtyard was suddenly full of pinpoints of light. It was 4.15 a.m. I made sure I had my phone and keys, slipped on my shoes and ran down the stairs.

'*Polizei!*' they screamed when they saw me. So loudly I was sure they must have woken the few neighbours who hadn't heard the commotion. I couldn't believe how many of them there were, maybe six, with three in the next-door courtyard kicking the bins around and shining their lights into the ground-floor windows.

'*Polizei! Halt!*'

'I called you! I was the one who called you!'

'Why did you come out? Go back inside!'

I turned and two of them followed me up to my apartment. Three others clumped further up to the floors above.

'Why did you leave the door open?'

I shrugged but felt nothing; I couldn't be more cowed than I already was. The big, blond, reassuringly brutish officer took a gun from the holster on his hip, and leant his back against the door to my apartment, which stood ajar. '*Hallo!*' he shouted. '*Polizei! Komm raus!*'

I realized he thought that the attacker might be in my flat, which seemed illogical, as I'd been in it moments before, but also thrillingly possible. He slammed the door against the wall to make sure no one was behind it. A female police officer had come up behind us by now, and they both went in ahead of me. She drew her gun. They switched on the corridor light and looked to the bathroom. The floor was covered with blood. The man tore the shower curtain back with such violence that the curtain rail fell to the floor and knocked over my jar of coconut oil, which smashed. Both police officers jumped but I didn't flinch. The adrenaline had bled out of me and I could barely bring myself to care about anything. The policeman pushed on to my bedroom, pulling the duvet off my bed, walking all over the plates and broken crockery which crunched like snails' shells. All the plates and all the glasses were strewn across the floor. I saw with relief that EG's more precious items – the tureens and salad bowls – had been spared. Officer Blondie looked under the bed and I so wished I'd tidied the night before. You'd think these kinds of petty miseries would vanish in such situations, but it turns out they don't. I felt crippled with shame. I'd left M&M wrappers and a Nutella jar by the side of my bed, and I saw Officer Blondie register them as he scanned the room. He opened and closed the front door and examined the lock. I could hear the rest of the policemen screaming, '*Polizei! Polizei!*' upstairs and knocking on my neighbours' doors. I heard the upstairs neighbour, Günter, opening his door and talking to one of them.

The policemen in the courtyard then came up to my apartment. The cluster of impeccable uniforms and fog of AXE deodorant made me suddenly conscious of my mini-shorts and the sweat under my arms, which smelt different from my usual smell, far more acidic, like curdled milk. Officer Blondie gestured for me to sit on the unmade bed and asked when I had discovered the damage.

'About ten minutes ago.'

At this the other officers sighed and went out into the courtyard as if I'd just wasted their time. I wasn't sure if they were giving up, or going to search for suspects in the area. I heard their cars pull away.

'Where is your home?'

'London.'

'How long have you lived here?'

'Four months.'

'Your German is good.'

This was thrilling.

'Do you have a pass?'

A pass? I wondered, as 'pass' in French means travel card. Don't they have a police car?

'No, I don't have a pass, I use a bicycle, but I can buy one if necessary.'

He rolled his eyes, immediately furious. 'No! *Ein Pass, PAssPORT, PAssPORT.*'

I fumbled in my drawer and handed over my French passport. I'm not technically British and I was scared this inconsistency in my story would throw off the whole investigation. But he didn't say a word, not even when he turned to my ugly passport photo. He looked from the picture to me without blinking and pointed to the blood all over my knees.

'Who did this?' he said, pointing to the blood running down my knees.

'I did it. On the glass,' I said.

'And who did this?' he said, pointing to the blisters on my chest. I looked down. The scabs had matured oddly, in very neat lines. I liked them, I thought they looked like tribal markings or war paint. But how to say 'sports clothes' and 'rubbing' in German?

'It's nothing.'

At this, Blondie and the two other remaining policemen turned towards me, looking at me with a dawning understanding.

'Did a man do it?' he said, a little more gently.

I blushed and smiled at this. They didn't understand *at all*. They thought I was the kind of woman who had a romantic life, someone who might plausibly be the victim of domestic abuse. Even more laughably, they thought I was capable of being coy and discreet about it.

'No! It is nothing, really.'

I saw his dark-haired stooge scribble something down. This was the most attention I had got in months. I loved it. The fact that it seemed credible to them that someone might feel possessive of me was incredibly flattering. Officer Blondie pointed to the broken plates. He muttered something to the two others who picked up some of the fragments bare-handed, which seemed very unprofessional to me. What about fingerprints? Where were the gloves and evidence bags?

'Have there been any other break-ins in this flat?'

'I don't know about that. But something strange happened a few months ago, around the third of April.'

'What exactly happened?'

'Someone threw a stone and cracked my window.'

'Did you report it then?'

'No.'

More swivelling of eyes and arching of eyebrows.

'Have you noticed if anything is missing?'

I looked over, and saw my laptop was still on my desk. I had nothing else of any value.

I opened the clothes and kitchen cupboards – it seemed all of EG's things were still there.

'No, I don't think anything is missing. I don't have any jewellery, or anything like that.'

'Hmm. Well, why would someone break into your apartment if they didn't want to steal anything? Do you have any idea who could do this? Someone who might want to scare you? Do you have a boyfriend?'

'No.'

'An ex-boyfriend?'

I thought with a lurch of dread of Richard Grausam, the stalker. It might be him, I thought. He was crazy and sinister. But the timeline didn't make sense since I'd met him a month *after* the first bricking. But then again, I wouldn't put it past him. He really was that crazy and sinister. Yet hypothesizing about complex psychological motives was really beyond my German at the time, and so I just said, 'No. But I think I know who did it. It was probably the neighbour downstairs.'

I didn't realize that I knew this until I said it, but then I knew it with *complete certainty*. Blondie signalled to the two others who ran downstairs and started banging at the door and screaming, '*Polizei! Polizei!*' in their menacing way. They came back a minute later.

'There is no one there. But the guy upstairs says he thought he heard something in your apartment earlier today, around lunchtime.'

'Günter said that?' I replied. 'That can't be. I was home then, I didn't leave until around six.'

Officer Blondie made a note, and then asked:

'Was the door open when you came back?'

'No, I unlocked it.'

'But the window was open?'

'Yes.'

'Did you leave it open?'

'I think so.'

He frowned and made another note.

'But it wouldn't be easy to reach your window. Are you sure no one else has a key to your apartment?'

'Yes, I'm sure. But I think it wouldn't be so hard to climb up. The downstairs neighbour could have climbed on to his window ledge and pulled himself up. He's tall.'

The policeman went downstairs to check something and then returned, frowning.

'You are correct, the distance between his window and yours is not very great, especially for a large man. But why would this man break into your flat? Is he your boyfriend or ex-boyfriend?' They were romantics, these policemen, desperate to make this into some kind of love story.

'No! We've never even spoken!'

'Why, then?'

'Because he gives me very unfriendly, nasty looks. It's just a feeling.'

'Is there any reason he would target you? Have you spoken to him before? Argued?'

'No, never. No, I'm always quiet.'

He looked dubious. He was nice-looking, and an expert at dubiosity.

'When did you last see him?'

'I saw him when I came home, and he saw me. He looked at me with an unfriendly look.'

'When was this?'

'Around three.'

'Where were you tonight?'

'Out with a friend.'

'Have you taken any drugs?'

'No!'

'Do you know this man's name?'

'No. But it might be on the doorbell outside.'

'Is there any other reason he would target you? Are you part of any political or special lifestyle organization?'

I had no idea what he meant. I thought he might be asking if I was an anarchist, or a lesbian.

'No. I just think he doesn't like me. I have a feeling he dislikes women in general.'

'Well,' Officer Blondie said, sceptically. 'Do you have any evidence?'

'No,' I said, 'but after I came home and found the flat like this, I heard a noise in the staircase. I think he was watching me, to see how I would react.'

'Well,' he said. 'There is not very much we can do without any evidence.' I looked at the mess in the apartment. I already knew they'd be of no help to me.

'Yes, I understand. What should I do?'

'Well,' he said, dabbing at his phone distractedly. 'I don't think it is a good idea if you stay here.'

They hung around for another ten minutes, asking for copies of my sub-rental contract, of EG's contract with Frau Becker, which I didn't have, and Frau Becker's number, which I also didn't have. Their bureaucratic investigations were far more thorough than the crime-solving aspect of their work. I offered them water and coffee, but they refused, reminding me of the men who'd repaired my window before. Officer Blondie gave me a card with the number of the local Kreuzberg police precinct.

'Call this number next time,' he said. 'It is better if you stay with a friend tonight. Good luck.' They left without saying goodbye. I double-locked the door behind them and sat on my bed, half relieved to be alone and half missing them already.

It was 5 a.m. by then and I had no idea what to do. I'd planned a run, but I thought my heart might really give out if I went. I stank but I didn't want to shower. I was too frightened. I kept thinking of that passage from *Stalkers: A Survivor's Guide*:

Your safety is your responsibility. At the end of the day, you cannot rely on the police, your parents, your neighbours to keep you safe. You must take measures to ensure your safety and protect yourself by any means necessary.

But I had no idea how to protect myself. I looked down into the courtyard. My heart was still racing. No one was around. I found it strange that not one of my neighbours had come out to see what was happening and to check if I was all right. This probably had something to do with German reserve, a quality I appreciated when I was left in peace in coffee shops or parks, but one that I resented that morning. They're just so 'private', the Germans, I thought. They're so respectful of the space between neighbours that if one day, Mr and Mrs Cohen are dragged out of their apartment in the middle of the night by the Gestapo, or Daphne Ferber is beaten to death by the downstairs neighbour, they'll pretend not to hear anything. I didn't know what to do. I thought about texting my classmates or my running friends, but I felt too ashamed. Not because of what had happened to me – I already knew it was sort of darkly glamorous – but because it was just so *embarrassing* to call them in such an intense moment of vulnerability. I couldn't bear to admit that they were in fact the best and only friends I had in Berlin, and my only go-to people in an emergency.

Instead, I sent three texts: one to my father, one to my mother, one to my brother. It was wonderful to text again, to see all the stupid smileys and selfie filters and all these things which confirmed the existence of a milder, friendlier world than the one I'd been thrown into.

[05:44:51] Daphne: Papa, something bad happened to me in the night 😔 I am OK but please give me a call when you get this message.

[05:45:07] Daphne: Ma, please give me a call when you wake up.

[05:45:53] Daphne: Hi brother. Please give me a call when you have a minute 🙂

My father is an insomniac. He is barely ever asleep, and so I could rely on him to call me at once. He sounded exhausted.

'*Oui? Alors?*' he said. 'So?'

'Papa, someone broke into my flat and destroyed all my glasses and plates.'

'What do you mean?'

I explained exactly what had happened, about coming home late (of course I didn't mention MatchTime or the date), about how the downstairs neighbour had looked at me and what the police had said.

'Are you sure it's him?'

'No.' I didn't tell him about my stalker. There is only so much reality a father can take.

'OK. Well, what are you going to do? Can you call a friend?'

'Yes, someone is coming over,' I lied.

'OK. Don't stay there tonight. Do you need me to send you more money? I'll book you a hotel room.'

'No, thanks, Papa.'

'Get out of there and send me a message when you are out.'

He passed the phone to my mother, who had been sleeping in the bed beside him.

'*Darrrrrling*,' she mumbled sleepily. The voice of milk and honey.

'Ma, I'm OK, I promise I'm fine.'

'My daaaaarling,' she purred again.

It was the first time I felt I might cry.

'Have you called your friends, my love? Are they coming over?'

My parents always think I have loads of friends. It's one of their delusions about me.

'Yes, Ma. They're coming over.'

'Good. Darling, what are you going to do? Are you going to move out?'

'I really don't want to! I've paid rent for the next two months. But I don't know if it's safe to stay here or not. I can't tell if I'm overreacting or under-reacting. Do you think I should move?'

My mother was silent. Poor woman, I thought. I've really put her through a lot in twenty-six years. As a child I was easily ashamed, terribly jealous of my big brother, and sobbed every morning when she left for work. As a teenager I was completely superficial. I wore Playboy bunny T-shirts and drooled over the little wankers in my class while she tried to make me take an interest in *Bonjour Tristesse*. I left at eighteen for Oxford and never called and seldom went home. I came back an emaciated waif three years later and did nothing with the excellent grades I'd nearly killed myself to earn. I ate stealthily, never giving her the pleasure of feeding me. I hid food wrappers and honey-crusted teaspoons in my sock drawer but she knew better than to confront me with them. They just disappeared punctually. She did that for me, my mother, discreetly evacuating my greatest shames, which were also her own. And there I was at almost 6 a.m. on a Saturday, making her responsible for my safety when she deserved to be asleep and dreaming.

'I don't know, darling,' she said at last. 'What did Papa say?' Unhelpful.

'Don't worry, I'll deal with it.'

'Don't get angry! What am I supposed to do! I don't even know where you live and I don't know how to help! Do you want to come home?'

'No, it's fine. Don't worry, I'll deal with it. I'll call you later.'

I'm often Estella with my mother. She loves me so much that I'm never guarded in my cruelty.

'Please don't be cross with me!'

'I'm not. It's fine. Speak later.'

And I hung up before she could answer.

I made myself an instant coffee with milk and real sugar. I felt calmer and more in control, after having upset my mother. I knew she would be fretting, but she wouldn't admit how worried she was, because I'd told her that her concern undermined my self-confidence. My phone buzzed with a message from her:

Please text me when you are out of there darling! Sorry we
had cross words xxxx

I ignored her and decided I felt brave enough to have a shower. I was frightened of the total silence. It reminded me of a landscape of virgin snow so perfect that the temptation to trample it would be impossible to resist, and the smashing would start again. I put on a podcast, the latest *This American Life* episode, and stepped around the smashed pot of coconut oil, which had begun to melt and spread. I didn't re-hang the shower curtain, because I didn't want to encourage the staging of a *Psycho* remake. I washed the blood-sour-milk smell off me. My cuts didn't hurt, but they looked impressive. I still felt sick with adrenaline. My brother called me just as I got out of the shower. I walked back into the bedroom and sat wrapped in a towel on the floor, cradling the phone between my ear and shoulder, watching the jagged edges of glass glitter as the sun rose.

'Pumpkin! What happened?!'

His tone was light, jesting. As always. I explained, and he laughed.

'I'm glad you seem to find it funny. What do you think I should do?'

'Berlin is a jungle. You need to get out of there.'

'Isn't that an overreaction, though?'

'Absolutely not. Whoever it is, he has made it very, very clear that he does not want you there. Do you need money?'

I wasn't paying much attention to him. I was googling 'crime in Kreuzberg' on my computer.

'No, thanks for asking.'

'Just move back to London! You can stay with me as long as you like.'

'Thanks, but actually I love it in Berlin,' I said, although the main reason I didn't want to return home was because it would have seemed like a capitulation. My parents had thought my decision to move to Berlin was a bad idea. They didn't think I could look after myself, and didn't like me to stray far from home. They had wanted me to make amends with my boss at Knights in Black Satin, reconcile with my flatmate, and take responsibility for Pringle, the kitten she and I had adopted together. They disapproved of the scorched-earth policy I'd carried out on my London life, and criticized me for deserting places and people whenever things didn't go my way. But then, if I left Berlin at this low point, I would prove them right. And I did love Berlin, in a strange dysfunctional way. Despite the bricking, the break-in, the stalker, the devastating loneliness I experienced so acutely that it resembled a gnawing, physical pain. I was convinced that it contained all the friends, lovers and stimulation I needed, if only I learnt to approach things the right way. I hadn't lost hope that I would soon be rewarded for my perseverance and that everything would fall into place for me. I have always been a very hopeful person.

I texted EG in Seattle, and Gabriel.

[06:40:07] Daphne: Hi dear EG, I am afraid I have bad news. I came home after a night out very early this morning, and I found that someone had broken into the flat and the police came but they were not very helpful. I'm not sure what I should do 😞 I'm so sorry for all this drama . . .
[06:57:38] Daphne: Hello Gabriel, can I ask you something when you wake up?
[06:57:56] Daphne: It is a bit urgent I'm afraid. So tell me when I can call!!

It was ten at night in Seattle but EG called me nearly at once. I explained, trying to sound normal. She was solicitous, reacting with proportionate horror to what had happened, but I was speaking in strange stale sentences that I don't usually use, saying things like 'It's no trouble', 'I'm A-OK' and 'I'm sure all I need is a good night's sleep', as if wheeling out such platitudes would trick reality into ordinariness, and force my life to become mundane again. She asked if I knew who might have broken in.

'I think it might be the guy downstairs.'

'Ah, really? God, he is pretty weird. Did I tell you about how he tried to give me a present on the first night I moved in, but it was late so I didn't want to open the door?'

'Yes, I remember,' I said, thinking that her un-neighbourliness had sown the seeds of my near destruction.

'Ah, but it makes no sense? Why would he do that?! It's so antisocial! Really, just antisocial! Did you do anything to disturb him?'

'No! Actually, he played music very loudly from the beginning.'

There was an awkward pause, which I interpreted as her

embarrassment for having sold her flat as being 'a cuddly nest in a nice neighbourhood'. She probably thought I would ask for my money back, which hadn't occurred to me.

'I just can't believe it, it is so crazy. Do you have any friends you can stay with tonight?'

'Yes, of course,' I lied. 'Would you mind telling Frau Becker what happened? I don't think I can explain everything in German.'

'Of course I will,' she replied.

'OK. Sleep well. Sorry for everything.'

My phone buzzed with streams of texts from my family, who were desperate to know whether I was out of there. I left them in suspense and checked my email, and saw that EG had already written to Frau Becker telling her that the flat had somehow been broken into.

Frau Becker did not answer the email, but a while later, I saw her in the courtyard sorting out the bins and I heard her mopping the staircase, resuming her *Hausmeister* duties as if nothing had happened. I found this behaviour incredibly strange, but I couldn't manage any more German, so instead I checked Facebook and WhatsApp again, sending out good mornings and smileys to various acquaintances to keep the flow of messages coming, keeping myself distracted like one of those old-fashioned telephone operators single-handedly manning the local telephone exchange, unplugging jacks and flicking switches, transferring between WhatsApp and Google and Facebook, asking my anxious parents to 'please hold' and juggling several lines at once. I spent the next few hours in this state, calm and efficient. A few hours later, Gabriel answered me.

[12:25:46] Gabriel Shamai: Hey hey
[12:25:54] Gabriel Shamai: I'm up

[12:27:54] Gabriel Shamai: I hope I'm not too late. 😞
[12:28:33] Daphne: Can I ring

He didn't answer my call and I almost began to cry in despair, but he called me back at once.

'Gud MOORRRN-ING, DARF-ne. Ow arrre you?'

He had just woken up and was with Nina. I was disrupting a nice, couple-y morning. They were probably lying bare-bottomed on lovely Nina's bed, spoon-feeding each other her homemade granola. I explained what had happened and asked if I could stay for a night. He immediately said yes. One of his flatmates was away for ten days, I could stay the whole time. Did I remember where he lived? Yes, Siegfriedstraße. I offered to pay for the room, but he said, 'No way,' and to come over whenever I wanted.

I pulled the big blue IKEA bag from under the bed and threw in my most precious possessions: running shoes, favourite underwear, the still unfinished *The Magic Mountain*. I looked around the room. I hadn't bothered to clean up the glass, nor had I swept up the broken dirty dishes and the remains of my coconut oil. I was desperate to get out, but I was also scared the neighbour might be waiting to ambush me with a flask of acid. I'd had a phase of googling 'women disfigured in acid attacks: before and after', and I kept imagining my youthful skin turned to waxy scar tissue. I tightened my backpack around my waist and hitched the IKEA bag over my right shoulder. I locked the door behind me and hurried down the stairs, shielding my face and eyes as I passed his doorway.

Frau Becker was loitering by the bins. Her hair was permed and more purple than the last time I'd seen her and she was wearing yellow rubber gloves, wellington boots, and an apron with yellow letters which spelled 'I'LL FEED ALL YOU FUCKERS'. This was her usual cleaning outfit.

'Ah! *Hallo!*' she said and pointed above me. 'Terrible!' To which I nodded. 'Something has happened twice already since you moved in and it never happened before,' she went on. 'I've never had any problems here and I've owned the building for sixty years.'

'It's not my fault,' I said, and felt my throat constricting against a sob. 'I didn't do anything.'

'*Naja,*' Frau Becker answered, which is the German way of expressing dubiosity without seeming too egregiously impolite. 'Well,' she added, suddenly whispering and confidential. 'I think the downstairs neighbour did it. Look at what I found outside his door.'

She beckoned me to come closer and pulled some tinfoil from her pocket. At close range I understood why her hair and hairline looked so strange. She'd had the most thorough facelift I've ever seen. Her skin looked like cling film pulled tightly over her bones. She unwrapped the foil and passed it to me. It contained the remains of what was unmistakably a joint. 'Drugs,' she said, pretending to smoke it and crossing her eyes, mimicking what she clearly thought a stoned person might look like. 'Bad boy!' She crossed her eyes again and took another pretend drag from her rubber-gloved hand.

I was quite impressed by her unexpected sleuthiness. She hadn't really been cleaning; the outfit was a foil. She was doing what the police ought to have done, snooping around, sticking her nose into things. Perhaps this was what she'd been doing all these months, pretending to clean but really keeping a watchful eye on the tenants. That would certainly have explained how filthy the place was. I agreed with her conclusion, in any case, but I found her evidence wanting. Weed can make you paranoid, but I'd never heard of it giving anyone the urge to break in and vandalize a stranger's apartment.

'Yes. I don't know . . .' I said, heaving the sagging IKEA bag. 'I'm going to a friend's now.'

'OK, well, here is a number for a locksmith, in case you want to change the locks,' she said, shoving it into the front pocket of my shirt. 'Call them at your convenience.'

As the doors slammed behind me, my heart lightened with relief. I scuffled sweatily towards the U-Bahn station, past the still full Der Kaninchenbau. I rode the train in the direction of Oberlandstraße, in South Neukölln. I wondered if I might run into Kat. My IKEA bag swung and bumped into me. What a feeble package I was, brittle china bones swaddled in sweating folds of silk. I remembered the good intentions with which I'd moved into EG's flat, how I'd thought I might use her special asparagus saucepan, learn to live with cupboards casually full of chocolate, start taking the pill like she did and get a boyfriend. But souls are not re-cast with a change of decor. Of course I'd always known this, everyone does, but to live it again and again in each new city and flat, to perform varieties of the same exhausting choreography only to find myself in the same spot, hating myself in the mirror, was draining me of the last reserves of optimism I had left.

I avoided my reflection in the U-Bahn window and stood aside to let the beggars past. A red-haired woman with a lovely kiss of a mouth got on at the next station. She was carrying a baby in a sling, and its round, buttony head stared up at her. I resented babies. I wanted to be them, and have them, but I was sure that my uterus was hostile to life, a polluted, acidic desert. The redhead was eating a cone of green ice cream, and every few licks she would point it into her baby's face, as if she was dabbing gouache at it with a fat paintbrush. The baby sucked at the green ice and flapped its buttery arms and legs. Will that ever be me? I thought. Will this nonsense ever end?

9

Habseligkeiten

To pass the time on our long runs, Ollie, Evan and I
would take turns teaching the others an interesting new
German word. On one hot Tempelhofer Feld day, Evan had
told us about *Habseligkeiten*, which he defined as 'the most
precious possessions a person has'. He tested our memories
every five kilometres or so, asking us to spell it and use it properly in a sentence. Whoever lost had to do a 100-metre sprint.

Back in EG's flat, I had looked it up. Evan was right, *Habseligkeiten* does mean 'the most precious possessions', but if
you understand some German, the meaning reaches far
deeper. *Hab* comes from the word 'to have', *selig* means
'blessed' and also evokes the word for soul, *Seele*. Together,
these associations compound to mean something like the
'dearest belongings of the soul', the 'very last items that the
homeless and refugees cling on to', the 'only things a victim
of a disaster will rescue before she flees'.

So there I was, riding the U-Bahn, my *Habseligkeiten*
stuffed into the IKEA bag, its weight burrowing into my
shoulder. I felt a murmur of that old optimism rising within
me. I was starting again. The tide was turning, a new chapter
beginning.

Gabriel buzzed me in. His courtyard was much bigger than mine and full of prams and children's tricycles. He too lived in the *Hinterhof*, but on the sixth floor. I clambered up like a loaded mule, and tried to reconfigure my features to hide the mask of terror I'd been wearing since morning. I only partially succeeded, however, because when Gabriel opened the door, he took me into his arms. He'd grown very brown in the sun and the contrast with his pale eyes made them seem still bluer. His hair was a mess of bleached curls. He looked and smelt like a cherub.

The flat was barely tidier than it had been during the party, but this time I found the mess of shoes and crumbs and coffee rings cheering. My bedroom was the closest to the entrance, to the left of the kitchen. It was pretty clean, with high blue scalloped ceilings. It looked out on to an enormous maple tree, which dappled the afternoon sun and cast dancing shadows on the bare walls. Gabriel had made the bed for me, cleared one of his flatmates' cupboards for my clothes, and put three yellow daffodils in the glass by my bed. All these small gestures were incredibly touching. I felt just as I had as a child when the school trips I hated going on would finally come to an end. The return home was like paradise regained. My mother would scoop me off the school bus and take me back home where she would stuff me with salami sandwiches and chocolate cake. Arriving at Gabriel's reminded me of coming back into the circle of love after days of anonymity and indifference. I began to cry.

'I'm sorry, it's not actually that bad,' I said, wiping my face with my U-Bahn crud-encrusted hands. 'I don't really feel scared or anything. I'm just really tired, sorry.'

I sat at the kitchen table while he prepared coffee, and we ran through the events of the night. Like nearly everyone else I was to discuss the case with, Gabriel's primary interest was in trying to figure out a motive. 'I discussed it with Nina,' he said, 'and she thought it might have something to do with gentrification or something. Maybe he hates foreigners, or is he some kind of extreme anti-gentrification Neukölln guy?'

'Maybe,' I said, though the man looked so blunt that I doubted he was capable of harbouring any kind of political sentiment. I was also disappointed by the implication that he might have figured out that I was a foreigner. I made super-human efforts to pass as a German. I never spoke English in public, I wore a German football shirt to run in, I ostenta-tiously displayed the German-language titles of whatever I was reading. I was currently reading *Der kleine Hobbit*, for God's sake.

'Well, anyway,' Gabriel said, 'it is an amazing and weird story. You ought to write about it.'

'Maybe I will. And if it's a bestseller I'll lob it through my neighbour's window.'

He smiled and asked whether I would join him and Nina for dinner later. I was about to say yes, but then I remem-bered my MatchTime date with Milosh.

I was meant to meet him in a few hours. 'It's too late to cancel now,' I said.

Looking back, I wonder why I didn't leave Berlin right then. As my brother had pointed out, the city hadn't exactly given me many reasons to stick around. I'd been stalked, bricked and had my flat broken into, and had no job. Although it was true that my German was coming along, I had no Ger-man friends to practise it with. My brother's invitation to move back to London was tempting. I liked Fulham, I knew a nice delicatessen in his neighbourhood where I might get a job, and if I really wanted to carry on with German, I could attend the Goethe-Institut.

But at the same time, the stalking, bricking and break-in didn't make me feel terrible about myself. There was something refreshing about bad things happening *to* me. In London all my miseries had been of my own making. Things had been incredibly easy for me there. I'd found a job in the cool coffee shop, which came with a ready-made group of friends. They invited me to house parties and to Sunday roasts. I lived in a flat in a beautiful house in Queen's Park, shared with a French-Canadian girl called Cécile who worked as a furniture restorer at Sotheby's. Two weeks after I moved in, we adopted a kitten and called him Pringle. She loved me and took me everywhere with her. She gave me massages when my body ached from waitressing. She taught me to wear pink- or orange-tinted sunglasses all year round to block out the gloomy greyness of London. Every Sunday we'd whip up big, airy Irish coffees for breakfast and then float headily through the Old Spitalfields Market, and return home ludicrously encumbered with old sofas and broken light-globes that Cécile would restore. Everything in the flat belonged to her. It was exquisite; my life was delightful. But I'd just spoiled it all in my usual way: suck up, lie, ghost, repeat. I spoke to no one from that time at all. Some disliked me intensely and wished me ill but others, I knew, including my old flatmate, were worried and wanted to get in touch with me. I ignored them, and felt guilty, but not so guilty that I ever answered. In Berlin, on the other hand, I was the innocent victim. None of the misfortunes were my fault.

The other thing was that these unfortunate incidents acted as tangible containers of the anxiety which was a perpetually present dimension of my life at the time. This anxiety never made any sense, really. I was lucky, young, with financially supportive parents and a good education. Nevertheless, for as long as I could remember I'd been plagued by a feeling of dread. It wasn't directed towards anything, but it was always there, a dark shadow over my life. The stalking and bricking gave my fear an object. They polarized all the small shadows of unhappiness that usually sullied everything, gathering them on to themselves like a big magnet, so that everything else seemed cleaner, clearer.

I was exhausted as I got ready to meet Milosh, showering quickly and using Gabriel's AXE Ice Chill body wash, its exaggeratedly masculine scent reminding me of the policemen. Only twenty-four hours earlier, I'd been on my way to meet Hans, and twelve hours before that, I'd been furious because I'd run out of instant coffee. All of it now seemed part of a more naive existence, one that I was no longer living.

I borrowed a green-and-white flannel shirt from Gabriel, and matched this with a denim skirt I had stolen from EG's. It was too small for me, and too short, but I felt that I needed a new outfit in which to turn over a new leaf. Mascara and concealer under my eyes to hide the enormous dark rings. I looked great, actually. The cut on my cheek and scars on my chest made me look sort of wild, and my face was pink and flushed. I always look my best when I am ill, hungover or exhausted. The tension slackens and something in my face opens up.

I had left my bike at EG's and was running late, so Gabriel lent me his. As I rode northwards, I sliced through the muggy, polluted air so fast that it felt like a sea-breeze, except that the biscuit factory had been going strong all day, so it tasted sweet instead of salty. I realized I was starving and thought of all the food I'd left to rot in the fridge of the old apartment.

I was a little late and so didn't have to run through the whole *Pretending* That One Is *Not Pretending* Not to Be

Waiting for a Blind Date performance, nor to invoke the nonchalant unfixed-yet-not-unhinged gaze. He was there. He was so handsome, I couldn't believe he was there for me.

'Daphne?'

'Yes, nice to meet you.'

We hugged.

'Have you been to the Tempelhofer Feld before?'

'Yes,' I said, and showed him my screensaver.

'*Krass!* It's the best place in Berlin. Do you mind sitting on the grass? I know the spot with the best view.'

He guided us towards a grassy patch near to the left of the central runway, far away from the grassy bank where I'd sat with Richard Grausam that one time. I pointed out the biscuit factory and told him about how I used to think the smell was caused by a mysterious chemical reaction between elements in the soil. He'd bought us Berliner beers and introduced me to what would soon become 'our' drink, what the English call a shandy and the Germans call a *Radler*.

I can't remember our conversation very clearly, but I do recall that his nose was perfect. I have always appreciated a good nose. His was pointed and spritely, a nose formed by a childhood spent inhaling fine, Black Forest air. He asked about my French family and my life in London. He told me about his Polish grandparents and his childhood in a tiny village outside Freiburg.

He had moved to Berlin to study for a master's degree in History. He played football with a mixed-gender team, and DJ'd in a few clubs. He had a twin sister called Ella and, more troublingly, an ex-girlfriend called Hedvig.

'We were together for five and a half years.'

'Oh, and when did you break up?'

'A few months ago. But it was complicated – we lived together, so then I had to move. We share the same friend group.' I wanted to ask him why they'd broken up, but I didn't dare. 'And how do you like Berlin, Daphne? Your German is incredibly good.'

By then the sun was beginning to set, which is always a dramatic occurrence on the Tempelhofer Feld. It is so flat and open that it affords a perfect uninterrupted skyline. A group of men behind us began to drum. People lit barbecues, drank and hooted with laughter. Smoke rose in spirals all across the field, and the red glimmers from the coal transformed the shadowy veldt into something strange and prehistoric.

He smoked roll-ups and after a few drinks, I asked him to roll me one. I love it when men roll me cigarettes. It's one of the very few things they can do that I can't, and it makes me feel damsel-y and like they might be of some use to me. He pulled another *Radler* out of his backpack. It was one of those Fjällräven rucksacks that the cool kids sport. Their symbol is a fox, my favourite animal. How do you say that in German? I asked. '*Fuchs*,' he said, and lightly touched the fox pendant I wore around my neck.

'Where did you get that?'

'My mother.' Then he touched my cheek and traced the cut running down it.

'And how did you get that?'

I still feel proud at the incredible self-restraint I had demonstrated in not having immediately divulged the whole brick-and-break-in story right off the bat. It went completely against my nature. Usually, if I want someone to like me, then I consider all my secrets as up for grabs, fair game in the trade of bargaining for affection. Come to think of it, I'm less ashamed of all the lies I've told than all the truths I've told. I've confided in near strangers the deepest, darkest things about me and my family. I've told them all about the infidelities, cancers, drug overdoses — the kinds of things other people don't like to talk about, told to only a handful of people who've earned their trust. I have always exploited my misfortunes for narrative purposes. If you have to live through something horrible, you might as well turn shit to gold by telling a good story.

And the bricking certainly made a good story. I told Milosh about it in my faltering German, drawing it out. I kept wondering whether we were going to kiss. Someone began playing a violin, and Milosh laughed and put his head in his hands. 'This is nearly too romantic, Daphne!' I had no idea what time it was, but it was already dark. I was dizzy from drink and giddy with infatuation, and the stars and moon and sky looked skewed and strange. I was beginning to shiver with exhaustion. 'I'm starving!' he said suddenly. 'Shall we get something to eat?'

He led me to a pizza place he liked in the Schillerkiez, a dark, leafy criss-cross of cobbled streets outside the eastern entrance of the Tempelhofer Feld. I saved our place on a bench outside and he came back with four big slices, three of them with meat.

'You're not a vegetarian, are you?' he asked.

'No,' I lied, taking a lascivious bite of pepperoni pizza. I hadn't eaten meat in years, but I don't really like to admit this to men I'm attracted to. It makes me feel fussy and cerebral, both of which are thoroughly un-aphrodisiac qualities. Despite all the strange habits I cultivated around food, I've always enjoyed sharing greasy food with boys I like. It feels sensual and risqué to nourish our lusty bodies together. I wanted to appear epicurean, capricious and original in my tastes. I didn't want anyone to know I was concerned about my weight, although it was probably the main focus of my life at the time.

I walked him to the S-Bahn station. Like Hans, who I never texted back, Milosh lived in the old East. We dawdled awkwardly by the station, the silence between us growing taut and tense. He moved towards me with heartbreaking hesitancy, eyes dancing between my eyes and lips, checking that he'd read me right and that this was what I wanted. Our kisses tasted of lemonade. His hand trembled at the base of my throat, my collarbone. I could feel my pulse beneath his fingers. He pulled away and we smiled at each other, shy and privately thrilled.

'This is the best first date I've ever had by far!' he said.

'I completely agree.'

'Will we meet again soon?' I nodded, and we kissed again. He had to run to make his train.

I smiled the whole way home, savouring the evening and his request to see me again, *soon*. In the darkness the streets looked strange and unfamiliar; I followed Google Maps all the way to Gabriel's. It took me a while to find Siegfriedstraße and the light in the staircase wasn't working, so I had to grope my way up to Gabriel's flat. I couldn't remember if he lived on the fifth or the sixth floor and forced my key into various locks, trying to find the right one.

[02:35:12] Daphne: R u still awake
[02:36:54] Daphne: Cannot remember which floor i am mad
[02:42:59] Daphne: All good found it
[02:44:14] Daphne: 🖤 thanks for all schlaf gut*

---

* Sleep well.

10

Vigilante Justice

I T FELT EASY TO run that morning, as I still had adrenaline fizzing through my system. The sky was clear, but the sun hadn't yet risen. The light felt soft and buttery on my skin and limbs. Here and there I spotted a prairie falcon perched on a fence post, its head sunk into its snowy breast-plumage, immobile and sleepy. I thought about Grausam. I enjoyed comparing him to Milosh and thinking about him cruelly. I was frightened of him, true, but I did get a kick out of ignoring his messages and witnessing how he humiliated himself for me. He was a horrid, sour old man and his life was already ruined, whereas mine wasn't. I was promised for wholesome things.

No one was home when I returned, and I made myself some coffee in the Bialetti and ate some chia seeds from the enormous jar Gabriel had, swallowing great black mouthfuls. They crackled between my teeth. Sweat trickled in rivulets down the backs of my knees. I spent all day pacing between my bed and the kitchen, wishing Gabriel would return so I wouldn't be alone but dreading his catching me with my hand in the cookie jar.

He didn't return that evening, nor the next morning. I

worried he might have been avoiding me and resolved to find somewhere else to live before the day was over. I enjoyed the unfamiliar walk to German class that afternoon, cutting across the south-eastern edge of the Tempelhofer Feld and through the Schillerkiez. I sat next to Leila, who lent me pens and paper and let me share her textbook, as I'd left mine behind at EG's. We tested each other on the *Wortschatz* section.* The theme of the new German chapter was crime and punishment and we had to fill in the gaps of a story about a robbery. I knew all the words, of course, from my recent brush with the law, and Leila seemed impressed when I got 'evidence', 'emergency' and 'suspect' right.

During the break, I followed Kat outside. She asked me to hold her mobile phone as she rolled a cigarette. She was wearing one of Lars's enormous wife-beater shirts and a Yankees snapback cap. She looked amazing. She began to tell me about her weekend. She had been to a club and hadn't slept since Friday night. Leila, Katya and the Venezuelans joined us. Eventually Katya spoke over her.

'You look bad, Daphne. So tired, what's the matter?'

'Well,' I said in German, 'I had a really mad weekend. I came back from a night out, and found that someone had broken into my flat.'

'God, I can't believe that this happened. I mean, first they throw a brick through the window, and then they break in? That's really unlucky. Do you think that maybe you might be cursed?'

'Thanks, Katya, that makes me feel much be—'

But Kat cut across me:

---

* *Wortschatz* is German for 'vocabulary'. It comes from the stringing together of *Wort*, meaning 'word', and *Schatz*, meaning 'treasure'.

'What the fuck, girl? What a stupid thing to say. What is your problem!'

'Oh cummon, I was just kidding!'

'Does she look like she wants to hear your dumb jokes right now?!' Break was up. Kat gave Katya a hateful look as we sat down. She, for her part, avoided making eye contact with anyone, blinking rapidly as if to hold back tears. She barely said anything for the rest of class, and ran out of the door before the teacher had finished reading out the homework. Kat took my arm conspiratorially as I got up to leave.

'Daphne,' she said. 'Let's hang out.'

It wasn't a question. We headed instinctively to the Tempelhofer Feld. She pressed me for more details about Friday night. She wanted us to find out 'who the fuck did it', and when I told her I suspected the downstairs neighbour she sprang to her feet and started pulling me up.

'Let's go over there!'

'No, we really shouldn't,' I said, trying to pull her back down.

'Why not?'

'What are we going to do to him?'

'Ask him what the fuck his problem is!'

'That's a terrible idea.'

'Why?'

'Because I think he might be really dangerous.'

'What do you think he'll do to us?'

'I don't know, but he could do something bad.' I didn't tell her about my secret acid-attack fear.

'Well, let's go with Lars, then. No, seriously, he knows some really scary guys, we could go there and just freak him out.'

'I don't want to drag Lars into this.'

'Trust me, he'll do it for me. He owes me a favour or two.'
She uttered this last sentence in such a lewd tone that I didn't
say anything in response, and after a pause she added: 'Let's
just go round there and freak him out.'

'But the police will know it's me.'

'So? Just say it wasn't. They'll have no proof. Anyway, he
probably won't call the police. If this guy is attacking sleeping
girls then I'm sure he's involved with some much more serious stuff too.'

'But he might hunt me down and hurt me.'

'You don't have to go with them. Anyway, if he sees you
with a big gang of Lars's friends he'll freak the fuck out. Seriously, Daphne, you can't let this guy disrespect you like this.
Just come over to mine. We can talk about it.'

I knew it was a mistake to have agreed just as soon as we
arrived at her apartment. The flat stank of weed but Lars's
pupils were enormous and he had clearly taken something
much stronger. Another boy who I'd never met before sat on
the floor. It was still only early evening, but I couldn't tell if
this was the middle, the end or the start of their night. Slices
of pizza lay abandoned on the kitchen counter. Lars was
wearing his signature tank top, and he pressed me very tightly
to him. 'Niiiiice shorts,' he said, and I looked around uncom-
fortably for Kat. She was sitting on the leather sofa. Her eyes
followed Lars's hands as they traced the hem of my shorts,
and then they rolled upwards to meet my own. She smiled
and nodded, as if to say, 'It's OK, enjoy him.' God, so strange,
I thought. It must be part of some game of sexual provoca-
tion they played together.

'But you're cold!' he said, rubbing the goosebumps on my
arms. 'Do you want to borrow a hoodie? Are you girls hungry?' He turned to Kat, who was already swallowing the stray
slices, but I said I was fine.

Kat took me by the arm and introduced me to the stranger.

'This is Daphne, my best friend in Berlin,' she said. His name was 'Blinker' or 'Blonker'. I sat down next to him, folding my feet beneath me. I was constantly worried that they smelt bad. I only had one pair of shoes, and seldom wore socks, and by the end of the day they'd brew up such a stink that I was sure everyone around me must be holding their breath. But no one said anything. In fact, Blinker shifted closer and turned the full beam of his attention in my direction. He looked like a greyhound: wispy-haired and lanky with a long thin face and pointed fingers. He offered me a sip of his drink and when I hesitated, he seemed to read my mind.

'Only beer in there.'

I smiled. I took a sip, and it tasted pretty normal, but I spat it back into the glass while he wasn't looking.

'How do you know Lars and Kat?'

'I met them in a club,' he answered. He had a way of making very bold eye contact, which I found charismatic, but I'd also read it's a classic psychopathic trait to watch out for.

'And now supplies Lars with the drugs,' added Kat.

'Yes, but I give him a discount price.' He smiled, and took a sip of his drink. 'Do you want something? I have Tor K.'

'No, thanks,' I said, with absolutely no clue what it was I was refusing.

'Daphne doesn't do drugs. But she's really a badass. Tell them about what your neighbour did.'

I told them the full story, embroidering a little, of course, making the first bricking seem more dramatic, and the break-in more sinister than it really was. I thought they'd laugh when I told them about the conversation with the police, especially the confusion about the 'pass', but they didn't seem to find it funny at all. Blinker twirled a lighter between his fingers as I spoke, and Lars turned down the music. In the sudden quiet I realized I'd been practically shouting. I stopped talking quite abruptly.

'And so what did you do?' Blinker asked.

'What do you think I did? I moved out!'

'No, I mean, what did you do about the neighbour?' he interrupted.

'NOTHING! What do you mean, what did I do? What could I do? The police were useless.'

'The police never do shit,' Lars said.

He plugged the speakers into his phone, and put on a playlist which must have been called something like 'panic-producing post-melodic electro'.

'No, but what about your friends?' Blinker went on. 'Probably you have friends you can ask?'

'Ask to do what?'

'To help you fuck him up!'

'I don't have those kinds of friends!'

'Yes, you do,' said Kat.

'Oh, that's nice, Kat, but you know, it's fine. I really appreciate the offer, but I think it's better to let sleeping dogs lie . . .'

'Yes, exactly, let the sleeping dog die!' she cried. '*Come on*, Daphne. I told you before! They are my brothers and my brothers are your brothers.'

I thought of my actual brother then, his avocados and gluten-free bread and safe, immaculate flat in West London.

'It's so nice of you, honestly, but I wouldn't want any of you to get in trouble because of me.'

'Why would we get into trouble?' Lars asked. He crouched down on the floor next to me and his knee was pressing into mine. I returned the pressure, and wondered where this was all leading. Blinker started emptying tiny ziplock bags full of white powder on to the low table.

'We're not going to hurt him or anything, we're just going to freak him out.'

'But what will we do?'

'Break his window,' answered Blinker.

'But we might get caught.'

'How? Do they have a security camera there?'

I thought about Frau Becker's refusal to fork out for a real *Hausmeister*.

'No, there is no camera.'

'Well then! No risk!'

'But maybe he will call the police.'

'I doubt this guy wants anything to do with the police.'

'So maybe a neighbour might call the police.'

'Did they call them when he bricked you?'

'No.'

Kat and Lars were bent over the table now, and I could see the deep furrow of her spine under her shirt. Blinker poured me another drink, and I guzzled it down. What's the worst that could happen? We got arrested? And if we were caught, or stopped, I suppose it would be a story to look back on. Kat came over and began to play with the zip of my hoodie, mesmerized as the little metal prongs weaved together then pulled apart like fingers. I could see the freckles and tiny hairs around her mouth. She leant against me and I could feel the pulse in her ribcage. She offered me a sip of her drink.

'Don't you want to go, Daphne?'

'Fine, let's go!'

They all seemed thrilled, and I didn't feel particularly worried. I was sure fate would turn in my favour – we'd get sidetracked, Kat would decide she was too tired, or they'd all get too stoned and pass out. But they weren't showing any signs of getting any sleepier. They sniffed cocaine off each other's index fingers, politely offering me some between each snort and rubbing the last white traces into their gums. They sprayed something that looked like nasal drops into their mouths, but which I found out later was Tilidin, an opiate derivative given to cancer patients. It made them whoop-y and frenetic. Suddenly we were all leaving, Kat ran back for a jumper, and we were streaming through the Tempelhofer Feld towards Huberstraße.

It was a mistake to take that path. The Tempelhofer Feld looks dramatic at the best of times, and that night it looked bombed out and apocalyptic. The three of them walked ahead of me, their black silhouettes like a garland of paper-chain people. I could hear music somewhere in the distance, but could not identify its source, as the night was moonless and very black. 'Good for cover,' I joked, 'we won't be seen easily.' They cast their eyes to the sky and nodded gravely in agreement.

We agreed to split up into pairs in order to look less conspicuous. Lars and Blinker were going to the Hasenheide park, to find some stones for us to throw, while Kat and I took a roundabout way to EG's flat.

My breath was shallow; I could smell myself, sour and a little sulphurous.

'Kat,' I hissed as we crossed the road, but my voice made her jump and her hands shot to her chest.

'God, I'm speeding, don't surprise me like that!'

'Sorry!'

'What did you want to say to me?'

'I'm worried about the guys.'

'Why?'

'Because they deal and if they get caught, isn't there a chance they'll get sent to jail?'

She rolled her eyes. 'Absolutely not. I once had to call the police when I thought Lars might, like, fucking kill me, and they didn't do anything at all, just told me to move out. The police really *don't give a shit*.'

'Lars hits you?'

'Yes. I mean, not often, but I mean, yeah, sometimes he takes shit out on me.' She pulled up the sleeve of her T-shirt.

'Is that a *bite* mark?'

'Mhm.'

'Oh God, Kat, why don't . . .' Before I could say anything else, we saw the boys walking towards us.

'So,' Blinker whispered, not quietly enough for my liking. 'We haven't done anything bad until we throw, so wait till the right moment, when no one is there.' He opened the backpack, which was filled with stones and broken-off pieces of concrete.

I pushed the key into the lock, only an easy half-turn before it swung open. The three of them flooded in. I felt anxious but very passive, too, as if the rope that tethered me to my normal life was running through my hands, and I'd already accepted there was nothing I could do about it. 'Guys,' I said, as they passed the second door and into the courtyard. '*Guysssss*,' I hissed. 'Please, I think I just heard someone walking past!' We stopped to listen but heard nothing at all. I followed them into the courtyard, careful to hang on to the doorknob before the door swung shut.

'Which flat?' Lars whispered, eyeing the windows. All the lights were off. The towels the downstairs neighbour usually used for curtains were nowhere to be seen, and his flat was dark. I pointed.

'It looks empty,' Blinker observed.

'Who first?' Lars said.

'I'll do it!' whispered Kat, and the stone flew from her

hand at the same time as the words escaped her lips. It was a clumsy throw, missing the window completely and bouncing off the wall just above the ground with a dull thump.

'Idiot!' said Lars, and took aim. He hit the middle window and smashed through the three layers. The impact rippled through the silent courtyard like waves breaking, first a whip-like crack of impact, the slap of the larger panes and then the delicate tinkle of scattering shards like water pulling back over smooth pebbles. But I was surprised at how quickly the sound was swallowed back into the night. When the stone had smashed my window, I'd felt the noise reverberate for ages. From out here, it passed in an instant. Maybe that was why my neighbours hadn't come out to check on me – they just hadn't heard it.

'Daphne?' Blinker asked.

'Sure,' I said.

The outer layer of the stone was crumbling into my hand, coarse and grainy like coffee grounds. I didn't want Lars to ridicule me so I threw it hard, aiming for the window to the left. The stone smashed through the window and big seg-ments of glass peeled towards us. I saw the neighbour loom into view and then hit the ground. A light in one of the second-floor flats, possibly Günter's, flicked on. I looked around at the others in the sudden brightness. Blinker and Lars had turned their faces towards the courtyard door.

'Let's go, *now*.'

We sprinted out of the courtyard, fumbling and bumping past each other to get out all at once. They turned right, towards the U-Bahn, but I ran towards the Hasenheide park and the Tempelhofer Feld. I was breathing hard and mechan-ically but I didn't know where the oxygen was going. It certainly wasn't to my heart, which seemed to be cramping, nor to my brain, which kept playing details of the evening on loop: taking a sip of Blinker's drink, Kat lifting her shirt to show me the bite mark.

I let myself into Gabriel's building. The courtyard light blinked on as I rushed in, as bright and blinding as a searchlight. Once inside the flat, I crept into my bedroom and powered my laptop on. There was a Ryanair flight for London leaving Tegel at 5.50 a.m., and an easyJet flight leaving at 7 a.m. I didn't know how badly the neighbour had been hurt. I thought about googling 'how easy is it to kill someone by throwing a stone?' but thought better of it. I checked my phone; it was 2.30 a.m. by then. I had a message from Kat: 'Fun night! Did you get home safe?' and a text from an unknown number, probably Blinker: 'Don't talk about tonight with anyone!'

What if the neighbour had died? We might be sent to jail for this. I googled 'prison time for murder in Germany': 'The penalty for *Totschlag* (manslaughter) is three to fifteen years in prison and in especially grave cases, lifetime imprisonment (minimum sentence fifteen years).'

But even if they did find me, they surely wouldn't give me fifteen years. I had no drugs in my system, and I'd been to a good university. I had potential. So, at the *very very* most, it would be five years. And honestly, I would have much rather spent a couple of years in prison, under the authority of laws and rational agents, than an hour hanging out with Richard Grausam or hiding from the downstairs neighbour. At least in prison I would have some externally imposed structure, and I would get *really*, *really* good at German, practically fluent. I would come out and really appreciate everything I'd lost a taste for – good food and family, individual freedom. And even if it *was* really awful there, it would be excellent grist for the story mill. This could actually be the making of me.

11

Clean-up

I MUST CONFESS THAT much of what I have just written is not true. It isn't really what happened. I don't mean the whole story is a lie – it is very nearly completely true. I'm referring only to the last chapter. Not all of it. I did go to Kat's and met her drug-dealer friend Blinker. We did leave the house and collect stones to exact revenge on the downstairs neighbour. But then I pretended to have lost EG's keys and although the others made a show of grumbling, we were all secretly relieved. We returned to the Tempelhofer Feld and stared at the sky, and after an hour I went back to Gabriel's flat, and spent the rest of the evening in my room, looking at my phone.

I'm not sure why I felt the need to lie. I suppose I wish that I'd done something truly daring like some character from a Western, and taken the law into my own hands. I wish I had taken decisive action and done something, even something stupid and regrettable. It might have snapped me out of the self-deceit that dominated my life. I wasn't truly awake during those months in Berlin. I was self-obsessed and thought about myself constantly, but I was completely in denial about how I really lived and acted. I thought of myself as a young decent-looking woman having the time of her life, living the Berlin Experience. I was strung along by ideas about myself. How I actually spent my time was immaterial, because eventually I could tell whatever story I fancied about those years of 'joyfully misspent youth'. That kind of self-denial is nearly a skill. No one would ever know I spent all day thinking about and avoiding food, and was mostly alone. I didn't even truly know it. An act of vigilante justice may have forced me to wake up.

The next morning, I asked Callum if he would help me move my things out of EG's flat, and he agreed to meet me at Huberstraße in the afternoon. I got my phone out again and logged on to Facebook, and scrolled through the pages of Berlin sublets. The only promising place was located in Neukölln and belonged to a woman named Cass Wolf. Her ad ran:

> I rent my apartment from 1st July till 30th January. It has a total of 38m² and is beautifully designed and decorated. The bathroom is spatial and has a bath and flawed heating. The kitchen is absolutely equipped – from the fridge to the dishes everything is available. From morning to afternoon, you can enjoy the sun on the south-facing balcony. The apartment is super quiet, due to the location in the Hinterhof.

I was wise to this quiet *Hinterhof* nonsense, but I liked the idea of a balcony and a bath and messaged immediately. She answered almost at once, suggesting I drop by in the evening. I went into the kitchen and chatted for a while with Gabriel. He had just finished making himself breakfast: chive-y eggs, tomatoes and lettuce stuffed into sweet little bread rolls Berliners call *Schrippe* and the rest of Germany calls *Semmel* or *Brötchen*. He made himself this kind of elaborate sit-down breakfast every morning. He ate slowly, squirting sriracha into the mouth of the sandwich and swilling orange juice between each bite. He offered me a *Schrippe*, but I told him that Callum and I were going to have an ice cream later. He made a face.

'I know, but I'm not very healthy like you, you know. I have baby tastes. I just like sweet and milky things.'

'Well, you have to look after yourself. Remember, nobody else will.'

'Yeah,' I said. 'I try.' Of course, I wasn't really trying. My whole life was a kind of montage for a rescue scene. I wanted someone to save me from my dysfunctional self. I didn't know what this rescue would look like exactly or who its instigator would be – I hoped for a kind of druid or monk figure. He would take me to a cabin in the Black Forest. He would bid me to sit. Serve me wine, bread, insist I eat. Lots of linen sheets, down coverlets and pails of fresh milk. I'd fill out and chill out and become a female version of Gabriel.

We drank coffee and did our German homework, but I couldn't concentrate. I kept checking my phone for a text from Milosh. I needed to get the rest of my things out of EG's flat. She and I had not communicated since the morning of the break-in. I was avoiding writing to her because I still hadn't cleaned up and she was avoiding me, I imagined, because she was scared I'd ask her to reimburse the remaining two months' rent.

The midday sky was a bright, ugly grey and it was hotter than I had anticipated. I caught sight of my reflection in the U-Bahn window. I looked like a broken umbrella. Because I am so inelegant, everyone always assumes that I'm 'relaxed', that I don't care how I look. I pretend to be above 'style' and 'fashion', but the truth is I am just incapable of it. I mind *terribly* about my appearance but am helpless to improve it. I try to plan nice, respectable outfits, but when I look in the mirror, I usually find myself grotesque. Nothing I wear looks as though it belongs to me. Often it actually doesn't. I tear the clothes off my back and leave them to wrinkle in piles all over the floor. My friends often comment on my un-put-together-ness, pointing at a coffee stain on the hem of my dress. 'You're so messy!' they say, shaking their heads as I rummage for my keys in the Aldi bag. 'You're such a *mess!*' And I guffaw and egg them on and say, 'Yes, yes, ha, ha. I'm such a mess, just look at me.'

I got off at Hermannplatz and walked over to Der Kaninchenbau. I felt naked and exposed on the street: I wondered if the bouncer would protect me from the downstairs neighbour if he happened to pass by. I had a message from Milosh, and one from Callum:

[13:03:11] Milosh: Hi beautiful Daphne. I see you tomorrow night, I hope 😊 How about we go and see a film @ Hasenheide Freiluftkino?* And maybe we can eat something yummy before?
[13:11:29] Callum: Going to be about 45 minutes late. Sorry, see you soon.

I sent them both a thumbs-up emoji. I didn't want to go into EG's flat alone. My shirt was sticking to my skin and I was longing for somewhere cool. I decided to go for a coffee at Karma Rösterei. I walked to the crossing, and was waiting for the light to turn green when I felt someone's hand on my shoulder. I turned, expecting it to be Callum, but it was Richard Grausam. I wondered if I was dreaming. I felt sleepy, suddenly, as if I were watching all this from far away, peering

---

* *Freiluftkino* translates to 'fresh-air cinema'. There are loads of outdoor cinemas in Berlin during the summer.

down the wrong end of binoculars. I stared at his hand on my shoulder. He had nubby, inelegant fingers, and his fingernails were dirty. His hand was warm and moist, and lay heavy upon me. I looked up at his face. He had very nice eyes – a restful, sea-green shade I've never seen in anyone else's. He seemed older – his head was so closely shaved that I initially thought he had gone bald. His thin lips were chapped. He looked delighted.

'Daphne! Why haven't you been answering my calls! I was so worried about you!' I shrugged his arm off my shoulder with a vehemence that seemed to surprise him.

'Daphne! God, what's the matter?!' The light went green, and he wheeled his bike beside me as I stepped off the pavement. 'God, come on, you're exaggerating, what's the matter with you?' I was moving away when he grabbed the front of my shirt. 'Hey! I'm talking to you!' I tried to pull away, but he had somehow managed to grasp the fabric of my bra through my T-shirt. 'I just want to talk to you! Why are you acting so crazy all of a sudden?' I pulled away again and this time I got loose. His bike clattered to the floor as the lights turned red, and I heard cars beep as he rushed to pick it up. I somehow made my way into Karma Rösterei. It was empty apart from the friendly barista – the one with red hair and spider tattoos, who still remembered my name.

'Daphne! *Alles gut?* Long time I didn't see you!'

'Hey! So good to see you! All good, you?'

'I'm good, I'm good. Keeping busy, you know, classes, and me and my girlfriend are going to Colombia in a few weeks so I've been working like crazy.' He manned the coffee machine as he talked, remembering my order. 'Have you ever been? Got any tips?'

'I'm afraid not. I really want to, though.'

This return to normalcy was a shock. Had I really just seen

Richard Grausam? The sores on my chest were throbbing. I wasn't imagining it; he had grabbed me. I realized that my legs were shaking. I steadied myself by leaning on the counter. The barista didn't notice, he kept prattling on in his friendly way. I sat down and took a sip of the coffee. It was sour and ashy and I could hardly bear to drink it. I didn't think he would follow me into a public place, but the door opened and he came in, ignored the barista's hello and sat next to me. He put his hand on my knee as if it were the most ordinary thing.

'Stop. Stop now or I'm going to call the police!' I said, loudly enough for the barista to hear.

'God, Daphne, calm down, please!' he hissed. 'Last time we spent time together you were so lovely, so affectionate! What happened to you? You don't look so well, did something happen to you?'

'Stop. Just leave me alone. I don't have to talk to you!'

'Is everything OK, Daphne?' The barista had overheard, and was leaning over the counter looking concerned.

'No, it's not OK. He won't leave me alone!'

'Argh, *Quatsch*,* Daphne.' Grausam spoke with so much emphasis that spittle flew in my face. I could smell his breath. His hand was still on my knee. I pulled his hand off me and his expression changed. For a brief, absurd moment, I thought he had felt the graze of my unwaxed stubble on my knee, and that he was grimacing in disgust, but instead he looked sad, and began to plead with me. 'What's the matter, Daphne, please. Please just explain to me what is wrong. If I did something then just tell me so we can make it up. I don't understand what happened!'

The barista had walked out from behind the counter and

_____
* Nonsense.

was now standing right beside me. I was reassured by his height. I saw Grausam register it, too.

'Do you want this guy to leave, Daphne? Is he bothering you?'

'Yes, he is. Leave me alone or I'm going to call the police!'

'Do you want me to call the police?' the barista asked.

'Hey, stranger, mind your own business,' Grausam replied, in a calm but firm tone. 'This is between me and my girl-friend here, OK?'

'Yes, please call the police.' I stood up. I felt unsteady on my feet. My body didn't really feel like my own, but like a haphazard collection of butcher's cuts. Grausam got to his feet, too. He was dwarfed by the barista, but there was something about him, a restless, dangerous kind of energy that made him seem more impressive.

'I'm the one who should call the police on you, Daphne. You're so crazy I don't even understand you. Do you have bipolar or something? One minute you're trying to come over all the time and telling me how lonely you are in Berlin, and now you want to call the police? I'm not allowed to talk to you any more? What is this, the Stasi?'

'Get the fuck out of here now,' the barista said. Grausam's gaze flitted between the barista and me, back and forth, appraising us. I braced myself for more aggression, but his face fell.

'I miss you so much, Daphne.' He was on the verge of tears. 'I don't understand what happened to you.' He turned and left. I looked up at the barista. I realized my hand was gripping his forearm.

'I'm sorry.' I let go, leaving white finger marks on his skin. 'I'm so sorry about that. He wasn't ever actually my boy-friend, I just . . .'

'Are you OK? Do you want to sit down?'

'No, no. I have to go. Thank you so much for your help. I'm so sorry for causing a scene.'

'Don't worry about it. Are you sure you are OK? You don't want me to ring someone? The police?' I thought of Officer Blondie and his useless sidekicks.

'No, I'm fine, really.'

He insisted on making me a hot chocolate to go, which I immediately binned when I was out of sight. I walked back towards EG's flat, my hand fluttering against my throat and neck as I continually checked my pulse. I wanted to get a locked door between me and Grausam but I was worried about running into the downstairs neighbour. I didn't think the neighbour would dare do anything in broad daylight. Anyway, it was a Tuesday. Frau Becker usually came to carry out her *Hausmeister* duties and 'clean' the courtyard on Tuesdays. He wouldn't dare try anything with her around.

I walked to my building and crossed the courtyard, keeping my eyes fixed on the ground as I passed his door. EG's flat was a terrible mess. The coconut oil had congealed, full of tiny pieces of glass, and all the bedding was still on the floor from when Officer Blondie had pulled it off the mattress. I threw the sheets, frou-frou pink cushion covers, towels and shower curtain into the washing machine with three Spring Meadow laundry capsules and set about cleaning the most offensive area: the toilet and shower. I was glad that Callum was late. I wasn't attracted to him, but I still wanted him to be attracted to me. My mirror was smudged with beige concealer and splatters of toothpaste.

The glass grated the tiles horribly as I scraped the coconut oil off the floor with kitchen roll. It smelt good, like macarons. I wiped up all the dust, unidentifiable things and hairs from all the nooks and crannies, vacuumed the shower, filled the loo with white vinegar (which I've since learnt doesn't work at all on toilets), and cleaned the mirror with bits of old newspaper. I'd learnt this trick while working in the cafe in London. My boss had been very particular about the windows and mirrors. She'd regularly sent us pictures of the fingerprints and other sinful omissions, followed by videos she took of herself cleaning with newspaper, showing us the proper way to do it.

By then it was 2.20 p.m. and Callum was still not there. I put the sheets in the dryer and began to clean up the kitchen. I threw all of my weird food, the *Rotkohl* and mustard and oats, into an enormous black bin bag, mixing it with glass shards and sodden paper towels. I sponged up all the insides of the cupboards, filling them with my showcase provisions. The freezer was frosted over, and I tried and failed to gouge out the shelf of ice with a bread knife. Although I was a little scared, I was enjoying myself. The dryer began to thud and whirr as it picked up speed, and the glasses on the shelf above rocked along with it, clinking together like chimes.

The doorbell rang. It was Callum. I opened the door and felt irritated by how great he looked. He'd obviously been going to the gym. I could see the muscles beneath the surface of his skin as he moved. He was wearing an immaculately pressed white T-shirt and aviator sunglasses.

'Hi! How are you? Good to see you! Come in! Do you want tea?' He was much bigger and stronger than my neighbour, so I felt safe. But I felt awkward. I'd only answered his texts a few times since the night he'd slept over, back in April, and I worried he'd think I was only using him for his body, which I suppose I was.

'Tea with milk, please. So what happened? Do you know who did it?'

'I promise I'll explain properly, but I can't *right now*,' I answered, pointing downwards and pulling a terrifying grimace.

'Oh,' he said. 'But do you think the neighbour downstairs did it?'

'Shhhhhhhhh!!!!!!!!!!!!!!!!'

'*Do you think the guy downstairs did it?*' he whispered.

'Yes, I'm sure he did, but *we can't talk about it now.*'

I boiled the kettle as he took off his enormous shoes and sat cross-legged on the sheetless bed.

'Aren't you going to have any?' he asked, as I handed him the cup and a plate of biscuits.

'No, no time. I have to get this finished.'

'Do you want me to help?'

'No, just sit there and be my bodyguard.'

'Can I read you a novel I'm working on?'

'Sure.'

He sat and read as I packed and emptied the cupboards, forcing myself to leave EG's dirndl dress behind. He read on as I swept up the tinkling glass confetti and sprayed and scrubbed the cabinets. He shouted the story over the vacuum cleaner and read it crouching on a chair as I made the bed. The cushions had dyed the sheets very slightly pink. I can't really remember what his novel was about. I think it was fine, even good, but I wasn't paying attention. I was itching to get out of there. At last I finished cleaning and his reading came to an end. The flat looked perfect, just as it had when I first moved in. EG would have nothing to complain about when she returned.

'Can you just help me with one thing?' I asked. 'Would you mind taking the bins down? I'm scared of running into him.'

The downstairs neighbour came out of his flat for a smoke just as Callum descended.

He brushed past Callum and leant against the wall facing my apartment. It was the first time I'd seen him since the break-in. He gazed up at me, looking stranger than ever. He smiled faintly, and put his finger to his lips, as if shushing a child. A nasty secret we shared.

'God,' Callum said, when he returned, 'that guy smells absolutely *terrible*! He looks so weird and spaced out! What a horrible person to have as a neighbour! I wonder how he can afford the rent here!'

I knew how. In Berlin, rich and poor live side by side in the same buildings. This is due to the distinction between 'old contracts' and 'new contracts'. If you have an old contract, the landlord is unable to charge a rent higher than 10 per cent of the neighbourhood's average price. If you have a new contract, however, the landlord can increase the rent as much as he wants. This means, effectively, that one person with an old contract might be paying 400 euros a month for a rather dilapidated 50 square metres, while the person living in a flat above might be paying 12,000 euros for the same space. Trustafarians and on-the-dolers live in the same buildings and dress from the same thrift shops. It makes social distinctions much less visible in Berlin than in most cities.

'Old contract,' I said. 'Let's go.'

Callum lugged the enormous suitcase down the stairs and across the courtyard. I glanced at the neighbour as we went past. He didn't look at us and didn't pull out a flask of acid. Could he really have done it? Was his apathy a sign of innocence, or psychopathic indifference? I felt relieved as the door swung shut behind me.

I was not in the mood to be social, but I'd promised Callum I'd buy him an ice cream if he helped me. We walked to Fräulein Frost, a lovely pastel-coloured parlour near the River Spree. I was surprised to see that Katya was working behind the counter. She smiled hesitantly, eyed Callum with a look of approval and winked knowingly at me. I didn't bother introducing him or setting her right. He chose mint and banana, which I thought was a terrible choice, and I had vanilla and pistachio. Katya gave me an extra-enormous serving, and I pretended to be grateful while inwardly wincing. He suggested that we try each other's flavours, and as we passed the cones back and forth between each other, I detected the faintest squeak of sexuality. I told him the full story of the break-in as we ate, but he didn't react as I'd expected. It seemed to upset him, and he looked sad and worried about me. Don't you understand? I wanted to say. It's not depressing, it's *interesting*. It makes a good story.

The ice cream swilled around in my stomach as I rode the U-Bahn back to Gabriel's. I felt a little sick imagining the white sweet paste coating all my organs. I heaved the bags up the stairs and then walked back to the U-Bahn, picking up a Diet Pepsi from the *Späti* on the way. Cass Wolf's apartment was near Boddinstraße, only two stops away from Gabriel's flat. At least it wouldn't be too hard to move my stuff if she took me on. I could do it in two trips, one if I got a taxi. I took a deep breath. You can do this, Daphne. None of that dark thinking now. Wipe your mind clear. Take this gift. Another immaculate fresh start.

12

Titania's Bower

FROM THE OUTSIDE, CASS's building looked run-down and depressing, wedged between a kebab shop and a laundromat. I searched the grid of names by the door for 'Wolf'.

'Halloooooo, Daphne! *Hinterhof*, left.'

I'd been sceptical about the *Hinterhof*, but this flat's charms had actually been undersold on the Facebook ad. The courtyard was *beautiful*, with three timber-trellis arches marking the doorways and a rough wooden pergola covering the bins and bike shed. There were a few raised beds full of yellowed plants, and a square of manured beds lining the courtyard's outer perimeter. These were barren, save for a wisteria vine, which climbed up the wall and clung to the window casing. There were three apartments per landing, each with defunct-looking square brass doorbells. Cass lived in the middle apartment on the first floor, and her door stood ajar.

'Halloooo,' I called.

'Hallo! *Komm rein!*' she called back.

I walked over the threshold and took off my shoes at once.

It was a wonderful flat. The bathroom was tiled green from floor to ceiling. It was the bathroom I envisaged for my adult self – a griffin-legged tub, hair straighteners, a blue kimono hooked behind the door. The cabinets, I felt certain, were full of the most luxurious beauty products: La Prairie Skin Caviar, algae brightening masks, Kiehl's Creme de Corps. Cass had canopied the corridor, pinning green and gold Indian silk to the ceiling to form three curved arches. They hung so low that the fabric brushed my head, and the canopy rippled as I made my way towards the bedroom, a square room lined with three tall windows. A fleecy white carpet lay underfoot, and I tried to bury my hobbit-like feet into it. A carved wooden Buddha with closed eyes and an all-embracing smile sat upon a low teak table. He looked impassive and blissed-out, a kind of good-karma version of the concussed-looking downstairs neighbour. Opposite him was a low white bed. The headboard was some kind of DIY Pinterest birchwood lattice, interlaced with fairy lights. It made me think of the description of Titania's bower in *A Midsummer Night's Dream*. 'I know a bank where the wild thyme blows/Where oxlips and the nodding violet grows.' Cass sat on the bed in *virasana*, her legs folded beneath her and her computer propped on her lap. Botticelli's Venus wearing Lululemon.

'I love your pregnant ceiling,' I said, gesturing over my shoulder at the canopied corridor. She made tea and we drank it on her tiny balcony, which she'd arranged with wicker chairs covered in blankets and pillows. I know so much about her now that it is hard to whittle it down to the bare facts I learnt on the day I met her. She was from Aachen; she was twenty-nine and a Pisces. She worked in advertising and had run campaigns for Coca-Cola and Deutsche Bank.

Advertising, however, was only her 'cash cow', as she put it. She was grateful for it ('money is a form of energy') but she had been called by 'spirit work'. She had done yoga-teacher training in India and regularly participated in ayahuasca ceremonies. At one point, she interrupted herself to ask me why I always covered my mouth with my hand.

'Do I?' I said, sliding my hand down my chin and laying it on my knee. I'm always flattered when people point out things I do, even if they are inaccurate or insulting.

'Yes. Normally, it means either that you are lying, or that you think the other person is lying. Do you think all this yogi stuff is bullshit?'

'No,' I lied. 'I think I'm just shy sometimes, and that's why I cover my mouth.'

'Hmm,' she said. 'Well. If you want, you can move in on the first of July already.'

'Oh, so I can have it?' I'd assumed I was still being interviewed.

'Yes, for sure. I trust you. I feel it in the gut,' she said, pointing to her Lycra belly. Well, your gut must have a very original conception of what 'trustworthy' means, I thought. But my cynicism lasted only a heartbeat. I felt hopeful about myself in Cass's company. I sensed that she could see beyond the pollution and putrefaction blighting my soul to the pure stuff hiding beneath it. She showed me how the oven worked (I never used it), explained how much water each plant needed and how to turn on the underfloor heating in the bathroom.

The only question I had for Cass was whether or not she knew her neighbours. She told me that a couple who were film critics lived directly opposite. Next door to them was a Syrian girl called Leila, who was a good friend. Reassured that there were no brick-flingers among the neighbours, I signed the sub-tenancy agreement there and then. The flat was expensive – it was a 'new' contract – but I was willing to pay. I would have promised her my and Milosh's first-born child if that was what it took.

13

A Kebab Mood

I SLEPT WELL THAT night, and woke early to the sound of Gabriel singing along to the radio. I felt waves of relief wash over me as I remembered the previous day. I was out of EG's flat, and I was going to move into Cass's place: another new beginning.

Milosh and I had agreed to meet at the Hasenheide park that evening. I arrived early and sat near the Gambians' bench. I wondered if they'd be jealous when they saw me with Milosh, or if they'd be happy I'd met someone at last. They'd often asked if I had a boyfriend, and seemed part delighted, part pitying when I panted 'no' as I ran past on endless solitary loops. They didn't care, as it turns out. They didn't even glance in his direction as he pulled up beside me on his bicycle. He was extremely sweaty, which he apologized for, but which I didn't mind. I quietened Estella from rising within me and told him how glad I was to see him again.

He was hungry, and we had a little time to kill before the film.

'I'm in a kebab kind of mood,' he said, so we walked to the döner place next door to Cass's. I told him about moving out of EG's apartment, and breakfast with Gabriel, and pointed out my new building. I remember distinctly liking him, as we sat in that ugly little place. He was so good-looking, even under neon lights, even with big skewers of greasy meat slowly rotating in the background.

I spoke much more than Milosh did that evening, and I would speak much more than him every time we were together, except for the last time. I provided the minced lamb, garlicky yoghurt and tomatoes of our conversations, while he provided the salad and flatbread wrap. I was the content, he was the structure. At the time I couldn't tell whether his silence was a reflection of inner depth, or just a sign that he was dumb as a box of bricks. I learnt later that he was perceptive, a kind of discreet genius who would under-stand me better than I understood myself. That evening he was quiet, and I was just happy to take a few bites of his kebab, to have my shoulder in the crook of his arm, and to let him pay for my cinema ticket. Sebastián had never treated me – he had been strict about always splitting the bill, even when I insisted that I wanted to pay. Splitting the bill was the extent of Sebastián's feminism.

I'd never been to an outside cinema before. Along with the Tempelhofer Feld, the Hasenheide Freiluftkino is one of my favourite places in the world. It is situated in a woody enclave in the middle of the park, very near to the rose garden. It is set up like a Roman amphitheatre, with rows of wooden benches sloping upwards, arranged in a semi-circle around a fabric screen, which hangs from an old oak. Milosh and I sat right in the middle. All around us, rivulets of smoke drifted upwards, and all the profiles looked elegant and old-fashioned. Milosh lit a cigarette himself and opened me a *Radler* using his lighter. I've never been able to master that myself, and along with cigarette-rolling, it belongs to a rep-ertoire of tricks which somehow really work on me. Milosh put his right arm around my shoulder and smoked with his left – that's another thing I am partial to, left-handed people – but before we could get properly comfy, it started to rain.

'What shall we do?' Milosh asked me, as everyone around us scuttled to shelter.

'We can just stay,' I said.

He pulled his denim jacket over our heads. The beam of the projector shone through the rain, like a police torch searching for something in the mist. The trees framing the screen shivered and nodded under the raindrops. It felt like we were alone in a tent deep in the woods.

For the first half I paid more attention to Milosh than to the film. I always do this when I watch a movie with someone – I watch *them* watching the film, searching for a cue to regulate my own reaction, because I trust their response more than my own. This is foolish and spineless of me, of course, especially because I've seen some brilliant films in the company of some real morons – but I can't help it, the mistrust of self is too deeply ingrained. It is why I usually prefer going to the cinema alone. He seemed to be enjoying himself, though. He was smiling and laughing and squeezing my hand and so I started to watch it too. By the time it ended the rain had stopped. Hasenheide was dark green and drippy. We walked silently and kept our voices low, as if careful not to scare off the complicity that had newly arisen between us. We walked past the pizzeria we'd been to on our first date, and through the Schillerkiez until we came to the language school, where I had locked up Gabriel's bike that morning.

'That is where I learn German,' I said, and felt as if I were showing him the place I'd been born. I rode ahead of him, and our bicycle lights formed a cell of luminescence rolling through the darkness like a sleeper train. It was nearly pitch-black and the lights mustered enough strength to illuminate

only a few metres ahead of us. We knew, I think, that w
sleep together. We just had no idea what to expect from o
another. I felt as if with each push of the pedals I was reeling
in a big spool of fishing line, shortening the distance till we
got to my bedroom, where I would find out if I had caught a
merman or a trout.

I am somewhat of a prude, so I will not share any of the
explicit details. But Milosh was more merman than trout. He
was quite suave and considerate, keen to please without being
obsequious. I could tell that someone, probably his ex-
girlfriend, had made sure he understood the rudiments of
female pleasure (thank you, Hedvig). Most of the very few
men I've slept with didn't have much of a clue, and I
was even more ignorant. Usually, during sex, I felt as if I was
expected to act in a porn film, but no one had shown me the
script. I have never watched porn myself – the few clips I'd
glimpsed by accident reminded me of the undercover foot-
age PETA makes to expose the inhumane conditions in
abattoirs. As a result, I am always completely baffled when
men start trying to contort me into strange poses. I often
have literally no idea what I'm supposed to do. This tribute-
to-porn sex is completely void of any duplicity and, on my
side, pleasure. Not that the men I've slept with were unkind
or selfish – they were always empathetic, considerate people
in real life – but they just didn't know how to act during sex.
I improvised as best I could, assuming I just had to sound
like I was having a whale of a time, like the upstairs neighbour's girlfriend.

If Milosh was a merman, and the other men were trout, I
was a starfish. Very passive, pretty useless, basically, trying to
look pretty but not doing much. I was mostly very self-
conscious. I felt towards my body what I imagine an anxious
pet-owner must feel when competing at the Crufts Best in

Show competition: putting her dog through its paces, hoping the training would pay off, trying to conceal the dog's defects while giving the appearance of enjoying herself.

Many of my friends feel more or less the same. Katya had once told me that, while she loved her boyfriend Chorizo and often instigated sex, she 'hates the actual penetration', and Kat had confessed that most of the tension in her relationship with Lars was born of her lack of interest in sleeping with him. The only woman I knew who uncomplicatedly adored sex was Cécile, my flatmate in London. She was always bringing men home – they were often much younger than her, invariably muscular. She would lock herself away with them for hours, and then fetch me from my room so that we could go to the chip shop together: 'I need to eat something greasy full of FAT after sex.' We'd eat fish and chips in the kitchen and she would talk about her proclivities. I suppose I found it awkward, but I loved basking in the glow of her pleasure. She was comfortable in her body, which was ruddy and fat-chinned but cared for, extremely feminine. I wish I was more like her.

Not that I dislike sex completely. I do enjoy some aspects of it. I want to feel like an object of desire. I want to feel wanted, essentially. It gives me a kick to think of myself as being someone's 'lover'. I just don't like it while it is *actually happening*. I feel that way about a lot of things, as a matter of fact – running, going to the dentist, visiting relatives. I'm glad when it's over, but I like knowing I've done it.

Anyway, the best part of sex with Milosh was that it took place entirely in German. I didn't say anything. But he spoke in German. He used all the correct cases and declensions, which I found astounding. Speaking German for me was such an act, such a mask, that I assumed that when Germans took off their clothes they'd revert to English, like the rest of us. This is not the case, I found out. They are German the whole time, even during sex.

I slept very well that night, far better than I'd slept in weeks. Although it was hot in Berlin in late June, Gabriel's flat was cool. My recent insomnia was due to the fact that I was often hungry in the night. I'd fall asleep quite easily, but I'd wake up at two or three in the morning, and then I'd have to eat something. I would creep out of my bedroom, stopping after each creak of the floorboards to listen for a sign that Gabriel was awake. It sounds so ridiculous, looking back on it, but it would not be an exaggeration to describe my state during those stealthy kitchen raids as one of terror. I was in mortal terror of Gabriel catching me eating his food at 3 a.m. I was in mortal terror of him realizing the food was missing. I was in mortal terror of myself, my rabid hunger, what it would do to my body. Yet despite this mortal terror, I was unable to put a stop to it. In the kitchen, which was far more abundantly stocked than my cupboards had been at EG's, I would eat white processed bread and spoonfuls of honey from the jar and cooking chocolate and walnuts and anything else high in fat and sugar. The food gave me more pleasure and shame than sex ever has. I'd never finish anything – but I'd take perhaps a 15 per cent tax on lots of different items so that no one would notice the difference. Then I would try to replace everything *exactly* as I'd found it, and creep back to bed, with every creak of the floorboards screaming, 'Wake up, Gabriel! Wake up, she's robbing you blind!'

But despite the fact that I'd only had a few bites of kebab the previous evening, I didn't wake up that first night Milosh and I slept together. He'd tell me later that he had this effect on his ex-girlfriend, too. He was a lovely person to share a bed with. He slept extravagantly, the sleep of a blameless German conscience. His gravitational force was so powerful that it drew more lightweight sleepers into his orbit and created an atmosphere of absolute peace.

When I did wake up the next day, around 10 a.m., which was far later than usual, it was only because I had an agonizing cramp in both of my calves. I had these pretty regularly, because I was always dehydrated and deficient in pretty much all minerals and vitamins, but they were particularly painful that morning. It felt like someone had seized the muscles and was slowly ripping them apart. I couldn't help uttering a gasp of pain, which woke Milosh.

'*Was ist los?*' he asked.

'Nothing . . . I just get cramps in my legs sometimes.' Still half asleep, he took my legs in his lap and stroked my calves, which was very sweet of him, but it did nothing to relieve the pain.

'I want to shower, if it's OK,' he said after a little while. I gave him my own clean-ish towel. While he showered, I hurriedly made the bed, flung open the window, and disposed of any evidence of the amorous night.

Gabriel was already in the kitchen, eating one of his sumptuous eggy breakfasts.

'Gud MOORRRN-ING, DARF-ne, ow arrre you? Did you have a gud night?' Oh God, I thought. Had he heard the German sex?

'Hi! Yes, it was nice, thanks. The film was really good,' and then, in a whisper, '*Milosh is here. He's in the shower. Sorry, I should have asked . . . I hope it's OK . . .*'

'Of course! Of course! Do you guys want coffee? Do you want some eggs?'

Milosh came in then, and they sat and drank coffee together while I showered. I could hear them talking. What might they be talking about! Could it be about me? This was proof! I was normal! I had a flatmate who ate breakfast and I sometimes slept with boys like everyone else! I was part of society!

Gabriel insisted on making each of us one of his signature sandwiches (with no sriracha for Milosh; he was very sensitive to anything spicy, one of his least attractive qualities). We wrapped them in some aluminium foil and packed them with a Thermos of iced coffee. We rode to what was now 'our' spot in the Tempelhofer Feld and spent the whole morning together.

'So why did you move to Berlin? Was it for a job, or something?'

'Oh no, I mean, mainly it was because I wanted to learn German, you know, and I wanted an adventure, too.'

'Nice, cool. And so, how do you survive? Do your parents help you with money, or a student loan?'

'Oh no, I work for a French family.'

'What do you do?'

'Oh, I babysit for two girls. Esther and Sylvia. I pick them up from school, drop them off. That kind of thing. Their mum is nice but their father is a bit creepy.'

'Really?'

'Yeah. He often makes remarks about my appearance, like, "I can tell you haven't had children, with a figure like that," and "My, my, what a wasp's waist you have!" And how about you, Milosh? Do you have a job?'

'I have a scholarship from the History faculty.'

I steered the subject away from my financial arrangements to what we were reading and to his studies. He'd just finished a book for his degree, something about Soviet Ukraine, and was re-reading *A Hunger Artist*, just for fun. I'd never read it before, and so he offered to read it to me. He pulled a copy out of his bag, along with the sandwiches, and read aloud as I sipped the coffee. It was good, compelling, everything you'd expect, but it was short, even shorter than *The Little Prince*. He unwrapped our picnic, and I tried to explain the Wittgenstein essay I'd written for my bachelor's degree, while he finished his sandwich and got started on mine.

'Are you sure you don't want any? Just have a bite?' I demurred. 'Aren't you hungry in the morning?' I shook my head. 'I know that the French prefer sweet things for breakfast – croissant and such.' I nodded. He went on about the Kafka. He was clearly capable of producing a refined interpretation of *A Hunger Artist*, but he was unable to spot a real one sitting right there in front of him.

But I didn't think any of this at the time. It's only now, after the fact, that I see the irony of the situation, of him reading that particular book to me at that particular time. I absolutely did *not* identify with *A Hunger Artist*, nor did I think he was stupid not to see through my 'I only eat croissant, I'm a French girl' nonsense, because hardly anyone ever did see through my lies.

I loved being read aloud to and I really *liked* him. He asked questions about my thesis which showed he'd really been listening. He was patient with my German, interrupting only very occasionally to supply the right word or to explain an idiomatic expression. He tucked the hair behind my ears and told me I had a beautiful profile. He was often quiet, but the silence between us was not uncomfortable.

At some point I heard someone call my name, but I was facing the sun and couldn't tell who it was. I didn't care. Let Richard Grausam or the creep downstairs try to bother me as I sat with this Black Forest elf. But it wasn't any of my foes; it was Günter, my old upstairs neighbour. He was looking especially blond and pink and piggy in his tiny running shorts, and as he panted over us, I noticed he smelt like he'd eaten *Wurst* for breakfast. He was friendlier than usual.

'Daphne! *Gut* to see you! I was worried because I never saw you after the police visited.'

'Oh, yeah, I moved out after that.'

'Did they ever find out who did it?'

'No!'

'Did they tell you that I thought I heard something? Around lunchtime that day, I am pretty sure that I heard a terrible noise of glass or something smashing in your flat. I was going to come downstairs to check on you, but I didn't want to intrude.'

'Yeah, I have no idea. I think it was the downstairs neighbour, though. I left my window open, and he could have easily climbed in.'

'Yes, he does seem a bit strange. I haven't seen him for a while. Frau Becker was knocking on his door yesterday because he did not pay his rent.' His watch beeped, reminding him that he should be running. 'Anyway, good to see you are safe. Have a nice day.'

'See you around.'

'*Tschüuuuuuuuss*,' he yodelled as he ran off.

'*Tschüuuuuuuuss*,' sang Milosh and I in unison.

I've made a major omission by failing to mention the word *tschüss* before now. It is the first word most foreigners learn after *hallo*. It is an informal way of saying 'goodbye', like *ciao* in Italian or *à plus* in French, except that *tschüss* is sung, not said, and always in a falsetto. I have no idea why the laconic, dark-clothed Berliners tolerate such a jaunty way of bidding farewell, but they do, and it is one of the only times they sound wholesome and jolly, and it always lifted my mood to hear it.

*

By then it was noon, the sun hung heavy and distended, and there were no free trees under which to take the shade. Milosh decided to go home, and we agreed we would spend the following night together.

'Why don't you come to my house? I can show you my room and introduce you to my flatmate.'

I knew, from my cursory exposure to women's advice columns, that this invitation was an encouraging sign, that it meant he was ready to take the relationship to the Next Stage.

14

LSD and Gnocchi

O N T H E I S T O F July I woke in a terrible mood and with terrible breath. I had slept poorly, eaten a whole can of Gabriel's peanuts in the night, and I faced the prospect of packing, cleaning, moving again. I scrubbed and wiped up any evidence of my presence from Gabriel's spare room. As usual, I did a botched job of it, slathering hand soap on the kitchen surfaces and blotting it up ineffectually with loo paper, leaving loads of gunky white lumps behind. I packed my bags and realized I was missing two of my favourite T-shirts. I'd probably left them at EG's. This happened whenever I moved. I'd leave behind a trail of my things like some kind of Hansel-and-Gretel tribute. There were probably millions of my hairs and flecks of DNA-rich dead skin floating all over the city. If I was ever accused of a crime, or someone wanted to track me down, I'd be easy to trace.

By the time Gabriel returned from lunch with Nina, I had changed the sheets, vacuumed, and was finishing the mopping.

'Wowwwww, Daph-neeee, it looks a-mayziiing, you did such a gud jo-oob.'

'It's the least I could do! Thanks so much for having me!'

'Can I help you with the bags?'

'Yes, that would be great.'

Gabriel rode the U-Bahn with me, and helped me lug the bags up to Cass's flat. As we were pulling the last things off the landing, Leila from our language class came up the stairs.

'What are you doing here?!'

'I *live* here!' she said.

'Oh! So do I now! I'm just moving in!'

Leila, Gabriel and I marvelled at the coincidence, and then began to discuss our German class, while Cass looked on rather impatiently. Finally she interrupted, saying she hated to be rude but she had a plane to catch, and she wanted to run over a few last-minute logistical things with me. Gabriel left, and Leila told me to come over some time. 'I hope you drink coffee,' she said, as she hugged Cass goodbye, 'not like this healthy freak – she won't drink anything unless it's green or blue.' I followed Cass inside, and she began explaining things. She told me when to water the plants. She gave me the key to her bicycle lock, and leant over the balcony to point out which bike was hers. She showed me how to work the thermostat, and explained exactly how recycling worked in Germany, and then led me to the kitchen. I thought she was going to say something about not dipping into her store of flax and chia seeds, but that wasn't it at all.

'You can help yourself to anything you want from the fridge or cupboard,' she said, 'but I have to talk to you about something first.'

'What?' I said, nervously. Had she figured out I was strange around food? Did she think I was too thin? Or maybe everything I'd eaten at Gabriel's was showing? Did she think I was too fat?

'You remember I told you about the ayahuasca ceremonies?'

'Ye-essssss . . .'

'And LSD and micro-dosing?'

'Nooooooo.'

'But you know what micro-dosing is, right?'

I did. Google Greg had told me all about it. He took tiny quantities of magic mushrooms, or LSD diluted in water, every time he wanted to work on his thesis or do some 'crazy math'.

'Yes, of course.'

'Well, see this?' She gestured vaguely to the contents of her store cupboard. 'And see this?' She pointed in the general direction of the fridge drawer. 'Well, that stuff has either LSD or mushrooms in it. You're welcome to have some, but if you've never done psychedelics, it might send you on a big trip.'

'Wait, what has LSD and what has mushrooms in it?'

She probably noticed I seemed concerned, so she hurriedly drew smiley faces on the bottles and jars she knew contained hallucinogens. Before long she had to leave to catch her train to the airport, and she hugged me very tight and told me not to hesitate to message her if there was anything I needed.

I unpacked my bags, trying as best I could not to ruin the atmosphere she had left with my ugly crumpled possessions. I rearranged all the food and drinks Cass had left behind in the two bottom shelves of the fridge and made a mental note never to touch any of it under any circumstances. I didn't trust her to have fully remembered what had LSD in it and what didn't. Along with swallowing glass, accidentally ingesting psychedelic drugs is one of my biggest fears. Though I was bad-tempered from hunger, I swore off all of Cass's food. I ran a bath, and I washed my pore-speckled face with Cass's sea salt paste, which smelt of mojito. I used Cass's clay face mask, her Mediterranean resurfacing scrub. I gargled and spat out a froth of her lagoon-blue mouthwash. I used her milk-thistle clarifying face oil and borrowed one of her collarless cotton shirts to wear with my pink shorts. I looked pretty, especially in the dim light of her flat. Not quite like Titania the Fairy Queen, but I could pass for a Peaseblossom or Cobweb, one of her low-ranking fairy attendants.

My temporarily lifted spirits crashed again the moment I stepped out of the flat. My moods had been terribly uneven since the break-in, cresting and troughing between ecstasy and despair at an ever-greater amplitude and increasing frequency. These extreme vacillations affected my relationship to the city. On good days, I loved everything in Berlin. Even the trash, the broken vacuum cleaners and toilet brushes and Häagen-Dazs cartons seemed fun and festive, happy garbage, like the leftovers from a grand banquet. On those days, I wouldn't have a word said against Berliners. I liked everyone. I found the beggars on the U-Bahn decent and resilient, and admired the boys with their complex haircuts and impeccable trainers. I even liked the men staring at me and felt as if their gaze landed on my calves and the backs of my knees as benevolently as a bumblebee alights on a flower. How civilized it felt to sit in cafes drinking *Radler*s, to say *tschüss* and to recycle correctly, while underneath the surface we were vigorous young animals capable of great disorder.

But with a change of wind my perspective of the city was transformed. I felt as if I'd been drunk for months and was finally sobering up. I detested Berlin then and could only see how poor and wrecked it was. I noticed all the horrible collaterals of human life and bunched them together to form a bouquet composed to exacerbate my hatred of the place. Walking around Kreuzberg felt like passing through a construction site manned by the criminally insane. It was extremely hot and polluted; breathing was like gulping air from the exhaust of an old diesel car. The streets were full of deranged perverts who should have been in jail. What are all these people hanging around all the time for, anyway? Doesn't anyone have a JOB to go to?! Of course, I didn't work either. But I was on a prolonged gap year. This wasn't my life!

The day I moved was such a day. I walked towards the station, malevolently occupying as much of the pavement as I could so that the bikes would struggle to get around me, throwing nasty looks at the men who looked at me and at those who didn't, hating them as much for objectifying me as for not finding me worthy of objectification. The station was full of organic-looking patches of wetness. The smell of urine was so strong that the odour seemed to bypass the nose; I felt I was smelling it with the insides of my stomach. Two minutes until the next train. A gaunt woman got on at Hermannplatz. She smelt of fermented garbage, her nails were long and yellowed, and her chin was crusted with what looked like yoghurt – disgusting. When she asked if I could spare some change, I didn't even bother to look at her, I just shook my head very slightly to make it clear that I had been in Berlin long enough to be hardened to her piteous state.

I got off at Ostbahnhof, and walked down to Milosh's flat on Straße der Pariser Kommune, pulling down the hem as the shirt rode up my thighs and stuck between my buttocks, trying my best to look relaxed. I checked Google Maps every so often to make sure I was on the right path. The area was pretty typical of the ungentrified old East – trafficky, charmless, the streets flanked by tower blocks and enormous deserted warehouses. Milosh's building came as an unexpected surprise, an elegant old *Altbau* sandwiched between bleak brutalist buildings.

I waited in the shady arch of Milosh's doorway until the sweat on my shirt had started to dry, and then pressed the bell. He lived on the sixth floor, and I was soaked again by the time I'd climbed the stairs. He and his flatmate had the landing to themselves, and they'd pinned pictures all over the wall. I inspected them as I kicked off my shoes, keen to catch a glimpse of his ex-girlfriend. One girl appeared in nearly half of Milosh's pictures. She was small, with dark curly hair. She had very large breasts and her skin was as white as the cream on the top of milk. But I wasn't sure if it was her. The wall was so full of exquisite epicene German faces, dozens of potential Hedvigs, that I couldn't bear to look at it for any longer, and I knocked on the door.

A pale, slight girl opened it.

'Uh, I am a friend of Milosh? I was looking for Milosh,' I stammered in terrible German.

'Daphne? He's just in the bathroom. Come in.'

She was much smaller than me, with very pale lashes and lachrymose eyes.

'I'm Daphne!'

'I know. I am Gracie.'

'Enchanted to meet you! How *are* you?!'

'Good.'

'*Really?*'

Sometimes I act strangely when I speak German. The few phrases I have memorized just shoot out of my mouth like a rapid-fire machine gun before I can really wrap my tongue around them, or adjust them according to the scenario. It was certainly odd to say I was 'enchanted' to meet her, odd to bark 'how *are* you' at someone I'd just met and then insist she told me how she *really* was. But after a pause Gracie answered with characteristic Berliner directness.

'I'm pretty sad, because my best friend's cat had kittens this morning, and all of the kittens died.' This seemed a bit pathetic. But then, I've never liked cats. I don't like the constant retching and the aloofness; they remind me of hairy reptiles. I'd loved Pringle, though. He was the exception. I often wondered how he was doing, and hoped Cécile was taking good care of him. Anyway, this exaggerated distress was representative of Gracie's incredibly sensitive nature, Milosh told me later. She was very fragile, the kind of girl who belongs to folk songs and cheesecloth dresses circa 1970, and not Berlin circa 2017.

'Oh, that is so terrible! I am so sorry!'

'It's OK,' she said, crossing her white arms, which were, strangely enough, freckled with sesame seeds. Milosh came out of his room then.

'*Na?* A little bit warm?' he asked, as he hugged me. 'Did you two meet?'

'Yes,' Gracie answered, before scuttling to her room.

'What were you talking about?' he asked me.

'Her friend's kittens.'

'Oh yes. So sad. Really terrible.' He nodded sombrely, without a trace of irony. 'I made dinner, but shall we go for a little walk first?'

Like the day we met on the Tempelhofer Feld, and the night we sat in the rain in the outdoor cinema, the third evening was a lucid dream. The most trivial things felt like the inauguration of a new ritual. We walked only a short while, past Berghain to a small park, and sat, talking and propping elbows on knees, resting heads on shoulders, indifferent to which limb belonged to who, making common property of our bodies. I spoke more than he did, as was customary, and we drank *Radler*s. The memories I have of us are no better than how it really was. We were so sweet together, so complicit, in each other's pockets. I think it was that evening that we first developed many of our long-standing routines. A walk, salty sunflower seeds, *Radler* and a story-telling game we referred to as *die allerbesten Menschen Spiel* (the best character game). Whenever we met, we had to tell the other about the most notable character we'd met since last seeing each other. He had a pretty good one that first time – he and his best friend, a jeweller they called the Milkman (because of the large quantities of milk he drank), had been walking in the street, when they smelt baking hazelnuts. They'd been trying to locate the source of the smell, when an old woman stuck her head over a first-floor balcony and invited them up to try her *Nussecken*, triangular nut pastries dipped in chocolate which the Germans go crazy for. He'd asked for an extra one, which he pulled out of his backpack, for me. 'Try it, I saved it for you.' I broke off a corner and tried. 'Mmmmm . . . so good, it tastes like chocolate crumble.' I took another bite, and then threw the rest away when he wasn't looking.

We walked home in the dark. Gracie was out so we had the flat to ourselves. Milosh put water on to boil for gnocchi and I started making vinaigrette for the salad, but not before we'd washed our hands side by side in the kitchen sink. I can't emphasize enough how hygienic Milosh was. He needed a full five minutes to brush his teeth, the nails of his hands and feet were perfectly clipped, he always washed salad and fruit before eating it. He wasn't neurotic or uptight – he was just very regular in his ways and looked after himself properly. I found this attention to detail very refreshing – I was too lazy to even peel the labels off the apples I ate, let alone wash the pesticides off them, and I usually just swallowed gum instead of bothering to look for a bin. I only wash my hands if I think someone is looking.

After dinner we went to his room. He and the Milkman had built a lofted bed, a desk and DJing table in the same dark wood. It looked like the Lost Boys' den, a secret nook in a tree. He put on a record ('Taste' by Rhye), lit some candles and a carved-gourd lamp, which cast a patchwork of scalloped leaves and fern-shaped shadows across the room. When we slept together, I was so close to the cusp of pleasure that I could trace the outline of its shadow. It was practically pleasure itself. Afterwards, he lent me a T-shirt and we sat on the floor knee to knee. He tucked the hair behind my ears, and I mirrored the gesture. We stayed like that a while, staring at one another, at once smiling and solemn.

He shook me out of sleep very gently the next morning. He woke early as he was going on holiday to Romania with the Milkman. His flight for Bucharest left at six thirty, so we had to leave the flat at four. He'd assured me that I didn't need to get up with him, but I knew I wouldn't be able to resist going through his things, and that I would probably pillage his and Gracie's joint muesli jar. We walked mute and tousled to the station, where Milosh bought a *belegtes Brot*, which literally means 'occupied bread' but translates to 'sandwich'. I drank a black coffee.

'Not hungry in the morning?' he asked.

'No,' I lied.

'But you never, ever eat enough. And you run all the time! You have to give yourself energy. You sure you don't want a bite?'

'To tell the truth, Milosh, I could eat the entire thing, together with all the other occupied breads in the whole of Berlin, and then devour your entire body like a praying mantis,' I wanted to say, but instead I just wrapped my arms around him.

'You're the best, Milosh. Come back soon.'

He squeezed me tight and looked into my eyes.

'You are the strangest and funniest person I've ever met. I'll miss you. Please look after yourself.'

I didn't answer, but felt my heart sink as he disappeared into the station.

15

Taking Care

I TRIED TO HEED this parting request. In the week of his absence I collected and curated all my memorable encounters. As soon as I started to look for them, lovely interactions rose up from nowhere to meet my attention. The day after Milosh left, I was walking down Parkhausstraße when I noticed a yellow beach bucket hanging from a balcony with *Etwas Hübsches macht uns glücklich* (something pretty makes us happy) scrawled across it in a toddler's hand. I looked up and saw two little curly-haired girls peering through the bars of the balcony. They pulled on the string to catch my attention and make the bucket sway from side to side. I searched my pocket, but I didn't have anything pretty, only a five-euro note, and packets of fake sugar I'd stolen from Karma Rösterei.

'Wait a second! I'm coming back!' I yelled up to them, and ran to Cass's flat. I plucked the flowers from her orchid and ran back to put them in the bucket, along with a packet of gummy bears from the *Späti*. They squealed happily as they reeled it up.

'*Danke, Fräulein! Tschüuuuuss!*'

Leila left a batch of inedible cookies on my doormat as a

welcome present. The barista at Karma Rösterei gave me a free coffee the same afternoon. The next day, an ex-Marine from Dallas joined Ollie, Evan and me for a very long run in the Grunewald. He cried at the end, because it was the first time he'd gone with his prosthetic legs, and he'd never expected to run again. On such days, I felt the city was changing from a grim dystopian fiction into one of the Grimm Brothers' cheerier fairy tales, with delights and kindnesses to uncover at every turn.

I didn't text Milosh about any of these interactions; I saved them for the night of his return. I'd expected him not to contact me at all while he was away, but he wrote to me every day, sent videos of the Romanian mountains and a few pictures of him and the Milkman eating slabs of meat in country inns. I ate one of the multivitamins he had insisted on giving me before he left every day for breakfast, letting it fizz and crackle on my tongue rather than dissolving it in water as directed.

I confess I didn't do much to take care of myself, unless memorizing German's many irregular verbs, running large distances in the heat, and eating lots of unpeeled raw vegetables counts as taking care. By the time Milosh returned in the middle of July, my skin was orange from the sun and all the carrots. We quickly slipped into a happy routine. He often stayed out very late DJing in clubs that I had no desire ever to go to, but I gave him the spare key to Cass's flat and he let himself in while I slept and crept into bed with me. We got to know each other a little better, and I discovered that he was very scared of horror films and he had a stuffed elephant called Butz. I hated such relics of childhood whenever I detected them in myself, but I liked these milk-tooth qualities in him. They were part of his contradictory Berlin charm. He was a popular DJ, and he would often go on big drug binges, but he wasn't dysfunctional and dark like Kat. He was able to go the whole way doing what he shouldn't – parties, cigarettes, MDMA; and the whole way doing what he should – paying his bills on time, washing his vegetables. He was a good influence on the days we saw each other. He made us do many of the touristy things I'd avoided: we went to the Holocaust Memorial, a cluster of tall concrete blocks that looked like broken, uneven teeth. We went to Checkpoint Charlie, and to the Nazi-era Olympic Stadium. I had told him that in November, I was starting a master's degree in Philosophy at the University of Potsdam, which was where he was studying History. He took me to the Potsdam Central Library. It was an enormous building and perfectly symmetrical, full of dark wood and dim lighting. Milosh spent a great deal of time explaining how I could take out books, and where the best, most private desks were for me to study. He bought me things: vegetarian *Currywurst*, which looked and tasted like the end-product of a disembowelment; a raspberry-coloured beret, because he heard me humming the Prince song.

But on the other days, when I wasn't with him, I was so unhappy that I wished I could sleep until it was time for us to meet again. As it was, I was barely sleeping, and when I did manage to drop off I would wake to the sound of muffled screaming coming through the wall. I never seemed to hear it when Milosh slept over, but the third time it woke me, I texted Cass. It was a complaint veiled as concern for her neighbour's wellbeing – but she claimed that she had never heard the sound. I asked Leila, who said she couldn't hear it either, but admitted that she was a deep sleeper. I tried to record it one night, as evidence for Cass, but the sound quality was too poor; all I managed to capture was the sound of my own breathing.

Thus were my black days. In retrospect, I am not sure what was worse, the insomnia or the heat. The temperature throughout July and August fluctuated between thirty-two and thirty-eight degrees, and it didn't rain for a month. There was no shade on the Tempelhofer Feld, and I became so dehydrated during my runs that my eyes would become crusted with flakes of white salt. I developed a heat rash on my thighs. I checked the weather forecast several times a day, as preoccupied with each upward fluctuation as a farmer watching his crops wither in a drought. The heat made me so grim that if the temperature was predicted to rise above thirty-five degrees, I would cancel plans with Milosh. I'd sit chewing ice on my bed, hunched over my computer, distracting myself until it passed.

16

Missed Opportunities

THINGS BECAME EVEN WORSE at the end of August, when Milosh went away again, this time to visit his parents in Freiburg and then attend a music festival outside Hamburg. He spent the night before he left with me at Cass's place. I filled the apartment with candles, poured him a glass of wine and ran him a bath. While he was in the bath, I made my grandmother's jewelled rice with cardamom pods, barberries, pistachios and almonds. I bought all the ingredients from the *Späti*. It was the only real meal I ever cooked in Berlin. A swansong of sorts. We ate sitting cross-legged on Cass's bed. Milosh was flushed and radiant from the bath.

'This rice, Daphne, it's the best rice I ever tasted!'

'It's not bad,' I conceded, pushing my own portion around my plate, 'but my grandmother made it much better.'

'Is she still alive?'

'No, she died last year. Do you want to finish my plate?'

'I'll eat half of it, if you eat the other half. You should cook more often, Daphne. I want to eat this again.'

We went to bed. Our nights together were always a complex compromise between our desire to rest and our desire to be close. I would wake up with a numb arm, or a painfully twisted neck, the collateral of falling asleep entangled in a perfect but unsustainable cuddle. That night, I woke every few hours and looked at his sleeping face. He seemed to sense my gaze, and would open his eyes and smile at me sleepily. He left very early the next day.

A few days after Milosh left, my German class ended. According to the Common European Framework of Reference for Languages, I was now at a level where I could 'understand a wide range of complex texts, and easily recognize their implicit meanings'. I could 'articulate my ideas spontaneously, communicate freely and express demands'. I've never been able to 'express demands' in any language, but I certainly felt as if my German was becoming more instinctive. Somehow, I'd memorized enough vocabulary that the German Grammar Gods had granted me access to the Teutonic ground source. German just welled up in me, and words I'd never consciously memorized spilt out of my mouth. It was immensely satisfying.

Most of my classmates – the Venezuelans, Katya and Gabriel – were staying on to take C1 level classes, where, presumably, they would learn how to compose great works of German fiction and read *The Magic Mountain* in the original. But I was bored of the same old routine of class every day, and I had lost hope that the 'friendships' with my classmates would ever develop into something substantial.

I did try to initiate a spontaneous hang-out with the Venezuelans. I was walking along the Landwehr canal one day, and saw them having lunch through the window. I stopped and waved to get their attention. They exchanged a look before Luis stood to open the window for me. He asked me if anything was wrong, and when I tried to explain that I was just casually passing by and wanted to say hello, he seemed cross. They didn't invite me in, and I felt embarrassed, as desperate and needy as Richard Grausam. Katya only ever wanted to talk about Chorizo, and things were awkward between us ever since Kat had screamed at her for saying I was cursed. Gabriel was too in love with Nina to be interested in hanging out with me. I had messaged him a few times, asking if he'd like to go to the cinema, or for a bike ride to catch up, but he barely replied. Kat had dropped out of class, and I hadn't seen her since the night of our failed revenge. I tried to call her once, but she didn't pick up and sent me a hurried text: 'Can't talk now. No privacy. Call U later.' A week had gone by, and I still hadn't heard back.

I was also running less often with Ollie and Evan, although they regularly tried to ferret me out of the flat to go to visit one of the many lovely lakes that line the outer limits of the city. One afternoon, I finally agreed to meet them for a few circuits of the Hasenheide park. But when I arrived, they were sitting on a picnic blanket and carrying plastic bags full of snacks from Aldi.

'Good to see you at last, Daphne! We thought we'd surprise you with a picnic. We could all do with a rest from running, don't you think?'

'Oh, that's so sweet, guys! Thank you, what do I owe you?'

'Nothing, nothing. Try these salt and vinegar crisps!'

I endured the picnic, and after a few hours pretended to go home. I cut back towards the Tempelhofer Feld and went for a short run, a sick, leaden feeling in the pit of my stomach. After that day, I didn't hear from either of them, though I once saw them running together, chatting away as we had when we'd all run together. I wondered why they had excluded me. Perhaps it was because my pace was too fast for them.

I was truly alone, and continued in just the same vein as I had begun the Berlin chapter in my life, unable to go the whole way doing what I shouldn't – drugs, clubs, vigilante justice; unable to go the whole way doing what I should – nourishment, honesty, employment. But things were getting worse, darker. I no longer hoped that moving to a new city would make me a better person, and I no longer enjoyed the guilty reprieve of midnight feasts. I was still too scared of Cass's LSD to break into her store cupboards.

I got so desperate that I decided to try to get a job. I printed off twenty copies of an extremely inflated CV and made the rounds of the local coffee shops. I focused on overpriced hipster places where none of the staff spoke German, so that my language skills might seem like an advantage. I started off at an Italian place near Weserstraße, and worked my way through the streets between Sonnenallee and the Tempelhofer Feld. At #Hashtag, they said they weren't looking for anyone. Karma Rösterei was shut for construction. At Bonanza, they said they required a minimum of five years' experience. The woman at ESPERA promised to call me if a vacancy came up. The barista at SoKaf told me that his boss never paid the staff on time, and when he did it was only in cash. The man behind the counter at Two Moons was so intimidatingly hipster that I was scared to speak to him. He was Australian (9 hipster points), had a septum piercing (8 hipster points), and wore white Veja vegan shoes (6 points). I didn't think I could bear to re-adopt my snobby barista persona from my time at Knights in Black Satin. The Australian looked like the kind of person who would meet a request for sugar with a superior sneer. But, hell. This was the only kind of work I was going to be able to get in Berlin.

As I approached the counter, he was finishing making a cappuccino. He spun the milk jugs around like a gunslinger twirling a pistol around his trigger finger, and slapped the steam wand into the milk as if smacking the haunches of a rodeo horse. He was like a barista Magic Mike. This mastery of the big, steel, glistening coffee machine sounds erotic, but the effect was irritating. He told me that they *were* looking for someone, and could I start straight away? I had just finished writing down my number when somebody tapped me on the shoulder: 'Daphne?!'

I froze, expecting to see Richard Grausam – but he was too mean to pay the price of coffee there – or Sebastián, who would definitely have hung out at a place like Two Moons. It wasn't Sebastián, but one of his flatmates from university, an American guy named Colton who I used to flirt with at the gym to try to irritate Sebastián. He was good-looking in an all-American-boy kind of way: big white teeth the size of tombstones, freckles, green eyes, a small if slightly reptilian nose. He was a category one (*The Little Prince* reader) masquerading as a category six (GI Joe), but his outfit gave him away. He wore Sperry Top-Siders, a plaid shirt, a Patagonia jacket, and the same pair of Veja vegan shoes as the barista, the only concession to Berlin fashion in his preppy East Coast armour.

'Colton!' I said. 'What are you doing here?!'

'I'm visiting Sebastián! How crazy, I've seen neither of you since graduation, and then I see you both on the same day! He never told me you were in Berlin!'

'Oh!' I feigned surprise. 'Sebastián is also in Berlin?! Wow. I didn't know!'

'Oh, really? Yeah, he lives just around the corner from here.'

'Wow, what a coincidence.'

'So are you here just for a visit? Or a job?'

I glanced towards the counter, where my CV still lay in plain sight. I resisted the impulse to snatch it up and rip it to pieces.

'Oh, yeah! I'm working for a human-rights lawyer based at the FU!'* (Where the hell did that come from?)

'Wow, that's awesome!'

By that point, we were holding up the queue. I let Colton order his macchiato to go, and stood by the door with him as he waited.

'And how about you, Colton? What are you up to these days?'

'Oh, I'm still working at the Oxford Immigration Fund. You know, the organization I set up when I was in my last year of university, to provide legal advice to migrants held in detention centres?'

'Yes, yes, I remember,' I lied. 'So you're just here visiting Sebastián?'

'Yes! Hey, you should come over tonight. He's throwing a house party! I'm sure he'd love to see you.'

'You know, Colton, we didn't really end on good terms. I think it's better if I don't come.'

'OK, well, let me have your number. You and I can get together.'

'I can't, I've got a boyfriend,' I said. 'He's German,' I added, as an afterthought.

I left Colton outside Two Moons, still waiting for his macchiato. I wondered if he would report back to Sebastián about my amazing job and my German boyfriend, and whether he had heard me telling the barista that yes, I was free all the time, and no, I had no other commitments. The nightmare scenario of one day running into Sebastián or any of my other university acquaintances while working as a waitress was so horrifying that I ignored the call from Two

---

* The Freie Universität, one of the major research universities in Berlin.

Moons when it came later that day, and never tried to get another job in Berlin.

On the 20th of September, I received an email from EG, informing me that she had moved back to Huberstraße. She didn't thank me for having given her place such a thorough clean, nor for paying her rent for an apartment I hadn't even lived in for the last three months. She informed me that she had returned my deposit, but subtracted 100 euros for the broken plates and cups, and for her IKEA bedsheets, which I had dyed very slightly pink. I fantasized about sending her a rude reply: 'Thanks for generously letting me live in your cuddly nest where I was nearly murdered twice. Consider the 100 euros your gratuity for providing such fine lodgings.' But I didn't. Instead, I released my passive-aggressive energy by agreeing to go for a walk with Callum, whose messages I hadn't responded to in quite a long time.

He was waiting by the U-Bahn entrance, tapping on his phone. Under his arm I noticed a bouquet of what looked like roses. The flowers were awful, dribbling water from their droopy mouths as if they had recently been plucked from a fridge-freezer and were beginning to thaw. What? He bought me flowers? So this is a date! No doubt about it . . . Well, he's noticed me now, nothing I can do, I'll just have to survive, I'll say hello and then I can disappear for ever and will never have to talk to him again. His face lit up as my heart sank and I put my arms around him in the hug of Judas. 'Sorry,' he said, as the sodden bouquet fell from under his arm. 'My boyfriend gave me these earlier today and now I don't know what to do with them.'

Of course Callum had a *boyfriend*. I was so self-centred that it never would have occurred to me that I was not the object of desire, that maybe he genuinely just wanted to be my friend. That sleepless night we'd spent together must have been a complete misunderstanding. Unless Callum was lying about the boyfriend and trying to save face. Maybe he had bought the flowers for me but chickened out at the last minute. Perhaps he'd realized I wasn't attracted to him and was embarrassed so decided to pretend to be gay. I could see myself resorting to that kind of strategy.

We ended up propping them in the doorway of an apartment building that had an especially large number of *Stolpersteine*. We walked through the Turkish market that runs alongside the Landwehr canal on the Maybachufer. Callum bought black tahini, flatbreads and triangular börek. He insisted I take a bite, and it was perhaps the most delicious thing I'd ever eaten – very light flaky filo pastry stuffed with feta and spinach. We sat on a bench with a view of the canal. He pressed another börek on me, and when I refused, he told me that he was worried about me.

'What do you mean, worried? I'm fine, Callum. I'm really fine.'

'I'm sorry to say this, Daphne, but you seem, I don't know, quite manic. I know you're running a lot but you look, I don't know, quite sad and unwell.'

'You know, Callum, you look pretty exhausted too. I've just been burning the candle at both ends. It's mainly the heat. I'm happy. Relax.'

Callum seemed momentarily overwhelmed by his own empathy, as if expressing concern had been an act of great bravery and unparalleled selflessness. I checked my phone while he chewed on his börek. I had received a text from Kat: 'Daphne, I have left Berlin.'

I got up, leaving Callum looking crestfallen with all the food he'd bought for us to share. That was the last time I saw him. When I was well away from the market, I called Kat.

She was vague about what exactly had happened, though she mentioned a threesome gone wrong, and money gone missing. After a violent argument with Lars, she had become scared, and her parents had driven from Stockholm to move her out that same night. That is what economic privilege means when you are in your twenties. If you have parents who can help you when shit hits the fan, things can only get so bad. I had suffered, and was still suffering, in Berlin, but it was thrilling in a way, dancing on the precipice without fearing the impact. I was one phone call away from help. How much greater my terror would have been if there wasn't this safety net. Kat had been careful about hiding hers. She had never mentioned her parents at all.

'I'm going to move back eventually. I just need a break. I'm so exhausted just from being there. How about you? You didn't seem so good, last time I saw you.'

'Oh no, I'm good. I'm great, actually. I've been seeing that German guy I told you about, Milosh?'

'Well, that's good. You two could come and see me, if you ever feel like visiting Stockholm.'

'Yeah, that sounds good, I'd love that.'

'OK, well, call me any time.'

'You too, Kat. I'm so sorry about what happened with Lars. I'll miss you. Speak soon. Bye.'

In a way, I would miss her. We could have been friends. I could have pushed her to take her studies more seriously, encouraged her to end her relationship with Lars. She could have taken me to nightclubs, and shown me a side of the Berlin experience I was missing out on. She could have called me out on my weirdness around food and over-exercising. We looked good walking down the street together. We were natural allies, but our relationship was tainted by jealousy and mistrust. We saw each other too clearly. Of all the people

I knew, she sensed that all was not well behind my bright, plucky exterior, and I saw through her party-girl pose. Her dysfunctionality was overt, whereas mine was covert. I knew she took drugs to make being with Lars bearable. She knew I was in trouble. We could have helped each other. But the shock of self-recognition is hard to bear. I was glad she was gone. Given our behaviour, it seemed statistically unlikely that we would both be able to make Berlin a success. I felt a strange sense of triumph that she hadn't. I thought, erroneously, that it improved my own chances.

17

Spätigate

IT WAS THE 25TH of September, the day before Milosh returned. I was munching on cubes of raw beetroot dipped in sriracha, and listening to a German true-crime podcast called *ZEIT Verbrechen*. I was having a hard time protecting Cass's sheets from the orange sauce – some of it dripped on to her cushion, which I flipped over in case Milosh came by later.

I was feeling ill at ease in Cass's flat. I'd infected the place with my own atmosphere, and my unpleasant habits. The flat was no longer an escape from myself, but a kind of landscape of my own mind: stained sheets, food wrappers stuffed in unlikely places, stray hairs everywhere, sticky finger marks on the fridge and light switches. I was constantly preoccupied with the thought of accidentally ingesting her drugs. I couldn't wait for Milosh to return.

My phone began to vibrate and my heart lifted. It was Gabriel. I hadn't hung out with him since moving out of his apartment. I was fond of him, and hadn't yet given up on our friendship. It was unusual for him to call. Perhaps he had locked himself out of his apartment, or broken up with Nina (if only); or maybe he had finally noticed that I had raided his food cupboards.

'Hey, Gab! How are you?'

He was in the street. I could hear traffic rushing past him and an ambulance in the distance. I got up from the bed and walked over to the window, where the reception was usually better. 'Hey, can you hear me?'

'Hey, yes, I can hear you! Hang on one second!'

I heard him talking to someone in German. The courtyard was empty, save for a cat sitting in a patch of sun opposite the letter boxes.

'Daphne?'

'Hey! Yes, what's up?'

'I'm calling because I ran into someone you know! He wants to have a word with you!'

Some more sounds of traffic as he passed the phone, and then:

'I've heard you've moved to the neighbourhood!'

I recognized the voice but couldn't match it to a name. Someone from our German class? Someone I'd met at Gabriel's party? I was always forgetting people's names.

'I am very sorry, I can't hear very well at all – the reception is terrible, who is this?'

'Ach, Daphne, you don't recognize me?'

The way he pronounced *Daphne*, and the raspy quality of his voice – something I probably found attractive when we first met – was unmistakable. It was Richard Grausam. I didn't hang up. I knew Gabriel must be listening to this exchange with interest, and I tried to think of what I could say to prevent him from becoming suspicious.

'I've been really concerned, Daphne. That day in the cafe you seemed really disturbed. Is everything OK?'

I hung up. My first thought was that Gabriel would assume that we were in a relationship and that I was two-timing Milosh with Grausam. The phone rang again but I ignored it, until I saw a text from Gabriel: 'Hey, it's Gabriel, give me a call, x.'

'Hey, Daphne. You good? Sorry, I hope you didn't mind me passing the phone to Richard?'

'Yeah, I mean, I don't mind, and it's not your fault because I didn't tell you, but he's actually been bothering me for the past few months.'

'What? What's he been doing?'

'Oh, I mean, nothing too bad, just emailing me and calling me, and he bothered me in the street a few times.'

'I'm so sorry. You should have told me, I never would have passed the phone to him if I'd known!'

'Yeah, sorry about that. You didn't tell him where I live now, right?'

'No, of course not. He didn't even ask.'

'Ah, then don't worry, no harm done.'

'I was meaning to call you anyway, actually. How are you at the moment?'

'Oh, I'm fine.'

'Really? I got a call from Kat yesterday. She's left Berlin, did you know that?'

'Yes, I know.'

'She asked me to watch out for you. She seemed quite concerned. Are you OK? Do you need help with anything?'

'No, honestly, Gabriel. I think she was worried because I told her I had a huge fight with Milosh. It's totally fine now.'

'OK.'

'I need to go, actually, because I'm going to meet up with him now,' I added.

'Oh, OK. Well, take care, Daphne. Let me know if you wanna hang out soon.'

'I will!' I lied, confident that he would continue to ignore my messages if I asked him to meet up. I threw away the rest of the beetroot cubes, and went to the bathroom and ran myself a bath. I didn't know if I entirely trusted Gabriel any more. Perhaps he really had given Grausam my address. What could Grausam have meant when he said 'you've moved to the neighbourhood' if Gabriel hadn't told him where I lived?

But Gabriel had only been to Cass's once, when he helped me to move in, and I wasn't convinced he would remember exactly where I lived. Perhaps he hadn't given Grausam my precise address, but only told him that I had moved from EG's flat in Kreuzberg to Neukölln. Grausam lived in the same city district, a few kilometres from Cass's place. I knew this because – despite wanting to forget I had ever had any connection to him – I had once been to his illogical, cluttered flat, full of broken radios and yoga books.* He had cooked something sophisticated, but confused – lemon linguine with bitter red radicchio and pistachios. His home was incoherent, uncared for, full of things but devoid of character. It had punctured the fantasy version of him I had constructed, and forced me to see him for who he really was – someone who'd never forgotten that he hadn't made the first football team in primary school; a guy who had lost his virginity a little later than the average because he was 'too nice'. A person who resented his bourgeois upbringing, but who would rather make a fatuous show of Marxism than use his luck to help others. A powerless, sad, thwarted, dangerous man – dangerous because like so many weak people, he would resort to coercive means to regain a sense of power. I

---

* He was only a substitute yoga teacher. There is something humiliating about having been stalked by someone so beta. If I'd had a choice, I would have been stalked by a legitimately threatening alpha male.

knew he would have approached Gabriel cleverly, casually, and extracted just the information he needed from him. If Gabriel had given him my address, I couldn't blame him. I hadn't given him any reason to keep it a secret.

I filled the tub up to the very top. The trick with very hot baths is to act as you would in freezing water. I lowered myself in, inch by inch, slowly letting each body part accustom itself to the heat before I submerged any more: feet, thighs, belly button, collarbones. I was beginning to relax when I heard the screaming again. It was barely discernible when I held my head out of the water, but whenever I dunked myself to rinse my hair, it was so loud that whoever was screaming might as well have been shampooing herself next to me. According to Google, sound waves travel further in dense substances like water than through air, and so it made sense that the water would magnify her wailing. The effect was weird: the quiet and peace of the bathroom contrasted with the desperate cries I heard whenever I let the waterline rise above my ears. I got into bed and went on to Facebook. Milosh had been posting pictures and videos of the festival every day for the last week. I watched the videos several times, focusing obsessively on the women who danced and bopped around him, who wore sunglasses and halter tops and seemed both put-together and carefree. I found their private Facebook pages, learnt their names and scrolled through their photographs. Effortless beauty, effortless happiness. In one particular video, a woman wearing a bikini top and a mini-skirt said something to him that he obviously couldn't hear. He moved closer to her, and she put her lips to his ear. He took her wrist to steady her. I imagined Milosh with them, and the thought filled me with violent jealousy tainted with desire. Finally, I fell asleep.

I sprang awake. At first, I thought something brick-y

might be happening, but I quickly realized that what had woken me was a fly, thudding against the windowpane. I rose to open the window, but the floor seemed to plunge upwards and suddenly I was lying on it, without the memory of having fallen over. Everything felt very strange and one-dimensional, as if depth and height had been pressed together like a flattened Coke can. My first thought was that one of my worst sci-fi nightmares had come true, that gravity had been dialled up and I'd soon be crushed into a thin disc of atoms. I tried to stand up, but my hands weren't working properly, and I couldn't get a proper grip on the side of my bed and the floor rose to meet me again. Perhaps I'd accidentally eaten some of Cass's LSD-laced food? My heart was fluttering, but the rest of my body felt like a muscle-less slab of frozen fat. I crouched with my head between my knees, and everything felt very distant and surreal, except for the electric fizzing in my chest and the frostbitten feeling in my hands and feet. I managed to drag myself to the sink and felt the water drip down into my stomach, but soon I had to fold down to my feet again. I could see the cleft between my collarbones pulsating. I tried to breathe it into a slower beat, but the extra oxygen only fanned the flames into a frenzied palpitation. My thoughts began to race to catch up with my heart and I felt on the edge of complete panic. I probably need sugar, I thought. I ought to get myself something to eat. I didn't want anything from Cass's fridge, so I decided to bike to the *Späti*.

The fresh air was helping somewhat, and everything looked a little more normal. The nearest *Späti* was only a few minutes away, but though it claimed to be open 24/7, I wasn't surprised to find it closed. It was exactly 5 a.m. I was sure that my favourite *Späti*, the one run by the Armenian family I'd been to with Kat, would already be open. I got on my bike and rode slowly. I felt calmer. The sky was low and the streets were completely empty; I felt as if I was gliding through a velvet stage-set. But I was having trouble catching my breath, and the pavement seemed to swim like melting butter beneath my wheels. As I locked up my bike, I realized that something was very wrong. The darkness seemed to fold up around me, like a moth closing its wings. I made it into the *Späti*, which looked as flat as a poster, but sank to my knees directly in front of the counter.

'*Alles gut?!*' the *Späti* man asked. I couldn't tell if my heart wasn't beating at all, or so fast that it was imperceptible, like a hummingbird's wings. I clutched my hand to my chest and to my left arm, which was painful and throbbing. I tried to smile to reassure him. 'Hey! *Bist du OK? Alles gut?*'

'I think so . . . can I just have something sweet?'

He fetched me a carton of strawberry-raspberry Durst Löscher from the fridge. I fumbled to remove the plastic from the straw but dropped it. My hands felt boneless, like blown-up rubber gloves. He picked it up for me and poked it into the carton.

'*Alles gut*, drink.' He held the straw to my lips. I took a few gulps, reassured by my capacity for ordinary bodily function.

'Shall I call an ambulance?'

'I don't know . . . do you think I need an ambulance?' He shrugged and looked completely helpless and very alarmed, which terrified me. This guy definitely did not know CPR.

'Yes, please,' I said, my voice suddenly breaking, 'Please, please can you call an ambulance.'

'Mane!' he cried, still holding the carton of juice and crouching beside me. 'Mane, come down.' One of the nymph-ish daughters came out from the back room, wearing a nightie. She looked sleepy and astonished. 'Mane, call an ambulance!'

I heard her speaking to them and felt suddenly completely filled with regret but also unable to maintain my grip on the little decorum I had left. My whole body was shaking so I laid my head on the floor, knocking over the carton of juice.

'Wow wow wow,' he said, trying to protect my hair from the pink ooze. 'Mane, get a blanket!'

'I'm so, so sorry,' I managed, in a voice I didn't recognize at first, but then I realized this strangled supplicating child's voice was what I really sounded like, and that my normal voice was a complete sham. I was shivering by then. Mane came back with a coverless duvet and dropped it on to me. Father and daughter looked down on me, so full of concern that I wondered if something was visibly wrong with my face. I shot upwards and groped it but it felt normal, the same big nose and combination skin. But perhaps the colour was wrong, liver-failure yellow or internal-bleeding blue. I tried to stand but my legs crumpled beneath me like an injured fawn. I realized that the enormous patch of wetness couldn't be attributed to a carton of juice. I pulled the duvet off, expecting to see a haemorrhage of blood, but saw only patches of diluted pink as pee ran into the gloopy juice.

'I am so, so sorry.' Head in my hands. 'So sorry!'

Mane made me lie down again, which I didn't dare tell them made me feel much, *much* worse. I rolled over on to my front and could hear my heart knocking against the ground. What if someone came into the *Späti*? It was too early for serious traffic, but what if some children of the night dropped by on their way back from a club? They'd probably feel sorry for the Armenian family, that they had to deal with such a certifiable case as myself, who belonged on a ward and had no place among the elements of air and light and youth. And perhaps they were right, I thought. The only thing standing between me and the certifiables on the U-Bahn was a conformist nature and a thick stack of cash bequeathed to me by my parents, one I was eroding with each passing day that I didn't get a job.

After a few minutes of lying on my stomach, I felt a further cardiac surge. I got up and began to pace around the shop, avoiding the patch of pale pink which trickled in corridors down the furrows on the tiled floor. From time to time I'd find a glitch in the matrix of terror, and then I would see things a little more lucidly and realize that I was probably having a panic attack, rather than a heart attack. But then I would become distraught, because I didn't like that version of reality any better. I wasn't at all sure that going insane was better than having a heart attack. What to hope for between a failure of the mind or a failure of the heart?

I was breathing hard but completely breathless, like the dying tubercular patient of *The Magic Mountain*. Perhaps my parents would find a sanatorium like the Berghof, somewhere high up with good air and sexual frolicking. At last the ambulance arrived, and then I really lost it. Goodbye, said the nymph-daughter, her plait brushing my face as she leant over the stretcher to tuck a carton of juice into my bag. She'd been so kind, easily the best character of the day yet. I saw Cass's bike, chained up outside the *Späti*. I would have to come back for it later, I thought, as they bound my arm and searched for a vein.

In the ambulance, the two men mostly ignored me, mumbling to each other about *hysterische Ausländerinnen* and *Drogensüchtige*.*

'I understand German!' I shouted hysterically. After that they were quiet until we arrived at the hospital, running the

---

* Hysterical foreigners, and drug addicts.

sirens extra loud as if to exaggerate my melodramatic behaviour. In a few minutes, we arrived at the Vivantes Hospital along the Landwehr canal.

I sat for hours alone in the waiting room, desperate to be compliant, but frightened I was failing to impress the urgency of what was happening to me. Now and then I'd bashfully ask if the doctor was coming, because my heart was still pounding painfully in my chest, or whether there was a nurse available, because the IV bag was empty and sucking the blood from my arm up the tube. The receptionist, who was typing away on her computer, just rolled her eyes at me, repeating in English that was poorer than my German that no one was available, that I just had to wait until I was called. I hoped that they were ignoring me because there was nothing seriously wrong.

Eventually a doctor appeared and called my name. I followed her into a curtained-off consulting room. She measured my blood pressure, palpated my stomach, and weighed me. She asked me about suicide plans, sleep and bowel movements, all in a mildly disapproving tone. She gave me a big white pill, with a glass of water.

'No Adderall? Speed? Cocaine?'

'No, nothing at all.'

'Well, there's nothing wrong with your heart. Your pulse is just a little high, but the Xanax should calm that down.' She glanced at her clipboard. 'Your vitals are in order. You are very underweight for your height. It is quite concerning. Have you been under particular stress lately? A personal loss, a death in the family?'

'I have had a few problems recently.'

'It seems to me that you had a panic attack. It's a kind of sudden terror. The symptoms can be severe, like yours – dizziness, numbness, a racing heart. People often think they are dying. If it happens again, you might consider going on anti-depressants. Do you have your family here?'

'No, they are in England.'

She looked concerned, but also worn out.

'Well, look after yourself,' she said as she readied my release papers, 'and try to relax. You need to find a way of releasing your anxiety. I recommend regular exercise, or meditation – there are many good videos online.' She passed me a prescription for Xanax. 'Otherwise these usually work.'

18

West Berlin

I RETURNED TO CASS's flat, still pacified by the Xanax, and knocked on Leila's door. She came out in her pyjamas.

'Hey, Leila. I'm so sorry to bother you, but the hot water isn't working in my flat. Would it be OK if I showered here?' The truth is, I didn't want to go back to Cass's flat, and I didn't want to be alone. I also wanted to find out if I could hear the screaming from Leila's apartment.

'Of course, come in, come in. You look destroyed. Did you party hard last night?'

'Something like that.'

In the bathroom I tore off the plasters from the inside of my arm. The wounds from the IV and from where they had taken blood had long since dried into invisible pinpricks, but my arms were tender and bruised from the paramedic's clumsy poking. Leila's bath was stained and old but perfectly clean. I put the water on and it was scalding hot, though I was so cold and numb that at first I could barely feel the heat, but my skin was turning red, warmer and redder, and then itchy as I began to thaw. I washed with mango body wash, white strawberry and sweet mint conditioner, and came out smelling like a rotting fruit stall.

Leila was leaning against the kitchen counter, watching over a Bialetti, wearing a black-and-white gingham shirt, denim shorts, and house slippers. I took a small polite bite of a brownie she'd baked the previous day. It was dry and tasted of nothing, like the homeopathic version of a chocolate cake.

'Delicious!' I lied.

'Really?' she replied. 'I think they are pretty bad. But you are polite, thank you.'

'How long have you been living in this apartment?'

'Since last year. My colleague helped me find this place. How about you? When did you move to Berlin?'

'About eight months ago.'

'How are you finding it?'

'A bit rough,' I admitted.

'In what way?'

I took another bite of brownie. What I wanted to say was that my life in Berlin was not what I had hoped. My existence and thoughts were dominated by indescribably banal worries. Does soya milk or oat milk contain more fat? Is Big Red gum sugar-free? Am I buying the right things? I had expected the tribulations of adulthood to be rather more . . . picturesque. I thought life would be like *The Lord of the Rings*: whittling weapons, facing foes, cantering through glades. I had, in short, great expectations. It's not that I wished something worse had happened – of course not – but I expected my suffering to feel redemptive in some way. I thought life was meant to be meaningful, even when it was hard.

I wanted to tell her that I was unhappy, but that my unhappiness had no noble cause, and was nearly entirely of my own making. It was slow, insidious self-destruction.

'Oh, I've just found it quite lonely here. I think I thought it would be easier to make friends.'

'I understand. You should come over here more. You must accept my invitations.'

We spent a few hours together. The conversation ebbed and flowed between us quite evenly. She'd moved to Germany in 2014, around the same time I'd graduated from Oxford. She didn't tell me much about her own family, nor the circumstances of her departure from Damascus. I imagined a constellation of horrors – the open sea, life jackets, camps in Turkey. I later learnt that she'd flown from Lebanon on a temporary visa. There had been nothing clandestine about it at all. My own covert departure from London had been far more furtive.

She worked as a designer for a furniture company. I admitted that I was jobless, and she reminded me of something Gabriel had said, about it being better to describe oneself as 'job-seeking' than 'job-less'. When she started yawning and rubbing her eyes, I stood up to leave and she pushed my uneaten plate towards me.

'But you haven't finished the brownie!'

'I'll save it for later.'

'Next time I'll make you some dinner.'

'I'd love that,' I said, but really I thought, 'Not likely.'

Back at Cass's I slept, at last, and woke to find a missed call and a text from Milosh, who wanted to know how I was and if I would meet him at the Schwarzes Cafe, a famous hang-out in West Berlin. I plundered Cass's cupboard as if it were a pharaoh's tomb, trying on beautiful girlish dresses which clashed terribly with my broad, manly shoulders, and looked like wisps of silk draped on a yeti. At last I found an oversized silky blue Dior shirt, which I thought passed fine as a dress. I hurried out of the courtyard, eager to leave. I kept imagining

195

Grausam showing up at my door. Part of me knew I was being paranoid. He had never actually threatened me – all he had done was to email me when I asked him not to, and call me numerous times from a masked number. Which is nothing. He hadn't turned up at my house. He hadn't been physically violent. 'He sends me emails and follows me into coffee shops' is not a prosecutable crime. This is what men do, if they like you. They pursue you.

And was I so different? I'd thought about Sebastián for years after he'd broken up with me. I had sent him messages – including the drunken one at Kat's – that he had seldom answered, and that he hadn't wanted to receive in the first place. Worst of all – and I am ashamed, deeply ashamed to admit it – I *had* known he was in Berlin before I made the decision to move there. I worried my actions were driven by dark, Grausam-esque motives. My own behaviour seemed like a lite version of my stalker's.

I got on the M29 bus headed westwards. It was half empty, and I sat by the window. We went up Oranienstraße, past Checkpoint Charlie and the Tiergarten zoo. I played with the Xanax packet in my pocket. It was hot; sweat trickled down my back and along the inside of my arm towards my sleeves. I tried to open the square window above me, but I couldn't work the latch. The other passengers watched me, placid as cows, as I struggled with the handle which swivelled around without any effect. I sat back down, embarrassed by my ineffectual fumbling. I tried to think about what Milosh and I could discuss. He provided situational novelty – he always found new, exciting places where we could meet – but it was on me to come up with fresh topics of conversation. This was proving increasingly tricky, because I did very little with my days, and also because we had nothing in common. Initially, this difference had been exciting. Our relationship was sustained by a deliberate process of mutual orientalization: we exaggerated differences, saw each other through a veil of appealing clichés and outdated cultural paradigms. He was fascinated by France, by my Oxford degree, and the lightness with which I alighted and left innumerable places. I was fascinated by him for the opposite reason: although he was born in Poland, to me Milosh seemed so German that he might as well have had MADE IN GERMANY © 1993 stamped on the soles of his feet. It was manifest in everything: his concern for the environment, his ease with nudity, his skill with a football, the natural, ungendered way he treated women. There was a certain quietism about him that I admired. He accepted his friends, his city and his life without ever questioning whether these were the best possible friends, the best possible place to live and the most fulfilling existence. Whereas I saw everything in my life as something that could be optimized: was Berlin really the best city? Was this the best part of town, was this the thinnest I could be, were these the coolest friends I could hope to have? Milosh reflexively, unthinkingly did what I find hardest: he accepted reality with ease and grace. He committed to and invested in his real life without fantasizing about the one he ought to be living.

I, on the other hand, was in a state of perpetual fantasy, not only about the life I might lead but about the life I was currently living. I told him detailed stories about my babysitting job, inventing sandpit dramas and awkward interactions with the 'pervy' father. I told him that Kat and I went clubbing and had taken MDMA, and that Gabriel and I went to the cinema together at least once a week. I pretended to belong to a football club, and told him stories of playing against tough girls in Marzahn and South Neukölln. I'd made light of the bricking and the break-in. I hadn't told him about Grausam. I wanted him to think of me as a happy, carefree person.

I got off the bus at Uhlandstraße and followed Google Maps to the Schwarzes Cafe, taking a large detour so that I wouldn't arrive too early. I made my way towards Savigny-platz, a lovely square which has somehow retained the old-world splendour of pre-unification West Berlin, without the gaudy pastiche of the rest of Charlottenburg. It was dusk; the streetlamps blinked on. Heat rose from the pavement like baking bread. Few people were outside, but the doors to all the bars and restaurants were propped open, and the smell of cooking onions and the tinkling of glasses drifted out on to the square. I was surprised Milosh had chosen the Schwarzes Cafe – it was quite different from the kinds of places we usually went to. I felt underdressed in my short shorts, oversized shirt and scuffed Adidas shoes.

There were a few tables downstairs, but I followed Milosh's instructions and walked on past a fridge full of cream cakes and shelves of Campari and Martini mixers. I climbed the curved staircase to a high-ceilinged room. It was dark, lit only by a flickering chandelier and tea lights on each of the small round tables. Milosh had not yet arrived, so I took a seat by the open window.

Closest to me was a very good-looking couple eating green pesto pasta. They were probably both around seventy, perhaps a little older. Their hair was completely white. He was wearing a grey single-breasted suit, with a square white pocket handkerchief, and she was wearing an immaculately pressed white shirt. Perfect lipstick, not even remotely smudged after slurping up spaghetti. They smiled at me with open faces, and looked as if they were going to strike up a conversation, when Milosh arrived. I felt such a rush of gladness to see him. He was dressed in a green hoodie and a wooden necklace the Milkman had given him, and looked like a hipster version of Legolas. The old woman looked at him approvingly, and nodded to me as if to say, *good job*.

'*Na*, Daphne? So, you found it?'

It turned out Milosh knew the woman behind the bar, and she brought us two Dark and Stormies and an enormous bowl of spicy peanuts. He rolled himself a cigarette, pinching the tobacco together, licked the paper and lit it. He took a drag, blew the smoke out of the corner of his mouth, and passed it to me.

'*Prost*, Daphne! Good to see you!'

'So lovely to see you! You look so handsome. How was Hamburg? How was the festival?'

'Ach, Daphne. It was such a good time. You should come next time I go. Me and my sister stayed in her van, which was so much better than camping. I felt sorry for everyone else, it was incredibly hot. But yeah, it was the best time, we saw Liveki-10, Ollie Krakenberg, Good Boy, the Flying Zobs. It was awesome. I played a bit as well, at the amateur stage, for, like, ten hours straight.'

'Wow. Amazing. You must be so tired.'

'Not really. But we did so much ecstasy, on the last day my sister was sick and I've been coming down hard.'

'That's so nice, that you got to spend all that time with your sister. And now I guess you can just recover and relax at home!'

'Yeah, although I have to work hard this week! My thesis is due in six days! I can't wait.'

'Ah, it will feel so good once you're finished, though. We must celebrate.'

'I'm going to have a party, actually, as soon as it's finished.'

'Oh?'

'Yes. Will you come?'

'Of course.'

Milosh helped himself to peanuts.

'You look a bit tired and thin, Daphne. Have you been partying too hard? Or working too hard? Is the French dad still creeping on you?'

I found myself telling him about the call with Gabriel, and about Grausam's stalking. I gave him an abridged, adulterated version of the story.

'I met Richard Grausam in a philosophy seminar. We went for a drink once and then he started harassing me, sending me loads of emails and calling me non-stop. He also followed me on the street twice. I've asked him to leave me alone but he won't.'

'God, that's so shitty,' Milosh said, crunching on the last of the peanuts. 'It reminds me of something that happened to Hedvig, my ex.'

'Oh yeah?'

'The last guy she was dating was super obsessed with her. SUPER obsessed. When she broke up with him, he contacted her constantly. He called her family. He used to show up outside her apartment all the time, even her work, threatening that he would kill himself and her if they didn't get back together. She had to get a restraining order. This guy, he never showed up at your house or anything?'

'No, not really.'

Damn you, Hedvig. More beautiful, more unambiguously the victim of harassment. Milosh often compared us, the new and the old model, contrasting our features and advantages. He had mentioned that I was 'much taller than his ex, even when she wore heels'. Many of the compliments he paid me – 'Wow, you don't take long getting ready!' or 'You aren't really into make-up, right?' – were subtle references to Hedvig, to the fact that she was well groomed and far prettier than me. It was only natural that she was on his mind – they had been together for many years – but still, it upset me. *Should* I start wearing eyeliner and painting my nails? *Should* I be more fussy about my clothes, more conventionally feminine? I knew I shouldn't let the comparison affect me. The manipulation of mentioning past girlfriends to condition behaviour in the current one was something I was familiar with. All the men I had dated found me radically different from their last girlfriends: less high-maintenance, less clingy, more willing to talk about their 'manly interests' ('I've never met a girl who is so into cars/football/video games!'). I always seemed to surprise them, despite the fact that they had groomed me to behave this way: they'd given me hints of what they wanted a woman to be like, and were astounded when I magically conformed to their preferences. Shame on them, shame on me.

Milosh's description of Hedvig's experience of stalking made me feel embarrassed that I'd brought it up. Maybe what Grausam did wasn't so bad. Perhaps I was exaggerating. I changed the subject. He ordered a slice of the Black Forest cake, and let me eat the maraschino cherries. Next time the subject of Richard Grausam came up, we would be sitting in a police station.

19

The Party

I SPENT THE NEXT few days taking Xanax and sleeping as much as I could. I went to Leila's a few times. She worked mostly from home, but one afternoon I knocked on her door just as she was on her way out. She seemed to sense that I didn't want to go back to Cass's.

'Just hang out here. Make yourself at home.'

The first thing I did was to look through her fridge and cupboards. I found some Soplica, a Polish vodka, in the freezer, and poured a generous amount, feeling adult and glamorously troubled, like a frazzled sixties housewife. It was hazelnut flavoured, very sweet, its effects immediate. The first sip went through me like an anaesthetic. After the second glass, everything within me slackened, dilated. I took a few deep, heady breaths. I helped myself to a cup of za'atar mix, which I ate with a spoon sitting at the kitchen table. I looked through my phone, rolling the sumac and sesame mixture on my tongue. Someone had posted pictures from the festival. In many of them, Milosh stood close to the bikini top and mini-skirt-wearing beauty. I would never have dared accuse him of anything. We hadn't agreed to be 'exclusive', and most Berliners seemed to consider monogamy to be a reactionary and antiquated concept. I took a Xanax, and fell asleep. I slept the whole day away.

Milosh's party was to take place on the 13th of October. I went for a long run that morning, 24km of Tempelhofer loops and the Hasenheide park to steady my nerves. I knew his friends would be scrutinizing every inch of me, comparing me to Hedvig as I'd compared Milosh to Sebastián. The grass in the Tempelhofer Feld had grown tall; it rustled in a restless silence, this way and that, so that the horizon seemed to shiver in the wind. I looked radiant upon my return, dehydrated, crusted with salt, rosy and bright-eyed. I always thought I looked my best after I'd gone for a long, draining run.

A few hours later, I was sitting on Cass's bed, overcome with anxiety. I couldn't face a whole evening of German strangers. I sent Milosh a text, explaining that I was not feeling well, that I wasn't great fun at parties anyway, and that I'd see him the following day as planned. To which he answered: 'Ah Daphne, no! I understand if you are nervous, but I would really love you to come! No pressure. Just decide for yourself after you think about it more, but I would love to see you there ☺'

I got to the party late, at around eleven, which wasn't very late at all by Berlin standards. Gracie had prepared a cake called a *Bremer Klaben*, the North German take on a Christmas stollen. It tasted like an English Christmas pudding and looked like a cowpat. Here and there, crumbling chunks of it lay around abandoned, and I stuffed them into my mouth when I was sure no one was looking. Milosh was busy DJing, so he couldn't spend much time with me, but he did pause when I arrived, to greet me, mix me a gin and tonic, and introduce me to his best friend:

'I've heard of you! You are the Milkman!'

'And I've heard of you! You're the French dream girl!'

Many of his friends knew who I was, it turned out, and somewhere between my fourth and fifth drink, I realized that I was a hit. I behaved impeccably – I fended for myself, never asking Milosh for help. I didn't check my phone once, I spoke with the Milkman about his diamond- and gem-based aspirations for what seemed like hours. I helped Gracie with the dishes and drank all the shots offered to me by Milosh's tall, broad-shouldered crew, and even danced for an hour or so with the more fucked-up contingent of the party. This may come as a surprise, given my strange body and generally frumpy manner, but I am actually a pretty brilliant dancer. I have this signature dance move called 'the crab' which I think makes me look funny and attractive at the same time.

I left the party at about four thirty, and it was still going strong. Milosh and I had an affectionate fumble on the staircase, and I was glowing the whole way home. Even the broken vending machine in the U-Bahn didn't dampen my spirits. The pride of my success was enough emotional nourishment to put me to sleep without an infusion of sugar. I showered and then wrapped myself in Cass's kimono, and twisted my hair into a towel. I walked barefoot down the pregnant canopied corridor, leaving a trail of watery footsteps behind me. I passed through the bedroom and grabbed my phone, which was still playing the latest *This American Life* episode. I rewound and started to listen from the beginning. I walked into the kitchen, flicked on the kettle, and stepped out on to the balcony. The courtyard light was off. It usually came on when I went on to the balcony, because it was motion sensitive – but I held myself still, and it remained dark, so I could see the night sky clearly. The moon was enormous, and cast a milky, galactic light which outshone the dull pinhead stars. I noticed what I thought were bats, wisps of silky black blindly dipping and flitting around the courtyard. The lights clicked on – probably because I had leant over the balcony railing, to try to see the bats – but I went back inside just in case it was a neighbour, as I was still only wearing Cass's slinky kimono.

I fastened the balcony door behind me, and was about to go into the bedroom when I heard the sound of a bird smashing into the bedroom window. I didn't see the bird itself, but I saw a shape collide with the glass, and heard the dull sickening thump. God, I HATE it when birds do that. I'd never heard of it happening during the night, though. Perhaps it was one of the bats. Poor gruesome thing. But then a moment later Cass's plant pots fell off the windowsill, and Cass's Buddha keeled over, and I thought earthquake, or a nuclear bomb. But I was still alive and the floor wasn't shaking. Then I noticed the glass flying away from the window, and I looked at it and thought, no, not the window again, smashed. I said, 'Oh no!' out loud. 'Oh no, oh no.' I rushed through the bedroom and into the corridor, the kimono flying around me. 'Oh no, I'm mad, I'm mad, this can't be happening.' I slapped my thighs, was relieved to feel their sting, yes, my brain is still tethered to my body. I'm not dreaming, I'm still alive. I'm alive, this is real, it really just happened, you have to do something now, call for help, but I had already run out into the corridor and the door had slammed behind me.

I immediately realized my mistake – all he had to do was walk up the stairs and he'd catch me. I'd left the key in my coat pocket inside the flat. I thought about running up to the second or third floor, but then if he came upstairs I'd be cornered. The spare set was at Leila's. I knocked on Leila's door with my left hand, and tightened the kimono around me with the other. I couldn't hear any noise from inside the flat.

But I could see the glimmer of light beneath her door. She must be there; why wouldn't she open? I was cold, too, in my bare, oddly dusty feet. I banged again. I should have taken my phone with me. Running outside wasn't an option; he was probably waiting to catch me in the courtyard. My stomach dropped suddenly, that feeling you have when you miss a step. And then the white-hot terror abated, and a feeling of futility came over me. Please, I thought. Just kill me now. If I'm going to die, let it be now. I mumbled this to myself, a kind of mumbo-jumbo of semi-formed sentences. My hands hung from the cuffs of the kimono as if they didn't belong to me. This can't be happening, this can't be happening. Then I realized that I was screaming, a long agonized cry of pain that sounded much like the screaming I had heard through the walls of Cass's flat. I slapped my bare legs. They felt so cold and numb, like the legs of a corpse. This cannot be happening, this cannot be happening.

Still no movement from behind Leila's door. Maybe she was out drinking with friends, and had just forgotten to turn her lights off. I wanted to call out to her – 'PLEASE, Leila, it's Daphne' – but I was scared that someone in the courtyard would be lured in by my shouting. But then I thought, I might not have actually seen the window smash. Maybe I'd had a nightmare, and had sleepwalked into the corridor. In any case, I was stuck outside. I knocked again, more gently this time, three polite raps. I heard some movement behind the door.

'Leila,' I hissed, 'Leila, it's Daphne!'

'Hello?' she called.

'Yes, it's Daphne, Leila! Please open the door!'

The door remained closed.

'Is everything OK?'

'No! Please, Leila, please let me in!' I sounded so desperate, like a drowning U-Bahn beggar. 'Please, Leila!' At last I heard the lock turn and she opened the door. She was wearing a white nightie and a pair of fluffy panda slippers, but she looked relatively awake. I pushed past her and slammed the door behind me.

'Lock it, Leila, lock it!'

She did, looking absolutely terrified. Maybe she thought I'd come to seduce her, in my sexy peignoir. I bent over at the waist, pinching the stubborn rind of flesh around my hips. This is happening, this is me. This is happening, this is me. You're OK, you're OK, you'll be fine. This is happening. This is me. I am me. This is happening. This is happening to me.

'What's going on? Do you need a doctor?'

'No, no. Leila, listen, someone threw something through my window.'

'Are you sure?'

'Well, no, I'm not sure, I think maybe I was dreaming. But no, yes, I think so, I think someone was in the courtyard, and threw a brick through the window.'

'When did this happen?'

'Just now, about five minutes ago.'

'Are you sure? Were you sleepwalking?'

'What do you mean?'

'Didn't I just see you standing downstairs in the courtyard?'

'What? No, I didn't go outside!'

'I thought I saw you in the courtyard! I was even worried because you were barefoot. I was just getting ready to come down and see you when you knocked!'

'No, Leila, that must have been someone else. Maybe you saw the bricker? What did they look like?'

'They looked like you! But maybe I didn't see properly.'

Leila put her key in the lock, and made as if to open the door. I pushed my arm against it to block her.

'What are you doing?'

'I'm going to go and check the courtyard!'

'Are you serious?'

'Come on, we can see who it is!'

She ran into the kitchen and came back with an IKEA bread knife. I slid my feet into a pair of her sliders, and hurried after her. Her slippers slapped down the stairs into the courtyard. It was freezing; I could see my breath. The light flashed on as we came down, and it seemed empty. Leila kicked off her shoes and ran towards the front entrance and out on to the street. I tried to keep up with her, but I was slowed down by my efforts to stop the kimono from flying open.

'Leila! Leila!'

She shouldn't be running like that while carrying a knife. I ran through the entrance, out on to the street, and sprinted after her. If you run very fast, time slows down. That's one of the laws of relativity. I felt like time had stopped entirely. I was moving, but exerting no effort, as if the road were gliding beneath me like a conveyor belt. Leila was running up the hill in the direction of the Hasenheide park. Ahead of her I could make out a bike light, glowing red like the tip of a cigarette. Just as I caught up with Leila, it disappeared.

'Ah, fuck,' she said, 'I couldn't see his face. Did you recognize him?'

'I didn't even see him. Are you sure it was a man?'

'I don't know. Whoever it was, they were wearing a hat. Green? Do you know anyone with a green beanie? Could that be someone you know?'

'No idea.'

A car drove up the street, slowing down as we passed. I

tensed up, but then saw it was two women. They looked as frightened of us as I was of them. We were quite a spectacle: Leila in her white nightie, carrying a knife, and me in my flapping kimono. We hurried home. The lights clicked on as we reached the courtyard. I looked up towards Cass's window.

'God,' Leila said. 'God. That's really a smashing.'

The flower bed below my window was covered with glass fragments. It looked as if someone had been smashing bottles.

I followed her up the stairs. I hadn't slammed the door behind me, and an awful thought occurred to me. 'Leila, do you think whoever did it could have been hiding in the courtyard? Maybe he's in your flat?'

Still carrying the knife, Leila checked the bathroom, kitchen and two bedrooms in turn. I followed her at a cautious distance. How come she was so brave? She wasn't any stronger than I was. She led me to the kitchen, and we sat at the table. I still felt incredibly disconnected, as if there was a delay in communication between my brain and body. I was working my jaw like a gaping fish and blinking my eyes. Every time I opened them, it took a while for the room to flicker into focus, as if my brain was a faulty TV screen. I wished I was alone. I wanted to measure my pulse. I needed a timer. I reached into my pocket for my phone, but remembered I'd left it in the flat.

'Do you think I should call the police?' I asked.

'If you want.'

'My phone is still there. But I don't know, I don't think I should call them anyway. There's no point, they're useless.'

'I'll get it,' she said, and went over to Cass's.

For the first time in my life, I thought: I want to die, I want to die, the refrain beating time with the thumping of my heart. This is awful. I want to die. When's it going to end? Even if I wasn't yet insane, if this continued I would lose my mind. Would this keep happening, wherever I went? I don't know if I can survive this. I don't have it in me. Life is meant to test you, but this was too much. I wasn't up to this. Not madness yet, but looming madness. I stamped my feet and slapped my hands together, and the sound and sensation reverberated back to me as if from a long way off.

20

Kommissar Faccini

L EILA AND I SPENT the morning together. We were both ill at ease – she because she did not know how to respond to my evident distress, and I because I couldn't summon the energy to mask my feelings. I tried to behave normally, but the effort of trying to remember what normal behaviour consisted of was making me panic. I accepted the glass of water she offered and held it to my lips, tilted my head, tilted the glass, let the liquid pool in my mouth and then swallowed, remembering to breathe in and out through my nose. Muscles and joints were functioning but all these normal gestures had lost their spontaneity. I felt like Frankenstein's monster pretending to be human. I formulated interesting questions in my mind – do you have weekend plans? How is your work going? – but I stayed silent, probing the inside of my mouth with my tongue. It felt sore. I must have bitten the inside of my cheek. I excused myself, went to the bathroom. I peeled back my lower lip. Crenellated teeth, pinkish gums, blood brimming from bite marks. Purplish slanted shadows drawing deep furrows beneath each eye. I seemed strange and disjointed, as if all my parts were designed by a dozen different architects, all with radically different aesthetics, and then were welded together in homage to Picasso's *Weeping Woman*.

It barely grew lighter outside as the day broke. It would be a windy, cold, shadowless day. I sat at Leila's kitchen table, looked at my phone, and refreshed my email. Ryanair were offering a fantastic November deal. Zara wanted me to look at their Timeless Basics currently on sale. I kept picturing someone staring up from the courtyard and looking into my window. I didn't suspect EG's downstairs neighbour. I didn't think he could have found out where I lived. I thought the man on the bicycle was probably Grausam. I could easily imagine him wearing a green beanie. Gabriel must have said something to him that gave away my new address.

I suspected Grausam. But I didn't know what to do about it. In *Stalkers: A Survivor's Guide*, Santiago Álvarez stresses that involving the police does not always work. 'Police contact sometimes causes the perpetrator to worsen his attacks, as he realizes he is unlikely to be arrested for his behaviour,' Álvarez writes. He adds the frightening afterthought: 'A restraining order will not restrain someone with homicidal intent.' But I worried that he would keep attacking me, if I did nothing. I posted my dilemma on the Reddit Legal Advice forum, and received the following answers:

Post Replies: Should I go to the police? Stalking, broken window (Germany).

From Tinkerbellend via /r/LegalAdviceEurope
First, do you seek therapy for your issues?
Second, at the very least report the crimes committed against you.

The last comment made up my mind for me. I texted Milosh: 'Hey, hope you had fun last night. I urgently need your help with something. Someone threw another brick through my window and I think I'm going to the police.'

He called me at once. His voice was croaky and thin, no doubt from staying up all night talking.

'Oh my God, Daphne. I'm so sorry. Tell me what happened. Do you want to come over? Everyone is still here. Or do you want me to come there?'

'Please come here. I'm at my neighbour's. Flat number four.'

'I'll be there as soon as I can.'

Leila poured me some orange juice and switched the radio on. I felt completely numb. To save from having to talk, I took a sip of juice, but quickly put down my glass. My hands were shaking so violently that I couldn't hold it steady. I looked through my bag and realized I'd left the last of the Xanax at Cass's.

'Leila, do you have anything stronger to drink? I need something to steady my nerves.'

'Of course.' She pulled the Soplica bottle from the freezer. She didn't seem to have noticed that I'd pilfered some last time I was alone in her flat. She poured me a generous glass of it. Thick and gloopy like children's cough syrup. I drank it in two gulps. We listened to the radio in silence. Two people were shot dead outside a synagogue in eastern Germany. The

London and New York police announced that they were opening a criminal investigation into the sexual assault allegations against Harvey Weinstein. This year's flu strain was especially virulent. A rare species of bat had become extinct.

The doorbell rang and I hurried downstairs. I burst into tears and fell into Milosh's arms.

'Daphne, Daphne, I've never seen you cry!' I pressed my face against his chest and shook.

'I'm sorry,' I managed. He was wearing jeans and a denim jacket, and carrying a skateboard under his arm. His hair was still damp from his shower. His hands felt cool against my cheek as he tried to dab my face. He gave me a pack of tissues and I wiped my eyes. I didn't want Leila to know I'd been crying. We walked up to her flat and sat in the kitchen. She made toast while I told Milosh about what had happened.

'So did you guys definitely see the person who did it? Was it definitely the person on the bike?'

'I don't really know,' I replied. 'I mean, I think so, but I guess it could have been a neighbour.'

'What about your neighbour, the guy you thought broke into your room at Huberstraße?'

'I don't think so. I don't think there's any way he could have found out where I live. I think maybe it could be Grausam, you know; the stalker. He lives quite near here. But I'm not sure. Leila thinks she saw a *woman* in the courtyard.'

'Really? What did she look like, Leila?'

'Blonde, quite tall. I didn't notice what she was wearing.'

'Oh my God, maybe you've got a doppelgänger, Daphne! Is there a camera or anything out there?'

'I don't think so,' Leila replied. 'I guess it could have been a neighbour. I could ask around.'

'OK. Well, we can explain it to the police, I guess. We

should definitely go, but to be completely honest, Daphne, I don't know if they'll really help.'

The pop of the toaster startled us. The bread was stuck. Leila rattled the lever, and when that didn't work, she prised out the slices with a wooden spoon. She pulled Nutella, apricot jam and a soft white cheese from the fridge. Milosh spread two pieces with jam and butter.

'These are for you, Daphne. You need to eat something. You don't look so good.'

Leila fussed over coffee and milk, and Milosh got up to help her dislodge the last piece of toast, but I felt him watching me with exactly the kind of concerned look my mother often gave me, as if I were a clueless lamb about to be slaughtered. I found it very anxiety-provoking. Why was he so concerned? He made me feel like a lunatic. My jaw clicked with tension as I chewed on my toast.

We left Leila's, walked up the mild incline of Parkhausstraße and crossed Hermannstraße. Milosh held my hand as we waited for the lights to change, as if to prevent me from running into the road like a wayward child. We walked by the pizza place, and past the language school. We crossed the Tempelhofer Feld towards the police station. The sky was grey, and the glass was turning sepia brown. Milosh skated ahead. Kick-push, kick-push, effortless coasting, and then the graceful C shape of his body as he leant to swerve back towards me.

The police station was located in the old Tempelhof Airport terminal. Despite my anxiety, I was curious to see what Speer's building looked like on the inside. The entrance was beautiful and imposing: the rows of perfectly symmetrical rectangular windows were encased in white stone and the building's limestone was luminescent, even on this grey day. We passed through a revolving door into an enormous hall.

The building had retained its original features from when it had been used as an airport: old-fashioned split-flap depart-ure and arrival boards; huge clocks and stationary carousels. The reception area looked like it had once been a check-in desk, except that now it was encased in bulletproof glass. Milosh explained to the police officer at the front desk why we had come, and she led us to a room and told us to wait. It was empty, save for a plastic table surrounded by three chairs. The walls were decorated with posters about the dangers of laced 'spiced weed' and domestic abuse statistics. A police officer came in, carrying a paper file and a can of Red Bull. He introduced himself as Kommissar Faccini. He licked his finger and opened the file.

'OK, so you are Daphne Ferber?'

I nodded.

'My colleague told me that you have an incident to report? Someone threw a brick through your window early this morning?'

'That's right.'

'OK. So here I have the report of another similar incident concerning you? Is that correct?'

'Yes.'

'OK, I'm just going to make sure all the information we have on file is correct. So you are Daphne Ferber, of 105 Huberstraße—'

'No, I've moved to 25 Parkhausstraße.'

'How long have you been living there, Fräulein Ferber?' he said, making a note.

'For approximately three months now.'

'Did you register with the *Bürgeramt*?'*

'No.'

---

* The local council.

216

'You know you can get a fine of a thousand euros if you don't register with the *Bürgeramt* within two months of arrival.'

'I'm sorry. I'll do it at once.'

'Everyone says that, but they never do it, HA!' He had a barking laugh, surprisingly high-pitched for a man of his girth and brawn. 'What is your profession, Fräulein Ferber?'

'I don't have a profession yet.'

'Well, she babysits,' Milosh interjected. 'She works for a French family.'

'Is that so?' Faccini asked, looking up from his notes.

'Yes,' I lied. 'I look after two little girls.'

'Is that why you moved to Berlin?'

'No, I came here to learn German.'

'Well, she didn't do a bad job, did she?' he said, winking at Milosh, who looked at me and winked. I winked back, awkwardly.

'OK, so you come to Germany, you want to learn German and you move into 105 Huberstraße. You were renting from Fräulein EG, it says here?'

'Yes.'

'How did you know Fräulein EG?'

'Through a flat-sharing Facebook group.'

'And the landlady, I see, is Frau Marie Becker, of 42 Cicerostraße, 10707 Berlin-Lichtenberg. This person knew you were subleasing the flat from Fräulein EG? You did it legally?'

'Yes.'

'Fine,' he said, making another note. 'So here it says that on April third, someone threw a stone through your window. But you didn't report it to the police at the time, is that right?'

'Yes,' I said. 'I thought maybe it had something to do with the change in temperature. But the repairman told me that it looked as if it had been broken by a stone.'

'OK. And at the time, did you know of anyone who might want to hurt you? Harm you?'

'No, I didn't know anyone in Berlin at that time.'

'So then there is a break-in, on the twenty-fourth of June. In the notes here it mentions that you suspected the down-stairs neighbour? Is that right?'

'Yes, at the time I did.'

'OK. Can I have this neighbour's name?'

'I never knew it.'

'Still, it would be useful to have his name for the sake of our files. But you think he broke into your flat? Do you think he was responsible for the incident which occurred last night?'

'No, I think that it was a man I met at a philosophy seminar.'

'OK, and what is this man's name?'

'Richard Grausam,' I said, and saying it provoked an uneasy stirring low in my stomach.

'And what was the nature of your connection to this man? Did you have a relationship?'

He reminded me of Officer Blondie, with his rom-com thinking.

'Yes, we went out very briefly.'

I glanced at Milosh. Until now, he had been staring at a fixed point on the table in front of him, without moving. It was as if he thought being silent and concentrated would make me forget he was there, and give me the illusion of privacy. He turned to me now, looking confused.

'What? You went out with him? Why didn't you tell me that?'

'I was embarrassed!'

'How long were you together with Richard Grausam?' said Faccini, ignoring this exchange.

'Only a few weeks.'

'From when to when was this?'

'Most of the month of April, I guess. We met the week after the bricking.'

'So you got together after the first incident on the third of April, and broke up before the second on the twenty-fourth of June?'

'Yes, that's right.'

'OK. And he knew your address in Huberstraße?'

'Yes.'

'Did he ever stay at your house?'

I nodded.

'What – once, twice, ten times?'

He fired questions at me with a swift, jolly panache, as if this were a joust-y game of tennis on a sunny Sunday afternoon.

'Two or three times.'

Milosh looked astounded.

'And did you ever stay at his house?'

'Yes, but only once.'

'And his address is?'

'15 Adalberstraße. I can't remember the flat number.'

'OK, and so then what happened? You broke up?'

'Well, we weren't really a couple.'

'OK, but how did it end?'

'I decided to stop seeing him,' I replied.

'And can I ask why this was?'

'Because I didn't like him, I guess.'

'Was he violent?'

'No, not really. But I mean, he was pushy. He tried to force me to let him move in with me.'

'OK, what do you mean by *force* you?'

I swallowed. I felt as if I was watching my own dissection, the good-humoured doctor occasionally raising his scalpel to ask, 'Does that feel like your spleen, or the intestine?' Repressed memories like toxic beads of mercury rolling around in my stomach, my chest. Too dark and heavy to rise to the conscious surface.

'He wanted to sublet his apartment and to move in with me. When I refused he got incredibly angry. I told him I wanted to stop seeing him, but he wouldn't leave me alone.'

'OK, and since then? He has been contacting you?'

'Yes.' I handed over my phone, and showed him the emails he had sent me. Faccini looked underwhelmed.

'He also called me all the time, and texted me. Until I blocked his number.'

'All the time, like every day?'

'At first a few times a day, then maybe two or three times a week. And recently, he persuaded a friend of mine to lend him his phone and spoke to me.'

'Did you keep a log of all his calls?'

'No.'

'Next time this happens, it's important to keep a log of the calls.'

I nodded.

'Anything else?'

'What do you mean?'

'No physical threat?'

'Well, he followed me into a coffee shop and grabbed me.'

'Did he hit you? Or hurt you?'

'No.'

Faccini took another sip of his Red Bull. The room was hot, and I felt incredibly thirsty and glanced at the water fountain but didn't dare to ask for a glass. Milosh gave me a wan smile. I wished I could have asked someone else to come with me. He looked overwhelmed. If only Kat were still in Berlin. She would have backed me up. The policeman was clearly so used to seeing such devastating brutality that he couldn't understand how I felt. Neither could Milosh, who was probably at this very moment thinking about poor Hedvig, and her own much more impressive stalker.

'OK. So when you were interviewed by the police officers on the twenty-fifth of June, you said you thought it was the neighbour who bricked the window, but now you don't think it's him any more?'

'No, I think it was him the first time, maybe the second, but not this last time.'

'What led you to suspect your neighbour?'

I turned to Milosh. 'How do you say, "he gave me a bad feeling"? And "he gave me a nasty look"?' Milosh explained to Faccini, and from then on he directed the questions to Milosh, who translated my answers from English.

'Let me get this straight. Someone throws a brick through the window at Huberstraße on April third. She starts a relationship with Richard Grausam around when?'

'She says around the start of April.'

'Until when?'

'Maybe the beginning of May.'

'So, they got together AFTER the first bricking incident?'

'That's right.'

'And then someone broke into her apartment at Huberstraße on June twenty-fourth?'

'Yes.'

'OK. And then she moves to 25 Parkhausstraße, on the first of July?'

'Yes, around that time.'

'And someone broke her window early this morning, this time at Parkhausstraße.'

'Correct!'

'But then, she thinks Richard Grausam was responsible for the third incident, but not the first or second?'

'The first couldn't have been him, as she didn't know him. She's not sure about the second – it could have been him, because he knew her address.'

'So she thinks that he did this to scare her?'

'Exactly!' I said, slapping my hand on the table for emphasis. '*Genau!*'

Faccini looked a little on edge all of a sudden, as if I'd vandalized state property.

'Is there a camera set up in the courtyard?'

'No.'

'And doesn't she think it's a little strange? First her neighbour throws a stone at her, then someone breaks in, and then her ex breaks her window today? Why are all the men in her life suddenly smashing her windows? Isn't it likely to be the same person each time?'

'Milosh,' I said. 'Explain to him that I told everyone I knew when my window was first smashed. And I told Richard Grausam. He knew the whole thing really affected me. It would make sense that he would do a copy-cat crime, if he wanted to get my attention!'

It was true, I had told the story innumerable times. It was my narrative currency. I had told Grausam about the bricking. He had made some weak displays of interest, asking what had happened and whether I knew a cheap window repairman, before changing the subject to the book he wanted to write, about 'neoliberalism and neo-capitalism in post-industrial utopias'. He was a bore.

'OK. But do you have any evidence that Richard Grausam knows where you live now? Did he visit you at Parkhausstraße?'

Milosh explained that it was possible Gabriel had given Grausam my address. This led to a whole wasted twenty minutes of questions about Gabriel, his country of origin, his family name. Faccini asked about the exact nature of our relationship, how long I had lived with him, whether I had registered at the *Bürgeramt* while living in his apartment.

'Well, I'm going to be honest,' he said, looking up from his notes and making eye contact with each of us in turn. 'Your girlfriend doesn't have much on her ex-boyfriend. It seems he was a bit pushy, but there isn't any sign of serious harassment. There isn't enough here for a restraining order. Now, if she wants, we could call him in and ask him a few questions, saying he is a person of interest in connection to the broken window. But unless he confesses, we have nothing on him. Is this her preferred course of action?'

Milosh looked at me. 'Do you want them to look into it?'

I answered Faccini directly.

'Will Grausam find out who brought the charges against him, if you look into him?'

'Well, if we take this further, then yes. But I wouldn't worry too much about provoking this guy. He doesn't seem violent, but I'll run a check on him now. Please excuse me. And help yourself to water.'

21

The Fake Nanny

MILOSH GAVE ME A euro for the vending machine. I pressed E5 for a Diet Coke Cherry, while Milosh helped himself three times to the water fountain. The Coke seemed to fizz straight to my brain. Delicious, aspartame-rich, coating my teeth in fake sugar. I had a sudden rush of energy, like a hyped-up athlete after a half-time pep-talk. Bring it on, Kommissar! Milosh, on the other hand, looked like he had just seen a corpse. He was pale, and when I took his hand, it was clammy and cold.

'I'm sorry this is taking so long.'

'Ach, *Quatsch*, Daphne. It's OK. You OK?'

'I'm fine.'

'Why did you never tell me you had a relationship with this Grausam?'

'Because it makes me feel sick to even talk about it, Milosh.'

Kommissar Faccini returned, carrying another can of Red Bull. He cracked it open, and the room filled with an irresistible smell of chemical flavourings and melted sweets.

'I have some news about your ex-boyfriend. Not so harmless after all. Two different women have restraining orders against him. He is also currently in police custody.'

'What for?'

'I'm not permitted to say, but if there was any sexual assault or coercion in your case, Fräulein Ferber, I urge you to report it.'

Milosh tried to take my hand, but I pretended not to notice. This was disturbing news, but I felt vindicated.

'No, nothing like that.'

'So he was in jail yesterday? Then it couldn't have been him!' Milosh said.

'Is there anyone else it could be, anyone who knows your address? Any other man in your life?' Kommissar Faccini gestured to Milosh. 'How about him? Is he your boyfriend?'

'Yes!' we said in unison, and both blushed.

'OK, OK. Busy romantic life!' He winked again. 'And is there anyone else apart from Grausam?'

'No,' I replied.

'What about that pervy French babysitting guy?' Milosh said, turning to me. 'Didn't you say he was harassing you?'

'Harassing?' said Faccini, leaning forwards. He had a tiny bit of white spittle in the corners of his mouth, and a tiny bit of stubble. But apart from this, his skin was perfect.

'Her employer's husband. Sometimes he behaves inappropriately with her.'

'Oh, but that was really nothing,' I said, 'really!'

'That is for me to determine, if something is important or not,' said Faccini. 'Who is this man?'

'The man for whom I used to babysit,' I said. 'I don't work there any more.'

'How long did you work there?'

'Maybe three or four months.'

'His name?' he said, as he fumbled in his pockets for a pen.

'I don't know his family name,' I extemporized.

'What's his address?'

'I can't remember.'

'But you were always at their house, Daphne!' Milosh exclaimed.

Faccini put on an expression of over-exaggerated confusion. 'So, you work for this family for a few months, but you don't know where they live?' he said, in a mocking tone.

I didn't reply, and he asked me again, more forcefully, 'Why won't you share this man's address? Are you working for him illegally? Is he making you do something illegal?'

In a perfect world I would have burst into tears or vomited at that exact moment, creating a diversion, or at least making them feel sorry for me. But I didn't.

I turned to Milosh, feeling faint. 'I didn't really babysit for this man.'

'What do you mean?' said Kommissar Faccini.

'I lied to Milosh. I didn't really work as a babysitter.'

Ich habe Milosh angelogen. I stared at the table in front of me, too scared to look at their faces to gauge the impact of what I had just admitted.

'You realize, don't you, that it is an offence to lie to the police?' said Faccini.

'I'm really sorry.'

'You can be prosecuted for wasting time, or for making a false report.'

'I'm really sorry.'

'Sorry won't get you out of breaking the law. Why did you lie about this? Where were you really working?' Faccini leant forwards with a knowing look. He probably thought I was a stripper or a prostitute. A rather unsuccessful one.

'I don't have a job.'

'How do you live, then? Is someone giving you money? Unemployment benefits?'

'No, my parents send me money.'

'Can you prove this?'

I unlocked the Revolut app, and passed him my phone. He looked through my bills, scrolling back months into the past: rent, language school fees, grocery bills, EG's returned deposit with the deducted amount for the stained sheets and broken crockery. A testimony of my unglamorous existence.

'Is there anything else you lied about? Are you still in a relationship with Grausam?'

'No!'

'And do you want to retract your description of Grausam's behaviour towards you?'

'No.'

'So you just lied about the job?'

'Yes.'

'OK.' He looked dubious. 'Look, I am still willing to make a report about the events of last night. But I have to warn you that if anything here is false, you will be prosecuted. We take false complaints incredibly seriously. They waste our time and our resources, and can end up with innocent people going to jail. Do you understand?'

'I understand.'

'Please excuse me for a moment. Think about whether you want to take this further.' Kommissar Faccini got up from the table, scraping his chair on the lino floor. The moment he left the room, Milosh grabbed my wrist.

'Take this further?' he hissed. 'No way, Daphne. We need to get out of here as soon as possible!'

'Fine,' I said. 'Let's go.'

'We have to wait for him to come back! Why are you lying all the time? What's wrong with you?'

'Oh, and you're perfect, Milosh!'

My face felt hot; I was suddenly full of adrenaline. It felt profoundly wrong to be unkind to him, a complete violation of my instincts.

'Well, I don't lie to you, Daphne.'

'Great. You are a saint, Milosh.' I got up to leave, just as Kommissar Faccini returned.

'So you are not filing a report?' he asked, looking pleased with himself.

'We'll leave it here,' Milosh said.

Faccini extended his hand to point out the exit, and thinking he'd been trying to shake my hand, I grabbed hold of his wrist. For a moment I held on, as if I were detaining him. He looked annoyed, and pulled away. He shook his head at me wordlessly, as if language could not convey the extent of my stupidity. Milosh and I walked out of the room, down the corridor, past the reception and out into the Platz der Luftbrücke.

I began to walk along Columbiadamm, the busy road which runs between the Tempelhofer Feld and the Hasenheide park. I walked so quickly that Milosh had to hop on to his skateboard to catch up with me. He rode alongside me and stared down at me, but I turned my face away. As usual, he was silent. I wasn't apologetic or remorseful. I was good at mental gymnastics, and managed to transform shame at being caught lying into fury at Milosh for catching me out. As if he'd barged into the bathroom without knocking when I was on the toilet. He hovered alongside me, his skateboard rattling. I was just waiting for him to build up the courage to ask me why I had lied before I launched into full Estella mode. I imagined saying: 'Well, Milosh, what else could I do but lie to you? You can't deal with anything. I had to filter reality to protect your delicate heart. If you wanted to know the truth you would have demanded it. You were just conveniently naive. You never helped me with anything. You gave me a few hours each week, you didn't ask about what I did all day, if I was lonely in this new city, why I never had any food at home. Don't demand "truth" now, when we both know that you were happy to accept my lies when they made your life easy.' But I didn't.

'Daphne, Daphne, PLEASE stop!' He was nearly shouting. 'What is it?'

'I have a problem with my board truck.'

'What?'

'It's to do with the wheel. I need to fix it. Can we sit down for a minute?'

We sat on a stone bench outside the Şehitlik Mosque, a beautiful Ottoman-style dome flanked by two tall minarets. I'd sat there many times before, as Evan, Ollie and I had regularly come to fill our bottles at the mosque's outdoor drinking fountain during long Tempelhof runs. Milosh flipped over his skateboard, placing it on the bench between us. He pulled a black tool out of his backpack. He began tightening the bolts of one of the wheels. His silence had neutralized my anger, and now I just felt anxious about what he would say next.

'See, whenever I turn, it's a bit too jumpy,' he explained, as if I was paying attention to what he was doing. 'I prefer it when it's a bit smoother, so I'm trying to see if I can just do that by regulating the back truck.' Milosh finished with the first set of wheels, and began loosening the other set. He stopped abruptly and looked up at me.

'Daphne, I don't understand why you lie so much. You've lied to me about everything. You lied about your job, you lied about the creepy boss, you lied about that guy stalking you. I don't get it.'

I didn't have the energy to put him right. I'd lied about so many stupid unimportant things that he wouldn't believe the one important truthful thing – the fact that Grausam had stalked me. From what Kommissar Faccini had said, Grausam was a dangerous person. But it was pointless trying to convince Milosh now. If only I hadn't brought him with me. I could have been honest with Faccini about my relationship with Grausam and about my job from the beginning.

'Why did you lie, Daphne?'

There really was no good answer. These lies felt like the countless others I'd told in various situations: no thanks, I've had dinner; yes, I am having a great time, thank you; no, I'm not lonely at all; yes, all my early promise is coming to fruition as I grow into a liberated woman.

I've lied because I found people's desire to know the truth invasive and their assumption I would tell the truth presumptive. People think they are entitled to honest answers, but I've never been very honest because I don't want to be depressing. Was I supposed to answer, no, I haven't had dinner, I'm stuck in a pattern of starving myself and I can't break the pattern because being hungry numbs me from the general pervasive feeling of failure and self-disgust which permeates my whole being? Yes, I'm so lonely that I slept with a disgusting man who treated me awfully and has been wrecking my life ever since. And no, I think my younger self would be utterly bereft if she saw me now.

I can anticipate the kind of soft-psychology replies people would give me: 'Daphne, we all need to talk about our bad feelings more. Let it all out.' But I don't agree. All we do is complain. I've done it all. I've had those boring, late-night tears with my university girlfriends about our body image issues and Eating Disorders (EDs). I've listened empathetically to my male friends whining about their EDs (Erectile Dysfunctions). I've complained about every minor thing that has ever happened to me to expensive therapists whose fees were being paid by the very devils I complained about for £180 an hour (my father and mother). I've moaned about the patriarchy endlessly. I've pontificated about the 'vacuity at the heart of things' in mediocre philosophy essays that earned me As, because my professor was scared that one of his students would have a mental health crisis if he gave anyone a B. We don't need more negativity. We need good cheer, optimism and courage. If I needed to tell a few fibs to give things a positive spin, I was willing to lie.

But then there remains the issue of lying about Grausam, and lying about having a job, and lying about my employer's harassment. Such lies can't be dismissed under the 'giving-things-a-positive-gloss' excuse-clause. They are good examples of the second kind of lies I told: the straight-out manipulative kind. I pretended that I'd been harassed by my boss because I wanted to seem like a victim. I wanted to awaken Milosh's protective impulses, and for him to know that other men want me too. I'd lied about having a job because I didn't want Milosh to know how privileged I was. I wanted him to think that whatever I'd achieved was due to my own efforts. In fact, I was the kind of child who never had to get a weekend job, had a tutor for everything, and a personal 'university application coach'. This meant that I had started life ten steps ahead of everyone else, and so naturally I felt illegitimate, a fraud, and pretended to my friends we'd all started from the same place.

If the first kind of lies I told were 'positive gloss' and the second kind were 'manipulative', the third category is the kind of lie I told inexplicably for no discernible reason. For example, I had told Milosh that I was twenty-four, instead of twenty-six. I'd told him that I owned a pair of roller skates, that I have an American passport, and I don't believe in God.

These lies make no sense and make my life more complicated without really making me seem cooler or helping me achieve any of my goals. They are the appendix or the wisdom teeth of the lying world – painful, and totally redundant.

The fourth and last category of lie should be called the 'addiction protection' lie. These lies were related explicitly to my 'food issues'. While I understood that my behaviour made me a good candidate for a psychiatric diagnosis, I was not willing to give up the advantages that these habits procured me. My odd daily rituals of running and roughage made everything else bearable. Think of it like this: you know that in the long term your covert behaviour will kill you, but the pain of not indulging in it is so awful that you think you'll die if you stop. I wasn't different from any other addict in that regard, and it is nearly impossible for an addict to tell the truth about their compulsions. It's like politely asking Gollum to hand over the Ring. He'll do anything to protect his Precious. I wasn't about to relinquish mine.

I did, however, resent Milosh and my friends for letting me tell all these types of lies and pull four layers of wool over their eyes. I held the mistaken belief that if someone truly valued me, they would care for me more than I cared for myself. I felt secretly superior, and hated them for how readily duped they were. Poor Milosh. He probably never lied. His words, thoughts and actions all beat in unison, faithful to the rhythm of his spirit. My inner arrangement was more like experimental jazz. Thoughts running to their own mad tempo. Action desperately trying to follow Word's chord progressions, while Word is thinking, fuck these guys, I want to make my own breakout band.

'Do you still have the tissues I gave you?' Milosh asked.

He was crying. I thought about putting my arm around him, but he was sitting at the other end of the bench, as far away from me as possible. I passed him the tissues, and he unfolded one of them, dabbed his face, and then used it to clean black marks off the underside of his skateboard. I was losing him, I knew. He was already hardening himself against me. I started crying.

'Milosh, I'm so sorry. I'm so sorry. I have no idea.' It was hard to speak between sobs. 'Something's wrong with me. I have no idea why I lied. I never meant to upset you. I'm just not a good person. I always lie, it's because I'm ashamed of myself.'

He softened immediately, and shuffled along the bench towards me.

'You're just not well, Daphne. I think you have a psychological problem. It's not your fault. You're not a bad person, Daphne.'

'Yes, I am. I am. It is my fault, Milosh. All I need to do is be honest. What's wrong with me? What's wrong with me?'

Milosh took my cold hands between his, and then lifted his shirt and pressed them against his stomach to warm them, flexing a little. It was unbearable to touch, because I knew I wouldn't ever touch him again.

'Daphne, listen. It's not your fault. But I think you are seriously sick and I think you need some help. I think that you lied about everything. I think it's possible that . . .' He trailed off.

'What?' I said. 'What's possible?' My stomach began to plummet again. He looked suddenly extremely uncomfortable and almost embarrassed, but pressed on.

'I think it might have been you who broke your window last night.'

'Milosh, I understand why you would think that, but honestly, I didn't, I'm not—'

'Leila said she saw a *tall, blonde* woman, Daphne. I said as a joke she sounded like your doppelgänger, but now I wonder if it wasn't you.'

'Milosh, I admit I lied to you, but I'm not that crazy. I wouldn't destroy Cass's apartment just to get attention!'

'But maybe it isn't conscious, Daphne. Think about it. In the last place when there was a break-in, no one even stole anything. And that upstairs neighbour guy, the dude we met jogging on the Tempelhofer Feld, said he heard someone smashing the plates that *afternoon*, *while you were still in the flat*.'

'He just heard some noise, it wasn't necessarily from *my flat*. It could just as easily have been from the bottle bank!'

'Think about it, Daphne. Nothing makes sense. Why would someone break into your house and not take anything? How could this person have found your new address? Why would Leila see someone who looks exactly like you outside just before it happens again?'

'But Berlin is full of people who look like me. It could have been anyone – it was dark, she wasn't even sure it was me.'

'So you really think all this is a coincidence, Daphne? Think about it. Think about it!'

'I have no idea, Milosh! I don't know, that's exactly what I've been trying to understand. But you're scaring me. You're really scaring me.'

I put my face in my hands. Something was tearing within me. Each heartbeat seemed to propel an ooze of poison into my blood. I could feel the pulse throbbing in my temples. It seemed possible, what he said. It seemed probable. I could picture myself smashing EG's crockery. I could imagine myself throwing a stone through Cass's window. It felt like memory, not fantasy. I wasn't brave enough for acts of vigilante justice or true revenge. But self-destruction was much easier. I cried, and continued to, my shoulders shaking.

Milosh held me and I felt his warmth radiating towards me. I loved him. I wanted to keep him as he was, real and so alive to me, a person rather than a memory.

'Do you think what I'm saying is true, Daphne?'

'I don't know, Milosh. I don't know. I love you, you know?'

'Daphne, I don't know, I can't—'

'Oh, I know, Milosh. I already know you're breaking up with me. I just want you to know. I love you.'

'You're a special person, Daphne, really, I just can't go on as if—'

'Please, Milosh. Can we not talk? Can you just hold me for a minute?' He wrapped his arms more tightly around me. I leant against him, rested my head on his chest. I held his wrist in my hand. I knew the moment would pass, that it was already passing. I tried to concentrate on all the details: the feel of his denim jacket, the sound of his heart beating against my ear. His scent, the shape of his hands. To pin the present to memory. He squeezed me tighter, and then let me go.

'I'm hungry, Daphne, and I'm really tired. I'm going to go home.'

I hid my face in my hands. I couldn't stop crying.

'OK. I understand. Thank you for everything.'

'Where are you going to go now? Are you returning to Leila's place? Do you want me to walk with you?'

'I'll be fine, Milosh. I'll be fine.'

'You're a special person, Daphne. Please take care of yourself.'

He left. I wiped my tears on my sleeve, watched as he turned the corner and disappeared from sight. Milosh left my life as gently as he had entered it; he had only wished me well from the very start. What a golden-hearted boy he was. He didn't have to be mine; knowing he existed was enough.

22

Lucky

I DIDN'T FEEL CAPABLE of facing Leila, and her questions about what happened, so I took a diversion via the Hasenheide park. I walked the same loop I used to run in my early days living in EG's flat. I felt as if I was walking backwards in time, rewinding all the blossoming I'd admired in the spring. The rose garden had shrivelled to a mass of thorny stalks; the leaves had crinkled and disappeared. The bare limbs of the trees intermingled, leaning against each other. I wished I could really rewind time, and start the Berlin chapter of my life from the beginning. What if things had gone differently? What if I'd moved into Cass's flat and not EG's, and met Leila on my first day in the city? What if I'd taken the job at Two Moons? What if I'd used Tinder instead of MatchTime? All along I'd been haunted by the thought of the endless possibilities, the myriad different lives I could have lived. And what had I gleaned, from the life I actually lived? What had I learnt in Berlin, apart from German, and that it is prudent to wash vegetables before eating them? How little I'd really taken advantage of the city, how little I'd achieved. I never went to a club, I never barbecued, I never went bowling or swimming in a lake. I'd just stewed in the fetid air of my own bell jar.

The only spot of colour in the park came from the Gambians, who with their enormous yellow, red and green puffer jackets looked like a flock of exotic birds. One of them noticed me, and started miming someone jogging.

'No running today?'

I smiled and walked on. One of the men began to follow me on his bicycle. He was wearing a red puffer, and a blue fisherman beanie, fashionably cuffed so that it ended just above his ears. I recognized him as the same Gambian man who I'd sat next to once after running into Grausam.

'Where's your boyfriend, runner girl?'

'He doesn't want me any more.'

He biked beside me, pedalling slowly to keep up, just as Milosh had on his skateboard a few moments ago. It made sense that everything had fallen apart just as I had fallen in love with him. As I had begun to depend on him, I'd lost what little remained of my ability to hold myself together.

'Stupid man! You're a very nice girl!'

'Thanks.'

'What's your name?'

'Daphne.'

I didn't know how to get rid of him politely. He continued to follow me as I left the park.

'You don't ask my name?'

'Sorry, what's your name?'

'Lucky!'

He followed me across the road and down towards Parkhausstraße, a silent chaperone. At my door I turned around.

'I'm home now, Lucky.'

He turned the bike around on the pavement, and smiled. 'Bye bye, runner girl! *Tschüss!*'

I waited until I was sure he had really gone, and then let

myself into the courtyard. I stared up at Cass's flat. The windows glittered black like the cracked surface of a frozen pond, the hole where the brick had gone through gaping open like a wound. It was me. I had done it. I remember the feel of the brick in my hand, a heavy but compact piece of concrete. Aiming right for the centre. Bullseye.

It took a long time for me to unlock Leila's door, as her keys were identical to Cass's, and neither had distinguished theirs with a key ring. It was around 6 p.m. Leila wasn't at home. I wondered if she was avoiding me. Maybe she'd guessed what I had done, just as Milosh had. Or perhaps she'd seen me do it and had known the truth all along, but hadn't wanted to confront me. I drank some of her orange juice. I opened a carton of egg-yellow salty margarine, and scooped some of it up with the leftover flatbread. I took a couple of large spoonfuls of mayonnaise, and a few smaller ones of Nutella. I heard keys in the lock and the door open, and Leila came in while I was still guiltily rummaging through her fridge. I pretended to be looking for milk.

'I'm having some tea. Would you like some?'

'Yes, please. Can you put in some toast for me?' She sat down and laid her head on the table. 'I'm soooooo tired!'

'That's because I woke you up so early. I'm so sorry.'

'It's not your fault! How did it go at the police station? Did they find out who did it?'

'Oh, it went OK,' I said lightly. 'It went OK. They're investigating now, I guess. Um, but I'm going to go home for a while. I just need a break. Is it OK if I stay with you until I leave?'

'Yes, of course, of course. When do you go?'

'As soon as I can. I have to sort out Cass's place, obviously. I haven't even told her what happened yet.'

'Oh, Daphne, I already told her. One of the neighbours

texted her about the window. She said she tried to call you but you weren't picking up, so she called me and I explained everything. I'm so sorry, I should have let you tell her, but I didn't know when you'd be back and she was worried.'

'That's OK, but what did she say? Is she angry with me?'

She had just taken a bite of her toast, and held her hand up to indicate for me to wait until she'd finished chewing.

'No,' she said, after a long pause, 'no, not at all, Daphne. Actually, she asked me to tell you not to worry about it. She guessed that you might want to go home. I'm going to let the repairmen in next week. Just get what you need from her place. I'll manage the rest.'

She accompanied me to Cass's flat to pack. The damage was worse than I'd remembered. Four of the plant pots had smashed, and had trickled muddy water on to the wooden floor and carpet. The room smelt sweet and fetid from the earth-manure mix, which had somehow got all over the bedspread. The Buddha was knocked over, prostrated as if in prayer, smiling impassively at the chaos around him. There were shards of glass shining in random star-like clusters all over the floor. I looked around for the brick, but couldn't find it. The flat was completely quiet, but there was something animated and threatening about its silence. Poor Cass, she would need to summon her most intense meditative powers to redirect this terrible energy.

Leila played with the canopied ceiling, ruffling it so that it rolled like a wave, and then helped me duct-tape the window. I righted the Buddha and the flowerpots, and then hurriedly hurled my clothes and books into the big blue IKEA bag. I attempted to tidy Cass's cupboards. I'd worn many of her clothes, and couldn't quite remember how they had been organized when I moved in. Leila stopped me when she saw me pull out the vacuum cleaner.

'No, Daphne, we're not doing that today!'

'You don't have to help, I'll do it.'

'No!'

'Why?!'

'Because we're both exhausted, and I want to chill.'

'But I'm going to get my ticket for tomorrow or the next day. I might not have time.'

'I'll do it later!'

'I can't let you clean everything.'

'Yes, you can. You are my guest now. I insist. It would be rude to disobey me.'

I opened the fridge, but it was empty, apart from Cass's jars and juices, still miraculously untouched. I checked under the bed, behind the headboard. No *Habseligkeiten* left behind.

23

A Gift

I LAY ON LEILA'S sofa, all my belongings sprawled on the floor, already falling out of the gaping blue bag. I booked an easyJet flight for the following evening. I treated myself to extra leg-room and Speedy Boarding. I was exhausted, but I was scared of sleeping in case I did something to Leila's flat. I lay awake and googled my symptoms. A few diagnoses seemed possible: dissociative disorder, dissociative fugue, psychogenic fugue. Not usually cross-diagnosed with exploding head syndrome. In a fugue state, a person does not remember who they are, or what they are doing. The state is often triggered by traumas or unresolvable inner conflicts. They often embark on bold adventures, or wake to find themselves behaving in an inexplicable manner.

But I couldn't understand these lapses in memory. I tried to make sense of it all. I lay on the sofa, not sleeping, and tried to remember. It was as if my entire life in Berlin were splayed out before me, each moment equidistant, a strange exhibit of objects and characters. There was the ballerina's flat. There was the ice cream I'd shared with Callum. There was my first run with Evan and Ollie in the Grunewald. There was Grausam, present and undeniable. There were the separable verbs. There was Kat, playing with the zip of my hoodie, and Milosh, plating up gnocchi. I could examine each in turn, an innumerable number of experiences, and feel as dispassionate as a biologist giving a class in dissection. 'This is the female *Daphnia magna*. On the left, the gut. The dark material is partially undigested food. On the right, the oesophagus, partially constricted. The white spot beneath it is an unfertilized egg. The heart is fluttering so fast it barely seems to beat.' Luminous and clear, perfectly exposed. Yet those moments of insanity, or fugue, whatever they were, those moments escaped me.

At 10 a.m., I got off the sofa and made some coffee, which Leila and I drank on the balcony. She hadn't slept either. We stood on her balcony, shivering and blinking in the light, steam rising from our breath and mugs. It was a bright, cold day in October. I asked Leila about her plans for the week ahead. We didn't discuss what I would do in London, limiting our talk to the city we had in common. Already, I felt a division growing between me and everyone else in Berlin. I wasn't one of them any more, no longer a 'Berliner'. Leila lit a cigarette. The smoke curled up. I leant over the ledge. From the balcony, the deep, sombre courtyard. It was Sunday morning, and very quiet.

Some hours later, I balanced the IKEA bag on my shoulder, and hugged Leila goodbye. It wasn't an emotional farewell. We didn't know each other very well, although I'd grown fond of her, and would miss the friend she could have been to me if I had stayed. She asked me to text her when I landed, and to get in touch when I returned. 'Of course I will.'

I walked down into Hermannstraße station. The trains ran only irregularly on Sundays; the next train in the direction of the airport wasn't coming for another sixteen minutes. The platform was not deserted, as I had expected. The kiosk was serving coffee and *Schrippe*, and silent crowds of people – many, it seemed, on their way back from protracted nights out – waited behind the yellow line. I was itching to send a text to Milosh. I kept opening and closing the app. I missed him already, I wanted to say, I'm so sorry.

The train arrived, finally, and I got on with all the other passengers. I sat down, fumbling in my bag. For one ecstatic minute I was sure I'd left my passport at Leila's, but then I found it in my back pocket, just as a beggar in a wheelchair reached me. He had falsely interpreted my gesture and something lively flared in his face as he held out his hand for change, murmuring quickly as if he was chanting or praying. His nails were semi-circles of dark mud, and a few strands of long hair hung down from his mostly bald head.

I found myself handing him my phone.

'Here,' I said. 'I don't need it any more.'

'*Danke schön*,' he said, bowing his head a little. 'Thank you, thank you.'

He slipped it into his breast pocket and for a moment I saw the outline of the lit screen through the thin fabric – the picture I'd taken of the Tempelhofer Feld was visible a moment before it went dark and he rolled onward.

As I boarded the plane, I had the sudden, terrible realization that I'd forgotten to go back for Cass's bike. I'd left it with the *Späti* man and his daughter before I had been taken to hospital. Now I wouldn't be able to text her, nor to ask Leila to pick it up. I had a window seat, 4A. As the engines fired and the plane took off with violent force, I felt a rush of adrenaline. I gripped my armrest. My thoughts turned to the first bricking in EG's flat. I remembered the optimism with which I'd moved in, and all my good resolutions. And then the terror on that night and my crazy hypothesis about exploding head syndrome. But I hadn't imagined it, and I know that I did not throw the first brick. I know the downstairs neighbour did it, and that he hated me, whatever his reasons. I know this with as much certainty as I know that Richard Grausam was a dangerous man. Kommissar Faccini had confirmed that. I was right to have feared him.

And then I wrecked EG's flat, and threw a brick at Cass's window. I had stopped eating and ran until I was bloody and faint. Violence and anger, finding no purchase without, turned within. I was sleepwalking in a toxic nightmare of my own making. But at least I was the heroine in the end. I threw the last stone.

In the seat next to me sat an Englishman with tiny, bloodshot eyes, who was undertaking some kind of suffrage campaign for the man-spreaders. As the plane straightened out, I began covert warfare, sprawling my legs and draping my arm nonchalantly over the armrest. I drank a can of Diet Coke, tried to read the last few pages of *The Magic Mountain*, but I was too tired to really concentrate.

From above, the city looked like a blacksmith's forge. The millions of lights flaring like fading sparks from the hammer and anvil. I tried to imagine what kind of person lay behind each light. It made me sick to think how many of life's variations I would miss out on. I would never know what it was like to have a man's body, to be a Muslim, or to have a child before the age of twenty. I'd never be an Egyptologist or a mountain climber or a ballerina, and I wished there was a way of trying on all these different possible lives, as one tries on different clothes, and to choose the outfit best suited to one's soul. I worried that I didn't know how to play the glorious possibilities of the hand I'd been dealt. Someone else would make great use of this characterful nose, the desire to please, would know what to do with my kind family, great education, and my sympathetic nature. All these gifts had gone largely wasted on me. But it was complicated, this feeling I had, as the sparks melted into a confusion of light – because while I did envy other people for being them, I pitied them for never getting to be me.

Acknowledgements

With love to my dearest friends and first readers: Noa Amson, Nir Ferber, Rainat Flanagan, Cécile Hubert, Dina Khadum, Zoe Reich-Aviles, Allegra Reinalda, Magda Rotko, Dana Sagi, Sally Tulaimat, Paul Doeman, Ben West. With gratitude for those who sheltered me in Berlin: Ed LeMonde, Michael Shamai, Mona Vogel, Mario Völker, the Ferber-Kedan home, Weserland, and the Amerika-Gedenkbibliothek (the American Memorial Library). With thanks to my ministering angels Bridget Bowen, Marina Cantacuzino, Louise Cardwell, Aurea Carpenter, Philip Connor, Emma Ferguson, Molly Meloy, Lucy Wadham, Elizabeth Wadham.

With thanks to my exceptional agent, Charlotte Seymour, for giving me so much support, and to my editor, Alice Youell, for her nurturing and creative input.

With gratitude to Ali Smith, who reached out to members of Newnham College and offered to give feedback to aspiring writers: her comments and encouragement were greatly appreciated.

With love to my family: Catherine, Olivier, Léon and Bobbot, who have been my number one fans since birth.

About the Author

Bea Setton was born in France and spent her early years in the Parisian suburbs before moving to the USA to study Philosophy. Upon graduating, she relocated to Berlin, and the city became the inspiration for this book.

She currently divides her time between London and Cambridge, where she is studying for a PhD, and working on plans for her second book.